IF HE'S DARING

Suddenly she was aware that she was seated very close to Orion and he had his arm around her. It was nice, the warmth of his body keeping away the encroaching chill of the night. It was also highly improper but then she was already doing a lot that was improper such as riding around the countryside with an unmarried man who was not related to her. She looked up at him to find him looking down at her.

His face was so close and so very handsome. She could see concern for her in his beautiful blue eyes. His mouth was almost as pretty, the bottom lip a little fuller than the top. Catryn could not recall the last time she had been kissed by a man and she suddenly craved a kiss.

Orion knew it was a mistake as he lowered his mouth to hers but the way she had looked at him had been a temptation he could not resist. There had been the glint of want and curiosity in her sea-green eyes and every part of him strongly encouraged him to answer both. It took but one brush of his mouth over her full, soft lips to tell him that he could be risking a lot just to steal a little taste but he ignored that warning . . .

Books by Hannah Howell

THE MURRAYS

Highland Destiny
Highland Honor
Highland Promise
Highland Vow
Highland Knight
Highland Bride
Highland Angel
Highland Groom
Highland Warrior
Highland Conqueror
Highland Champion
Highland Lover
Highland Barbarian
Highland Savage
Highland Wolf
Highland Sinner
Highland Protector
Highland Avenger
Highland Master

THE WHERLOCKES

If He's Wicked
If He's Sinful
If He's Wild
If He's Dangerous
If He's Tempted
If He's Daring

VAMPIRE ROMANCE

Highland Vampire
The Eternal Highlander
My Immortal Highlander
Highland Thirst
Nature of the Beast
Yours for Eternity
Highland Hunger
Born to Bite

STAND-ALONE NOVELS

Only for You
My Valiant Knight
Unconquered
Wild Roses
A Taste of Fire
A Stockingful of Joy
Highland Hearts
Reckless
Conqueror's Kiss
Beauty and the Beast
Highland Wedding

Silver Flame
Highland Fire
Highland Captive
My Lady Captor
Wild Conquest
Kentucky Bride
Compromised Hearts
Stolen Ecstasy
Highland Hero
His Bonnie Bride

Published by Kensington Publishing Corporation

IF HE'S DARING

HANNAH HOWELL

ZEBRA BOOKS
KENSINGTON PUBLISHING CORP.
http://www.kensingtonbooks.com

ZEBRA BOOKS are published by

Kensington Publishing Corp.
119 West 40th Street
New York, NY 10018

All Kensington titles, imprints, and distributed lines are
available at special quantity discounts for bulk purchases
for sales promotion, premiums, fund-raising, educa-
tional, or institutional use.

Special book excerpts or customized printings can also
be created to fit specific needs. For details, write or
phone the office of the Kensington Special Sales Man-
ager: Attn. Special Sales Department. Kensington Publishing Corp., 119 West 40th Street, New York, NY 10018.
Phone: 1-800-221-2647.

Zebra and the Z logo Reg. U.S. Pat. & TM Off.

First Printing: October 2014
ISBN-13: 978-1-4201-3499-5
ISBN-10: 1-4201-3499-X

First Electronic Edition: October 2014
eISBN-13: 978-1-4201-3500-8
eISBN-10: 1-4201-3500-7

10 9 8 7 6 5 4 3 2 1

Printed in the United States of America

Chapter One

England, Fall, 1790

The groan echoed through the small house, every note of it filled with pain and helpless fury. Catryn tossed her cloak on the hook near the front door and rushed toward the room she was certain the sound was coming from. Her heart pounded with fear for her family as she cursed herself for leaving them alone. She never should have given in to her friend Anne's pleas to join her at the morning salon on the servants' day off. She certainly should never have lingered there as long as she had.

She found her father on his knees in the library, one hand on the settee as he struggled to get to his feet. Catryn ran to his side to help him stand and then urged him to sit down on the settee. Blood stained his pale cheek as it seeped from the side of his head, the red of it stark against the white of his hair. The knuckles on his right hand were scraped and his left eye was already swelling. A quick look around the room revealed a knocked-over table and a smashed vase. Who would attack her father? The man was just a quiet, somewhat reclusive scholar.

A demand to know what had happened burned her tongue with the need to be uttered, but she bit it back. Her father needed tending to first, the dazed look in his gray eyes telling her that he was not ready to answer all her questions, not even the one now screaming in her mind. *Where is my son?*

Catryn quickly dampened her handkerchief with a little of the spring water her father always brought to the city from their country home and kept in a decanter on his desk. Her heart still twisted with fear, she gently bathed the blood from his face. By the time she was finished, his wound did not look quite as bad as she had thought it was, and his eyes had cleared. The first words he spoke chilled her to the bone.

"He took Alwyn."

"Who took him, Papa?" she asked, although she already had a very good idea of who would commit such a crime against her.

"Morris." He took the damp handkerchief from her hand and held it against the small wound on the side of his head. "He and some hired brute came into this house, marched right into this room whilst I was reading a story to Alwyn, and demanded that I give him the lad. Told the man he was a daft fool and to get out. Then we had us a tussle and I lost."

She could see how that shamed him and patted his knee. "It was two men against one, Papa. I know, with all my heart, that you did all you could do to stop him. Now I will do what I can."

Lewys Gryffin looked at his daughter, his only

child, and wished he had shot Sir Morris de Warrenne a long time ago. Since her husband, Henry, had died nearly two years ago, life had become one vicious, unending battle with the man's younger brother over who should have control over the heir, her son, and all the riches the little boy now had claim to. The months of strife had left them all weary and angry. It was clear to see that the fight over Alwyn had now turned truly dangerous and it hurt him to be of so little help to her when she needed him so badly.

"I should be the one to fight this," he muttered. "'Tis my place as the man in this family, as the head of this house."

"Ah, Papa," she said as she sat down next to him and kissed him on the cheek. "You *have* been fighting and doing a fine job of it. Fighting since the moment Henry took his last breath. And as soon as I get Alwyn back home with us where he belongs, you will be fighting again. Now it is my turn to take up the fight. I will go after Morris and retrieve my child."

"It will not be easy. Do not forget how they took him from us. This was an attack. He demanded, and when I said no, he attacked. He came prepared to fight us for the boy. I think Morris has lost his mind, most probably when he lost the last court battle to be named Alwyn's guardian. I ne'er considered Morris a very clever fellow, but I did not think he could ever be as lack-witted as this."

"Neither did I. I had no warning at all, no sense that this could happen. This tastes of pure desperation, Papa."

"It does. I thought the same when he showed up with the obvious intent of taking the boy no matter what or who stood in his way. I have heard that he is having some financial difficulties, but this was still a very drastic action to take."

"That would depend on how deep his financial troubles run." She resisted the urge to tell him all she had discovered about the dire condition of Morris's finances, for the man needed no more weight added to his worry about Alwyn. "All this trouble with the courts and lawyers cannot have been cheap for him. It certainly pinched our purse hard. The why does not matter," she said as she stood up. "He had no right."

"No, he did not, but now he does have the boy and he may well think that is enough to help him win his case."

"Then he will be wrong. All he will get from this is a prison cell."

Lewys cursed when she hurried out of the room. He placed the damp handkerchief she had left behind over his throbbing eye. He should be at her side in this fight, but he knew he would be useless, his sight still affected by the blow to his eyes, and the blow to his head made it throb so hard and constantly that it scattered his thoughts. Good sense did not stop him from being infuriated that his barely five-feet-tall, not quite eight-stone daughter was about to confront a man who had just revealed how violent he could become when he did not get his way.

Catryn was unfastening her gown even as she strode into her bedchamber. She hastily changed into something far more serviceable and then began to stuff two more sturdy gowns into her saddlebags. It took her only minutes to pack a few other things she considered necessities and then she hurried down to the kitchen to gather some food. There was a good chance she could confront Morris right in his town house in the city, but she had been taught to always prepare for the worst. There was a chance she might have to chase him down.

They had been prepared for Morris to try and take Alwyn almost from the moment her husband died, for they had known he would heartily dislike the fact that her father had been named Alwyn's guardian and, along with a few trustees, given control over Alwyn's inheritance. Yet, as the months dragged on and all Morris had done was drag them through probate and the courts time and time again, they had lost that cold fear. They had been foolish to drop their guard.

Racing toward the front of the house, she paused when her father yelled out, "Take your pistol!"

Peering into the library, she was relieved to see that his color was better than it had been. "I have it with me, Papa. I will be very careful. Do not worry. And have Eccles look at those wounds when he returns. I will return when I have Alwyn and not before," she vowed as she hurried away, confident that their clever butler would care well for her father.

Lewys wanted to argue that but heard the front door slam. He made an attempt to stand up but swayed with the dizziness that assaulted him and quickly sat down again. As he took several breaths to recover from nearly swooning and sprawling in an undignified heap upon the carpet, he thought about Catryn going after Morris, armed for battle with no strong man to protect or aid her. She was a true red-head in all the ways people thought of the breed, although her temper rarely showed itself. She was also a mother about to fight for her child. Morris had no idea what he had just unleashed.

Catryn checked her saddle and saddle pack to make certain both were secure before swinging up onto the back of her mare. She had packed enough to sustain her if she had to chase Morris down to the de Warrenne country house, but sincerely hoped she did not have to. Although she was a good rider, she had not ridden any great distances for a long time.

Fury warmed her blood as she rode through the cool, misty streets of London toward Morris's town house. The man had been a thorn in her side from the moment her useless husband had breathed his last, but this act went far beyond being a nuisance. For a moment she considered setting the authorities on his trail, but she was not sure who to go to or if she could even afford such help. Legal help of any kind did not come cheaply and, after so many court battles with her brother-in-law, both her and her father's purses were painfully light.

Just as she rode within sight of Morris's town house she saw him shoving a thrashing, screaming Alwyn into his carriage. Shouting at him to halt gained her only a hard glare before he joined her son in the carriage, which began to move. The heavy traffic upon the road made a swift escape impossible, but it also slowed down all her attempts to catch up with him.

Cursing softly, she did her best to gain enough speed to overtake Morris's carriage, but the only thing she was able to do was to keep him in sight. Catryn knew he would soon reach a road that led out of the city. If she could not catch him before then she would quickly lose sight of him. Her mare was a fast, sturdy creature, but the animal could not outrun a carriage pulled by four strong horses.

"Never expected him to actually leave the city, Sorley," she muttered to her horse. "Am certainly readied for a journey but truly did not expect, or wish, to make one."

Ignoring the curse shouted at her by the man she splattered with muck as she wove her way through the crowded streets, she struggled not to lose sight of Morris's carriage. It troubled her when she realized they would soon leave the part of the city she knew well, might even pass through the more dangerous streets. Even as a child she had been sternly warned about the dark, filthy, and dangerous streets where the desperate poor and the criminals lived. Catryn prayed that Morris's carriage would soon turn away from that rapidly approaching peril.

A moment later Morris's carriage took a left turn and she breathed a silent sigh of relief. She quickly moved to follow him, only to see several small boys rush into the street to pick up the coins Morris had tossed out of the carriage. In her frantic attempts to avoid trampling the children, Sorley reared and then stumbled as its hooves hit the cobblestones again. Once she was safely through the crowd, Catryn realized that the hasty prayer she had uttered that they would all survive the brief confrontation unharmed had not been answered. Sorley's gait was no longer smooth.

Moving to the far edge of the street, Catryn dismounted and began to walk her horse, closely studying the way the animal moved. The injury was not a bad one, just soreness in the muscle or hoof, but there would be no chasing Morris on horseback now. Not only would continuing to ride Sorley worsen the mare's injury, but she would have no chance of catching the man while riding an injured horse. She would have to come up with another way to chase after the man. Fighting the strong urge to weep or scream, Catryn walked along trying to think of what she could do.

Then she saw it. It was like a miraculous answer to her prayers. The carriage stood in front of a pleasant town house, ready to be driven away. It was being idly polished by a liveried servant as the man waited for the passenger to arrive. Catryn's heart pounded with excitement and terror as a desperate plan formed in her mind. Stealing a carriage was a hanging offense, she reminded herself as she approached the vehicle and the servant, but she might find some mercy for her actions since she was attempting to rescue her kidnapped son.

"Can I be of help, ma'am?" asked the servant when she halted in front of him, and yanked her saddlebags off of her horse.

"Why, yes, I believe you can." She pulled her pistol from a hidden pocket in her skirts and aimed it at the man. "I have need of this carriage."

The man took a step back and blinked. "Ma'am?"

"It is of the greatest urgency that I have this carriage. I must chase down a man. As you can see, my mount is no longer able to serve me in that endeavor. Her name is Sorley. She is a very good mare. I will leave her with you in trade for the carriage."

"But, ma'am . . ."

"I am very sorry," she said and moved toward the front of the carriage, keeping her pistol aimed steadily at the man. "Truly, truly sorry, but I really must do this. I will return the carriage, but if something goes awry and I cannot, you may keep the mare as payment." She tossed her bags up on the seat and scrambled up after them. "If it is not enough to cover the cost then go to Lord Lewys Gryffin, Baron of Gryffin Manor in Chester. He is residing now at Gryffin House here in London. Tell him Lady Catryn Gryffin de Warrenne sent you to get recompense for the loss of the carriage."

She snapped the reins just as he lunged toward her. Catryn nearly screamed when the horses darted forward. The pull on her arms was far greater than she had anticipated. It hurt, a lot, and she had to brace herself just to stay on the seat. A quick look back showed her that the man was not chasing her, however, so she turned her full attention to making her way through the busy, narrow streets. A few shouted queries to people she passed were enough to keep her on Morris's trail, for the man's fancy blue-and-gold carriage caught the eye of nearly everyone it passed by.

When she was finally free of the crowded streets of

the city, Catryn breathed a hearty sigh of relief. That
relief was short-lived, however, as she realized that
Morris was headed southeast. If he was taking Alwyn
to the coast, he could be planning to take her child
out of England. It would make it all that much harder
for her to find her son.

A rush of fear left a sour taste in her mouth before
she could push it back. Morris could just as easily be
taking her son to his country home in Easebourne.
Catlyn scolded herself, determined not to keep falling
into a deep mire of panic. Such fear clouded the
mind and she needed hers to be clear and sharp. Her
thoughts needed to be fixed upon one thing only:
getting Alwyn back, no matter where Morris went or
what obstacles were put in her path.

Catryn's arms ached and her back wept with pain,
but she kept the carriage moving along the road at as
fast a speed as she dared. She was not surprised by the
occasional look of shock she saw on the faces of the
people she passed. Driving a carriage was not something women were supposed to do. She had only
learned the skill because she had had to. Everyone at
Gryffin Manor had had to work hard in the two years
before she had married Henry, learning as many skills
as they could to try and save the estate after a hard
loss in an investment scheme her grandfather had
foolishly made. They had succeeded, but during those
hard times she had lost both her grandfather and her
mother. Grief had stolen her father from her in many
ways, too, leaving her carrying far more weight than a
girl her age ever should have had to.

The pain of those losses still lingered, though the

good memories came far more often than the sad ones now. Catryn did not regret all she had had to learn, either. She wished she had continued to use those skills from time to time, for now she was not sure how much longer she could continue without a rest. She had been racing along for nearly an hour and her whole body was protesting the exertion. Morris's carriage had long been out of sight, but she was certain she was on the right trail. It would help if she had some idea of how far behind him she actually was, however.

Worry was a constant ache in her heart. She did not think Morris would hurt her son, but then she had never thought he would resort to kidnapping Alwyn either. Morris had never spent much time with her son and knew nothing about him. She doubted he had ever spent time with any child. Catryn feared what the man would do when he became aware of Alwyn's habit of talking to people who were not there, such as his dead father. She had worked hard to make Alwyn understand that he needed to hide that little quirk, for it bothered, even frightened, too many people, but he was only five years old. She could not be certain he truly understood the danger.

The first of the obstacles she had worried about arrived an hour later, and she had to wonder if the Fates were working against her. The team was beginning to lag. Shaking free of her troubled thoughts, she briefly considered pushing them harder and then softly cursed. Catryn knew she now faced the same choice she had been forced to make with her mare

Sorley. The only difference was that these horses simply needed a rest.

She pushed aside all thought that she was doomed in her quest to catch Morris, as well as the unkind thoughts she nursed about the man whose carriage she had stolen and the lack of stamina in his horses. It would do her no good to run the animals until they could run no more. She might gain on Morris for a little while, but she would lose him again when she was forced to stop and hunt down a new team. Morris would also have to rest his horses at some point along the way. Catryn began to search for a safe place to allow the horses to rest, perhaps one with both water and some grazing space.

An hour passed before she found the perfect spot. Catryn carefully drove the carriage off the road onto a grassy clearing near a brook. The moment she got down from the driver's perch, she knew it was not only the horses that needed a rest. She had to hang on to the side of the carriage for a moment until her legs stopped shaking. There was not one single place on her body that did not ache, but her arms and upper back pained her the most. She was going to pay very dearly for this adventure.

Just as she was rubbing her aching bottom, a young voice said from behind her, "Arse hurting you, is it?"

Catryn spun around so quickly she stumbled back several steps as she struggled to keep her balance. A young boy stood there, grinning at her, his blue eyes shining with laughter. With his thick black hair tumbling around his face in waves that came perilously close to being curls, he was an astonishingly pretty boy. She judged him to be several years older than her son and wondered where he had come from. It was late in the day for a boy his age to be wandering the countryside all alone.

"Who are you and where did you come from?" she asked.

"I am Giles Wherlocke and I was sitting in the carriage you nicked. Who are you?"

"Lady Catryn Gryffin de Warrenne."

By the time she finished telling him her name the full import of what he had said had seeped into her mind. Catryn stared at the boy in growing horror. There was no denying the truth that now blazed across her mind, however. In her blind desperation to get her son back, she had stolen away another person's son.

"Sweet mercy," she muttered. "Your parents are going to see me hanged for this."

"Only have the one parent, m'lady. Only have my father, Sir Orion Wherlocke. Truth be told, a fair number of people have taken to stealing his carriage of late, though those people were all his own kin. You are not kin, I am thinking. Not with that red hair. So why did you have such need for my father's carriage? And, I do say, you held off Cody right fine, you did. Did not know a proper lady could hold a pistol that steady."

Even though she was a little bemused by the way he spoke with an odd mixture of proper and not so proper English, Catryn did notice that the boy did not assure her that she would face no punishment for what she had done. "I needed it."

"Why? You be a proper lady and all. You must have one of your own."

"My horse came up lame and I needed the carriage to continue my hunt for the man who stole my son. I could not afford to take the time to return home to get another horse or the carriage."

"Why did some man take your son? He want money for the boy?"

She dragged her hands through her hair, idly noting that it had fallen free from the neat style her maid had spent a great deal of time perfecting. "I need to see to the horses right now."

Giles did not push her for an answer to his question but moved to lend her a hand. As they worked together to unhitch the team, rubbed the animals down with handfuls of grass, and then watered them, she told Giles all about Morris and his fight to gain control over Alwyn and his inheritance. Her openness with the boy surprised her, but she decided she just had a deep need to speak her thoughts aloud to someone and he was there, watching and listening, his pretty eyes sharp with intelligence. At times Catryn felt as if she spoke with an adult while at other times, especially when the boy asked why again and again, she could see the young boy beneath the air of toughness and maturity.

Just speaking of all Morris had done stirred her anger. The moment the horses were tethered so they could graze, she began to pace as she talked. Spitting it all out, her father would call it, and that was just what she was doing. She cursed Morris for his greed, his inability to accept what was right by law and his brother's will, and even for his fanciful blue-and-gold carriage. Even telling herself that a young boy should not be subjected to her fury at Morris and her fear for her child, she could not stop talking. Or pacing.

"Morris is headed to the coast," she said, abruptly changing from ranting about all of Morris's past crimes and thinking only of the one he had committed this time. "He may be trying to take Alwyn out of the country. He may even be thinking to just toss my baby overboard once he is out to sea."

"No, he would ne'er do that," Giles said as he paced alongside her. "He wants what your boy has and that means he best be keeping that boy alive until he gets it. That is how the game is played."

She paused to stare at him. "How old are you?"

"I think I am eight."

"You think?"

"Well, no way to be certain since my mother left me in an alley in the city when I was a babe still swaddled and all."

Catryn did not know what to say and stared at him in silent shock for a moment. "And your father?"

"I told you; I just found him. Me and my mates were helping his cousin and then he came to help, too, and one of the older ladies said I was his. No one argued with her, said she knew what she was about, so he took me in. My mates are all staying with his cousin and are at their country house now. We are going to better ourselves and not have to live in the dark alleys, maybe thieving a bit, maybe going hungry. I begin to think the lady knew what she was talking about, too, because my father and I do well enough."

"But how did you survive until you found your father?"

"My mates. There was a woman or two along the way who helped, but it was mostly my mates who raised me. As I told you, they are all at Penelope's now and that was where my father was taking me. Lady Pen is my father's cousin and she used to have a house where all the other Wherlocke bastards stayed. My father named it the Wherlocke Warren. Now that Lady Pen is wed, she has kept the ones she has and deals with whatever new ones appear as she thinks best."

It was impossible for Catryn to envision the life he spoke of. So hard, stark, and dangerous. That a mother would leave her babe in an alley as if the child were nothing but trash to be tossed away was also impossible for her to understand. Without his mates, Giles would have died and she had no doubt that he knew that well. It was no wonder he often seemed to be so much older than he was.

She was not so certain he had improved his lot much by being taken up by his father. A cousin who had run a house for the bastard children of her family? Who still took in the occasional new one? It was very good of the woman to care for the children so many just tossed aside, but how good was such a scandal-filled life for a young, growing boy? Better than living in an alley, she told herself firmly, and shook aside her concern over his future. She could look into that later, when she had Alwyn safely back at home.

"You were very lucky to find them."

"I was. And you will find your boy soon and take him home."

"If Morris has not hurt him."

"Why do you keep thinking the man will hurt your son? There is no gain in it for him. You have to see that."

"I do. But Alwyn is just a little boy, and Morris has no skill with children. He would not understand Alwyn's ways, his little quirks and the way he plays." Catryn had seen how people had reacted to her son carrying on full conversations with people who were not visible, even telling others what had been said to him, and knew Morris would have no patience, might even be afraid, which could prove very dangerous for her son.

"What do you mean by his quirks and how he plays? Was this Morris ne'er a lad himself?"

"Of course he was."

"Then what does the boy do that you think will make Morris hurt him?"

"Alwyn talks to people who are not there," she replied, surprised at her own candor. "It is but a child's game. He has few other children to play with and then only rarely, so he has made up a few of his own. That is all it is. But people find it alarming and I have taught him to be quiet about it. He is only five though."

"So he has some boys he has thought up to play with."

"Not all boys," she reluctantly admitted. "He claims he is talking to his father, who has been dead for nearly two years." She shook her head. "It is just a game."

"I suspect it is. The lad is lonely, is all."

There was something in the way the boy said the words that made Catryn think he did not really mean them, but she did not press him. "It would upset Morris, but you are right, there is still no gain in his hurting Alwyn."

She realized that caring for the horses and talking to the boy had eased her fear for Alwyn. It was still there but was not as sharp. The boy was right. There was no gain in Morris doing any serious harm to Alwyn. That did not mean the man would not hurt him or frighten him.

"It will be well, m'lady," said Giles, and he patted her on the arm.

"It has to be. But for now, we shall let the horses rest and have ourselves something to eat. I fear I brought very little with me as I had thought Morris was taking Alwyn to his town house, not out of the city."

"Not to worry."

Giles went to the carriage, climbed in, and quickly returned with a basket. The way he carried it told her it was well stocked. It made sense that such a thing would be in there as the man had been taking his son on a trip to the country. She sat on the grass beside him and opened the basket to find a bounty of bread, cheese, cold meat, cider, and apple tarts.

"At least I shall eat well before I am tossed into Newgate," she murmured.

Giles chuckled. "You will not be tossed into a prison, m'lady. You had good reason to steal my father's carriage. He will understand."

Catryn was not sure of that but just nodded. She hated that time was passing and all she could do was sit, eat, and hope the horses were ready to pull the carriage again before the sun went down completely. The sooner she got her son back from Morris the better.

"It will be the man who took your son who will rot in prison," said Giles.

"I truly hope so." She also prayed that Giles judged his father well and that the man did prove to be as understanding as the boy thought he would be.

Chapter Two

Sir Orion Wherlocke took a last look at his image in the mirror, adjusted his neckcloth a little, and then started out of the room. It was foolish to be so precise about his appearance when he was about to take a long journey to the Radmoor country home, but he had once promised himself that he would always look his best and could not seem to break free of that vow. It was a vow born of a humiliating experience in his childhood and he should have overcome that by now.

Promising himself that he would work on freeing himself of that emotional chain, he stepped outside and stared at the place where his carriage should be waiting for him. Orion heard Cody shout and turned in that direction to see his carriage disappear into the heavy London traffic. That brief glimpse he had gotten of his rapidly retreating transport told him that the driver did not look anything like one of his many kinsmen and -women, who had lately taken to stealing his carriage with an irritating regularity to perform some act of daring that required immediate access to transport. Unfortunately, that had usually proven to be his carriage. As far as he was aware, there were no women in his family with such brilliantly red hair. He looked at Cody and the pale worry on the man's face reminded Orion that he had told his son to wait for him in the carriage, the carriage that had just vanished.

"Giles?" he asked Cody.

"Inside the carriage, sir," replied Cody, and then he looked briefly at the mare standing placidly at his side.

"The carriage that has just been driven away, the one you do not appear to be chasing after."

"The lady handed me these reins and aimed a pistol at me. I was that shocked, sir, that there was never a thought in my head about fighting her. Cannot chase her on this horse, either, as it is lame. I was just trying to think of a way to set after her."

"I believe I can understand not fighting with her, although I do wish it had been otherwise. So, a woman has just stolen my carriage and my son."

Cody frowned. "Well, aye, she took the carriage, gave me this mare in trade until, so she said, she returned the carriage. I do not know why I think it, sir, but I could swear on my mother's grave that the woman had no idea the boy was inside. Lad never made a sound, either."

Orion sighed. No, Giles would not sound any alarm. The boy would think it all some grand adventure, confident in his ability to get free of any tangle. Giles still thought like a boy allowed to run free on the streets, one encouraged from time to time to steal or aid in some fraud, and one whose life had been charmed enough that he had never suffered much for that. It was going to take a while to teach the boy that the comforts of home and family he now enjoyed came with the responsibility of not leaping headlong into any trouble that was around. Orion decided he was going to have to remind Giles that he was no longer without family, and that his family possessed the kind of funds that many a criminal would covet. He could not be so free to risk himself. The boy also had to be made to understand that the family he was now claimed by would worry about him.

"Fetch me a mount, Cody, while I go and gather a few things for a journey," he ordered the man. "I will leave a message for you to deliver to my hostess for this evening's event that will adequately explain my absence."

As Orion returned to his bedchamber and quickly gathered what he would need for the hunt he was about to go on, he felt no regret over missing the ball he had planned to attend after leaving Giles with his cousins. He did, however, experience some annoyance over missing his chance to woo the fair Beatrice, a buxom widow well-known for her skills and appetite in the bedchamber despite all her efforts to be discrete about her affairs. He was very close to success there and missing the chance to meet with her could set his seduction back some. It had been a long time since he had enjoyed the pleasure to be found in a woman's arms and he had been looking forward to the chance to do so again.

The woman had been out of reach for quite a while and only recently available. Beatrice had been involved with a rich, older man for months, and Orion never poached on another man's territory, no matter how great the temptation or need. When Beatrice had indicated her interest in him while still on the other man's arm, and in his bed, Orion had responded with nothing more than politeness. The chance to do more had come only last week, and he had wasted no time in acting on the opportunity after learning that Beatrice was free to be pursued.

The delay in that game could not be helped, he told himself as he hurried back outside. Giles was his son. The boy was not legitimate and had only recently been discovered, but the bond was already there. Even if it had not been, Orion knew he would still go after the boy. Every Wherlocke and Vaughn was taught the importance of caring for one's progeny, even if that progeny was a half-wild street urchin. There were a few who tried to ignore that rule, ones who occasionally needed a harsh reminder of their responsibilities, but most followed it without hesitation. Too many of them had been victims of a parent's desertion and neglect themselves.

His concern over Giles's fate was not as strong as he thought it should be, but he quickly shook off a sense of guilt about that. Giles was clever and had grown up on the dangerous streets of London. His son was no tenderly raised, overly protected child of the gentry. He had not even had a life as easy as Orion's other two sons, despite how those boys had been cast aside by their mothers. Even if this woman proved to be a threat, Giles had the cunning and strong self-preservation instincts of a London dock rat. The boy could easily keep himself safe until Orion could rescue him.

The last shadow of the worry that had gripped him

was eased by reminding himself of his own skills. His family and his colleagues in the government did not call him The Bloodhound as a jest. He could, and often did, find anyone with only the mere hint of a clue to lead him. No one who knew him would gamble with him or play chess or cards, even just for the sake of passing time. He could figure out a person's next move, his entire strategy, with ease. He would find this woman and retrieve his son. Orion swore to himself that he would also find out just what game she was playing. If someone had discovered who he was, what he did for the government, and then discovered how closely Giles was connected to him, it was possible they would try to use the boy to get information. Giles's connection to him had become a great deal more well-known than young Paul's or Hector's. Someone discovering it and using it against him was a distinct possibility. He hoped that was not it, for then it would mean he might have to get the blood of a woman on his hands.

The note to his hostess took only a moment to write. There was no need to concoct any elaborate excuses. He simply spoke of some undefined family emergency. Most of society knew that the Wherlockes and Vaughns were an extraordinarily close family. It was one of the many things that had them all marked as odd. There were those amongst the two families who had deserted their husbands, wives, and children; some people wondered if the rumors of a close family were actually true, but only a few remained doubtful for long. Nor did it take a determined person long to discover just why there were so many desertions. What he had always considered sad was the vast number of

people who believed it was perfectly acceptable for
those women, and a few men, to walk away from such
a strange family even when that included abandoning
their own children.

Orion shook his head free of such thoughts for
they stirred too many unhappy memories, left the
message on his desk for Cody to deliver, and walked
outside. He was still caught in the shock of finding out
he had another son. Paul had been less of a surprise,
for he had been keeping the woman who had borne
him. Hector had been the result of Orion's first few
years of breaking free of the bonds of family duty
and living the life of a wealthy young man in the city.
The surprise had come when he had found himself
responsible for this boy in ways far beyond visiting
him now and then and giving his mother money. He
still thanked the Fates for Penelope, who had taken
Paul and Hector into her care without hesitation.

Now there was Giles. Orion was becoming a family
man and he did not think he was ready for such responsibility. He was still far too young for such a thing.
He grunted in irritation as he stepped outside and
tried not to curse when he saw a horse instead of his
carriage.

"Did the woman give her name?" he asked as he
handed Cody his saddle packs and the man secured
them to the horse.

"Lady Catryn Gryffin de Warrenne," Cody replied.
"She told me to take that mare in payment—"

"That lame mare."

Cody ignored the muttered interruption. "—but
swore that she would return the carriage when she
was done with it. Then said that if she could not, and

more was due us, I was to go to her da, Lord Lewys Gryffin of Gryffin House, here in the city, and he would pay the rest."

"I have never heard of the man."

"Nor have I, but I could find out who he is if you wish it done. She told me he was the Baron of Gryffin Manor."

"I do wish to know all you can find out about him, even though I mean to recover my carriage and my son very soon. I would also like to know all you can discover about the lady. What I do with Lady de Warrenne remains to be seen. Knowing more about her, her father, and her family could help me decide."

"She was most polite."

"You said she aimed a pistol at you."

"Aye, she did that—"

"Politely."

"—but she did not shoot me, did she. Said she had do this, that she had to chase down a man."

"What man?" Orion hoped all this trouble had not been caused by some lover's argument.

"She did not say. I just cannot believe she would be any danger to the boy. I am still near certain she did not know young Giles was inside."

"I do not intend to go and shoot the woman," Orion said as he mounted his horse. "I will leave the judging of her until I catch her."

As he kicked the horse into a careful trot, Orion nearly grinned at the frown on Cody's square face. If it had been a man attempting to steal the carriage, pistol or not, Cody would have fought like a tiger. It was why he had hired the fellow. With the sudden tendency of his kinsmen to steal his carriage, he had decided a strong guard was needed so that they at least had to endure a solid beating before they robbed him. Cody had the brawn to stop someone and the skill to do so without inflicting too much damage. He did not, after all, wish to maim or kill his thieving cousins.

But Cody had a weakness. It was women. He could be twisted around those soft little fingers far too easily. Orion was not hindered with such a weakness. If this woman was a threat to Giles, him, or anyone else in his family, he would make sure she never caused anyone any trouble again.

It did not take him long to find the woman's trail. A small redheaded woman driving a carriage was a sight few missed. The fact that she was headed away from the city worried him. There were too many dark reasons to steal a boy and run with him. It was both sad and reassuring to know that Giles was aware of every one of them.

One man he spoke to talked of seeing a grinning face in the window of the carriage and Orion was relieved at the news that Giles was still unharmed. He did not bother to correct the man's opinion that it was the face of a spirit, a grinning death's-head. The man was certain that she was fleeing from that spirit; that was why the woman was behaving so scandalously as to drive a carriage herself and travel with no man attending her. Nor did he intend to warn the little redheaded thief, as the man had suggested, that the demon she fled was sitting in the carriage she drove. Aside from the fact that it was an idiotic idea, he knew Giles would enjoy hearing that far too much. When he caught the woman, Orion also intended to make certain that if the woman thought of demons, she thought of him.

A familiar voice hailed him when he reached the more open road outside the heart of the city. "Halloo, sir!"

Orion looked at the young man who moved up to ride beside him when he slowed the pace of his horse. Trenton Cotter was a new man in the group Orion worked with in the government, a group so intent on remaining secret that even Orion and his fellows were not completely certain what it was called. The younger man was eager, patriotic, and still very green. There was not yet any blood on Trenton's hands. He rather hoped service to the Crown did not steal all of that away. It had certainly jaded Orion, but he had always told himself being jaded was far, far better than being dead.

"Where do you ride off to, sir? Anything I could help you with?"

It was tempting to ask Trenton to come along, but Orion resisted that lure. "'Tis but a personal matter. If you would be so kind, I would appreciate it if you would tell our captain that I may be unavailable for a while."

"Will do. I was surprised to see you, but then it has been a day rife with strange sightings."

"Has it now? What else have you seen?"

"A redheaded woman driving a carriage all by her dainty little self. It had a grinning boy peering out the window as it raced by me, and he looked a lot like that lad you just claimed as yours. I believe he may have recognized me because he waved merrily as they passed me by. Truth to tell, that carriage and the team looked a great deal like yours, as well."

"That is strange." Orion inwardly cursed his bad luck, for he had wanted to keep this matter a secret if only because it was embarrassing to have a woman steal his carriage from right in front of his home. "I would strongly suggest you do not mention this vision, for it is bound to cause you trouble. Why, sounds much akin to the tale told me in the city by a man who swears it was a demon with Death's head peering out of the carriage window."

Trenton's gray eyes gleamed with laughter and his mouth twitched as he fought to suppress it. "No talk of demons and death's-heads shall pass my lips."

"Thank you."

"Nor of little redheaded ladies driving your carriage while your grinning child waved merrily at all the people they passed by."

Orion stared up at the sky for a moment before narrowing his eyes and looking at Trenton again. "I have my pistol on me."

"Good thing, too. I have heard that redheads can have quite the temper."

"You are enjoying this far too much."

"I fear I may be. It but begs to be thoroughly enjoyed. There was one other odd sight."

"You appear to have had an interesting ride."

"Very interesting. There was a carriage that rattled past me before I saw yours. It was a startling shade of blue with gold trim, pulled by four speckled gray mares. It, too, was going somewhat fast and it, too, had a face in the window. Another child, but this one was not smiling. Little lad with a head full of black curls, and he looked quite frightened. I almost turned about to follow them and see what was going on, but I need to get back to the city."

"Could just be a child who does not like traveling."

"It could be, but I thought I would make mention of it since you are headed in the same direction. If I am recalling it right, that garish carriage belongs to one Sir Morris de Warrenne, and I did not think he was wed or a father. He has been far too busy trying to gain guardianship of his brother's child."

"And how have you come to learn that? Is this de Warrenne someone the Crown is interested in?"

"No, but my brother is de Warrenne's solicitor, and he came by my place to sup with me a few nights ago. Complained a lot about the man, for he just would not give up and made a lot of unnecessary work for my brother and the others in the firm." He shrugged. "Just wondered if he had finally won his court case, or perhaps decided to go around the decisions of the court and take matters into his own hands." He shrugged again. "I will look into it when I can. May not be my business, but I have a strong distaste for men who try and take an inheritance away from a child and that appears to be what this is about."

"I believe I will do the same." Orion wondered if the theft of his carriage had something to do with Sir Morris and that frightened boy Trenton had seen. He was not sure a custody battle was all that much better to deal with than a lovers' quarrel, however. Either one could be messy and fraught with the sort of emotional morass he always did his best to avoid.

"Are you certain you do not need a hand?"

"With one small redheaded lady?" he drawled, and Trenton laughed briefly before giving Orion a darkly serious look.

"She should be no problem if she is on her own, but there is always the chance she is not acting alone. You have enemies, sir. It is not beyond possible that this is a trap."

The younger man might not be as green as Orion had first thought. "I have considered that, but I have it on rather dependable authority that she does not realize there is a child in the carriage."

"Ah, well, good luck then." His pleasant voice suddenly grew hard and cold. "If by chance you discover otherwise, be assured of my assistance. The people who work for the Crown need to believe their families are safe and protected. If this matter grows more serious, I would ask you to call on your compatriots for help. Good hunting!" He turned his mount and rode back toward the city.

Definitely not so green after all, Orion thought as he urged his horse forward again. For just a moment he considered bringing the younger man back to ride with him but then dismissed the idea. He wanted to do his best to see this matter settled and put aside without too many people knowing about it. If nothing else, it would not do to have the world know all about Giles yet. Too many knew already. He also did not want his enemies to think that the boy could be easily grabbed and used as a weapon against his father. Orion never wanted to face the choice of his son or his country.

It might be time to end his service to the Crown,

Orion thought. He had a third child now and could
not keep three children hidden away forever. Nor was
it good to continue to go away on assignment as he
had been doing, leaving behind no information on
how to reach him or even what name he might be
using. His work forced him to keep too many secrets.
It was satisfying to work for the Crown, even exciting
at times, but it certainly was not convenient nor was
it conducive to raising three sons.

Cursing softly, he turned his thoughts back to hunting down Giles and the little redheaded carriage thief.
Now was not the time to make important decisions
about his future. He would do that later. The fact that
he was puzzling over such matters showed him that it
would probably be wise to leave the service or at least
curtail his missions. He now had a family to worry
about, and to leave them behind, unprotected, could
easily prove fatal.

Several times he paused to speak to people he encountered, but it was not until he stopped to greet a
young farmer leading a calf down the road that Orion
heard anything more than an acknowledgment of
having seen the carriage. He had a very good idea of
where the woman was going, but confirmation never
hurt. When he asked about his carriage, the farmer
eyed him with suspicion and idly scratched at the thin,
ragged beard on his sharp chin. That display of mis-
trust told Orion that he had a chance of getting some
useful information.

"Which carriage are ye asking about, milord?"

"Sir, not m'lord. Just sir. I ask about the one being
driven by a small redheaded lady."

"Why?"

"Because it happens to be my carriage the woman is driving. She took it without my permission."

"That little woman stole a carriage from a man as big as you?" the famer asked, his skepticism clear to see.

"I am reluctant to use the word *stole*. It is a private matter. I just need to find her and my carriage. I am quite certain that she has no idea that my son was sitting within the carriage when she took it."

"The lad looked to be having a fine time when I saw him. Smiling and waving at me as the carriage passed me by. Not like the wee lad in the carriage that passed by before yours."

"A blue one with gold trim and four speckled grays pulling it?"

The farmer nodded. "Foolish to buy something so pretty, all blue and gold, only to drive it on roads like this one. It were not looking so fine when it went by me. Driver had to stop because old Jude was taking his sheep across the road. Man inside the carriage was hanging his head out the window and yelling at old Jude and them sheep as if that would be making them move faster."

Orion smiled faintly when the young man laughed at the memory of the incident. "That must have been a fine sight."

"Oh aye, it were that. But then I saw the boy. Little lad with a lot of black curly hair and big blue eyes. He was looking out the window at me and he was fair sad, he was. Poor wee fellow looked some scared, too. Odd and all, for I thought I saw some light behind him, but that must have been something else, for the fool shouting at Jude and his sheep would have been blocking the light from the other window. The boy looked to me like he was trying to get the door open and I do swear, I think he was saying *help me*. Thought to go a little closer, but then the fool yanked the lad away from the window and, from what I could see, slapped him fair hard."

"So they moved on after that?"

"Moved along just as I was thinking I would still go talk to the lad and see what was wrong. 'Bout two hours later that lady came by driving your carriage and your boy did not look sad at all. Nay, he did not. Was grinning like a fool, he was. As I done said, having himself a fine time."

"Yes, that would be just like Giles."

"You thinking she stole the boy, too? Took your son?"

Orion hesitated only a moment before shaking his head. "No, I do not. As I said, she just did not know he was in there and he does not seem to be inclined to let her know." Honesty weighted his words for he was beginning to think Cody had been right. "I begin to believe that she is chasing the man in the blue-and-gold carriage because he took her son."

"A sad business."

"It is that."

"Well, you will be getting him back soon enough. The team pulling your carriage was looking weary, it was. She will have to be stopping soon."

Now he had to worry about his team, Orion thought, and silently cursed before asking the man when he had seen the second carriage. He left the young farmer and traveled on after discovering that his carriage was not all that far ahead of him. The more information he gathered the more he began to think Lady de Warrenne was doing just what she told Cody she was doing. She was chasing down a man. Orion had the sinking feeling that the sad boy in the first carriage was her son. It was not a mess he wanted to be dragged into, but he had to get his son and his carriage back.

As he rode on he began to notice a difference in the trail he followed. The farmer had been right. His horses were tiring. The team was never intended to pull the carriage at a rapid pace for so long. He had intended to set an easy pace when taking Giles to Radmoor, and an easy pace back to the city after allowing the team a rest or perhaps even changing horses at Radmoor. Orion did not believe he could count on a woman to have the experience to judge when her team needed a rest, and the thought of how she could harm his team stirred his anger anew.

When he caught sight of his carriage pulled off to the side of the road, he feared that she may have irreparably damaged one of his horses, but then he saw his team. The horses were placidly grazing beneath a tree. His son and the little redheaded woman he had been chasing were seated on the ground enjoying the food he had had packed for him and Giles.

It was more than his barely leashed anger could tolerate. Orion reined in next to the carriage, dismounted, and marched toward the woman who had caused him so much trouble. The look of fear on her face as he approached her both satisfied and disturbed him. When she leapt to her feet and put herself between him and his son, he refused to allow admiration to dim his anger. He did not like frightening a woman, but she deserved it. Orion decided it might just teach her some much needed caution. He would make certain that next time she would think twice about what she took without permission.

Chapter Three

Catryn stared at the tall man striding toward her as she leapt to her feet and moved to put herself between the man and the boy in case this man was a threat. The way Giles moved to her side and grinned told her that this man was his father, or at least someone he knew, but her unease did not fade much. Her first clear thought was that no man had the right to look so handsome, especially when he also looked so furious. His clothing marked him as gentry as clearly as his fine horse did. At some point during his pursuit of her, his midnight-black hair had come undone and flowed back from his finely carved face in thick waves as he moved rapidly over the grass. Straight dark brows met in a vee over his perfect angle of a nose and, as he got near enough for her to see, his eyes were revealed to be a very stormy blue.

"I believe you have something of mine," he said and placed a hand on Giles's shoulder. Then he glanced at his horses and carriage. "Two somethings."

Those statements deserved a reply, but it took

Catryn a moment to think of one. The man's voice was deep and a little rough. It stirred her in a way that made her heart beat faster. She wanted to think about why it did that, and how a man's voice could affect her so, but quickly shook aside her fascination and curiosity. Now was a bad time to succumb to some odd feminine fluttering over a very handsome man.

"Yes, I do, and I can explain that," she said and watched one of his brows cock upward. "I borrowed your carriage but had no idea at all that the boy was inside. I would never have taken the carriage if I had." A little voice in her head whispered that that was probably a lie, that she would just have made sure the boy got out before taking the carriage.

"So if you had known that my young son was within the carriage, you never would have stolen it."

His tone left her in no doubt that he thoroughly disbelieved her claim. "Exactly." She frowned and fought down the guilt she was feeling over her actions, for that guilt could weaken her defense. "And I did not steal it. I borrowed it."

"Taking a man's possessions without asking his permission is theft."

"Only if one does not intend to return those possessions, and I left you my mare in trade."

Orion realized his anger was rapidly waning. The woman stood there arguing earnestly with him, yet there was a hint of fear to be read in her wide, sea-green eyes. Her beauty had caught his eye from the moment he saw her, but he had refused to allow it to dim his righteous anger. The somewhat ridiculous defense she was making was doing just that, however, and his appreciation of her beauty was rising to the fore again. He had to struggle to cling to at least some scrap of his rapidly fading suspicions about her.

She might, if she stood up very straight, reach his collarbone so that he could rest his chin upon the thick curls of her dark red hair. Short and slim though she was, he could see the womanly curves shaping her travel-stained gown. Considering the aids a woman could employ beneath her clothes to add to her shape, he knew he could be misjudging the true curve of her hips, but there was little doubt that she possessed a magnificent bosom, the curve of her breasts full and smooth above the neck of her soft gray gown. Being a man who unabashedly favored a magnificent bosom, Orion had to force himself to keep his gaze on the woman's face.

There he saw a sweet innocence beneath the beauty, which made him quell the fleeting thoughts of seducing her. Orion divided women into two groups—those he could seduce if he chose to, the ones who knew how to play lovers' games, and those he would never try to seduce because they could not separate their hearts from the pleasures two bodies could share. This woman might be a thief, but instinct told him she was one of the latter sort. That was the type of woman a confirmed bachelor avoided at all costs, and he was a very confirmed bachelor. And that, he thought, was a damned shame.

"You believed a maimed horse was an even trade for a team of horses, a carriage, and my son?"

"Sorley was not maimed. She will heal with a little care," Catryn said.

"And she did not know I was in the carriage," Giles said and shrugged when Orion frowned at him. "If you could have seen her face when I appeared, you would know the truth of that. Near scared her out of her skin when I stepped out and showed meself."

"It still does not exonerate her from the charge of theft," said Orion.

"She had a good reason for doing that. Someone kidnapped her son and she is chasing him. She could not do that on a lame horse, could she, and there was your carriage all set and ready to be driven off. I am thinking you need to stop leaving it there so ill-guarded and ready to go."

"Are you now?"

"Well, it does get borrowed a lot."

"Which is why I hired Cody, but she pulled a pistol on him when she stole my carriage."

"She just needed to stop him from stopping her from borrowing it."

Orion decided he would not get into an argument with a boy over the distinction between borrowing and stealing, especially a boy who had done quite a bit of both in his meager eight years of life. "Who are you?" he asked her, wondering if she would give him the same name she had given Cody.

"Lady Catryn Gryffin de Warrenne," she replied. "I told your man to speak to my father, Lord Lewys Gryffin at Gryffin House. He is the Baron of Gryffin on the Wold. He would willingly compensate you."

"I doubt he could compensate me for the plans I had made for the evening, the ones I was forced to cancel to chase you down." He smiled faintly when, after a brief moment of frowning, she blushed, revealing that she had understood his implication. "Who took your son?"

"His uncle, Sir Morris de Warrenne. The man has been fighting us over the inheritance left to Alwyn by my late husband and just lost yet another fight to gain control over my son, the de Warrenne lands, and the money. He did not take it well, but I never expected him to do this. By custom, I suspect he should have been named Alwyn's guardian, but my husband never trusted his brother Morris, so he named my father Alwyn's guardian in his will. My husband may not have been the best husband, and actually he was a terrible husband, but he was careful to do all that was needed to make sure Alwyn got all his birth gave him the right to. He knew Morris would never do that, or honor his wishes."

"Do you fear for your son's life?"

Catryn opened her mouth to reply with a resounding no, but the words would not come. It was something that had worried her briefly, but she had pushed that concern aside and then talked herself out of it, if only for the sake of her sanity. She could not do so this time. The thought of how Morris might react to Alwyn's childish game of speaking to his unseen friends had obviously brewed in her mind long enough to be a deep concern now. There was also the simple fact that Morris could gain a great deal of wealth in land and money if Alwyn was gone. The panic such thoughts stirred in her heart was difficult to subdue.

"I believe I do, although I have never had such a fear before," she replied, tasting the truth of her own words. She could not thank this far-too-handsome man for putting that worry in her mind, either.

"The man never took the boy from you before,

either, did he? Or try to. Perhaps this latest defeat in the courts has made him see that he can never win his case there and must now take a more drastic action."

"I need to talk to my father," Giles said as he grabbed Orion by the hand and started tugging him away from Catryn. "We will be but a moment."

"I still have questions for the lady, Giles," Orion said. "Can this not wait?"

"Nay, it cannot wait."

It was not easy, but Catryn stood where she was as Sir Orion and young Giles walked away from her. For a moment she glanced between the boy and his father and the horse the man had ridden up on. The gelding was strong and made for speed. It could help her catch Morris and get Alwyn back.

She shook her head, crossed her arms over her chest, and silently cursed. The horse had been used as hard as the team pulling the carriage had been. It needed to rest as much as the other beasts did. Her heart urged her to grab the horse and race after her son, but common sense told her that she would not get far. All she would accomplish was to run that horse into a state of dangerous exhaustion and end up stranded on the road as night fell, still without her son. Yet she could not be certain this man would allow her to use either the carriage or the horse once the animals were rested. It was an untenable situation and she had a strong urge to scream.

As she waited for the boy to finish speaking with his father, Catryn struggled to recall anything she could about the man. He had not done her the courtesy of introducing himself, but Giles had told her all she needed to know. Sir Orion Wherlocke was not anyone she knew, however. She had heard some bits of gossip about the Wherlockes and their close relations, the Vaughns, but could recall very little of it and certainly nothing that inspired her to believe this man would help her.

It appeared that she was going to have to go to whatever authorities she could to try and get her son back. She had hoped to keep all this trouble private and settle it herself. The few people in authority she had dealt with since her husband had been attacked and died of stab wounds had not been very helpful or capable. Catryn suddenly had an urge to sit down and cry, for she could foresee weeks, even months, of waiting to get her son back.

"Look, you done made her all sad," said Giles, frowning toward Catryn.

"She stole my carriage and you," said Orion. "She disrupted my very carefully made plans for the day. And night. She held a gun on Cody."

"Pfft." Giles waved a hand in dismissal. "You can charm another skirt, and she would never have shot Cody."

Although his son's confidence in his skill at charming women was rather flattering, Orion was a little discomforted that the boy knew exactly what he had been planning to do tonight. "How can you be so certain that she would not have actually shot Cody?"

Giles shrugged. "I just am. I know these things. Always have. She is no danger to anyone. Not even the bastard who took her son. Well, unless the fool actually hurts the boy, and then I think she would show him a fury that would scare the biggest brute alive. Dockside rats would probably run from her."

Orion did not have Giles's apparent skill at knowing how people felt but believed his son was right about how the woman would react if her child was harmed. "This is not our business, not our trouble to deal with."

"I think it is, and not just because the man took her son and it would only be right and honorable to help her get her child back."

"That was well said. A palpable hit."

"Thank you."

"What other reason could there be?"

"I think her son may have some Wherlocke blood."

Orion frowned and looked toward the little redhead pacing the ground over near the carriage. "I see none in her."

"I could not say where it might come from, but I think he has a gift like Lady Pen has. He can see spirits." Giles nodded when his father looked at him in surprise.

"She told you that?" Orion wondered if he was in danger of being taken in by a pretty face, a woman who knew all about the Wherlockes and thought to use some false connection to get to one of the family for her own gain.

"Nay, not exactly. She was ranting about how she would never catch that Morris fellow now and worrying out loud about what he might do to her boy. Said the man never spent much time with little Alwyn and might not be kind when her son played his little game of talking to people no one else could see."

"Children do that from time to time. It does not mean they talk to spirits. Just a make-believe friend. I believe it is common among children who have few playmates."

"Nay. This is more than that, and not all of the ones he talks to are children, playmates, or friends he makes up in his head. He also has hair like mine."

"How do you know that?"

"I am fair sure I saw him. That blue-and-gold carriage went by and I saw a little boy peering out of the window. It was a real quick look but he had black hair. That is the carriage we are after."

Orion softly cursed. His son was the third person to mention that the boy had black hair, something the child had certainly not gotten from his mother. Yet, if her son truly was speaking to the dead, and at such a young age, then his connection to the Wherlockes or the Vaughns was not in doubt. If the boy had a gift, it was definitely the mark of one of his kin; far more of a mark than his black hair. It was now not just a need to help a woman rescue her child that would motivate Orion to assist her, but the need to save one of his own.

He looked at his newfound son and inwardly grimaced. Here was yet another one who was showing early signs of a strong gift. Most of his family showed hints of the gift they had been born with while still in their childhood, but it did not usually grow strong until puberty; although just lately there appeared to be a lot more children revealing a strong gift early in life. Giles revealed a true skill at knowing how people felt, what was in their hearts and minds. He might need to go to Elderwood, the family seat, and train with Aunt Dob, as Modred, the Duke of Elderwood and the head of their whole family, was. God help the boy, he thought, if he was to be cursed with Modred's gift. It would be difficult for him to find peace anywhere. His future could well be to live as reclusive a life as poor Modred did.

Shaking aside his growing concern for his son, Orion thought about the woman who was trying to retrieve her own child. Inheritance battles were far too common and very messy. It also usually ended badly for the one who held what others in the family wanted or thought should be rightfully theirs. This time the heir was a small boy, one who could well carry Wherlocke or Vaughn blood, and every instinct he had told him to join her in getting the child safely home. He suspected he would have decided to do so anyway for it was a crime he could not, in all good conscience, ignore, but the possible connection to his family only increased his desire to help her.

"She fears the man might hurt the boy?" The easiest way to get one's hands on an inheritance was to kill the true heir, he thought, and he knew it happened more often than people knew.

"She does, but I cannot see any gain in that for him. Not yet."

"Perhaps not, but there will be at some time during the next few years if he can gain control of all the boy holds. So, I suppose it behooves us to put a stop to this thievery."

"Aye, since the one being stolen, and will be stolen from, is one of ours."

"You do seem very sure of that."

"I am." Giles smiled and shrugged. "No use asking why, either." He slapped his hand over his heart. "The knowledge rests here and that is enough for me."

"Enough for me as well. Let us go and tell her of her great good fortune in gaining us as allies." He smiled when Giles laughed and they both walked over to Lady Catryn.

Catryn watched the man and boy approach. They shared a look. No one who gazed upon the pair together for long could ever mistake just whose son Giles was. Although she found just a bit unsettling the way Giles too often seemed more adult than child, she had to admire the way Sir Orion treated the boy with respect, not like some errant child or one who had not yet faced all the hardships life had to offer. There was a sharp mind in that child's head and it was good to see that his father respected that.

"I need to tend to my horse, have a little of that food you and Giles were enjoying, and then we shall be on our way," Sir Orion said.

"I cannot return to London," Catryn said, trying desperately to keep the panic out of her voice. "That would allow Morris to succeed in getting away with Alwyn. I need to stay close on his trail or I may never find him."

"You will not be returning to London. Giles and I have decided that we shall lend you our assistance in retrieving your child."

Catryn opened her mouth to thank the man kindly but refuse the offered help and found herself staring at his back as he walked away to tend to his horse. She was not sure what to say anyway. The offer of help was extremely tempting. Caught up in chasing Morris, she had given little thought to the fact that she was a woman alone on the road. Any woman traveling alone faced a great many dangers. It was not a lack of ability to handle the matter of travel that had women dragging men with them everywhere they went, but a simple acknowledgement of the need for one to keep the many potential dangers at bay. Yet she did not know this man, and for all she knew, he could be one of those dangers.

She looked at Giles, who just smiled that cocky little grin he so often did. He had won her trust quickly, for there were no shadows in him. Giles did not hide behind a pretty face and practiced words; she wondered if he had the wit to know if his father did. A boy who had just found a family, been claimed by his father, might be blind to the man's faults. Children did not wear masks but grown men did. Sir Orion had a very pretty mask, one that could easily beguile a woman, but there could be something ugly lurking behind it. Catryn wished she was better at seeing through such pretense. Her choice of husband had definitely revealed a weakness in that area.

"I am not certain it is wise for you and your father to assist me," she said.

"You cannot be traveling alone," Giles said in a tone that would have done a dictatorial father proud. "Women should never do that. I am no true protection, although I am very good at slipping away and hiding. My father can protect you as we look for your boy."

"He must have other business to attend to."

"I do," said Orion as he walked past her and Giles and sat down to help himself to some of the food. "It is nothing that cannot wait, however."

Catryn moved to sit facing him. "This is my battle. You do not even know who I am or if my story is true."

"As it happens, I do know that the story you told me is true. I met a colleague on my way here and his brother is a solicitor in the firm that your brother-in-law has hired. Seems your brother-in-law is considered a very troublesome client."

"Society is an annoyingly small word full of gossip," she grumbled, hating the idea that everyone knew of her fight with Morris, even if he was the one considered the villain in the tale.

"It certainly is. You, I do not know, and I believe I neglected to properly introduce myself when I arrived. I am Sir Orion Wherlocke, the father of this boy you ran off with."

"I truly did not know he was in the carriage." She frowned at Giles. "And he made no sound, did not cry out at all."

"I was curious about what you were about," said Giles when both adults looked at him. "Knew you were no threat to me."

"How could you be so certain of that?"

"I know things."

Catryn wanted to ask what he meant by that but decided it was not what was important now. Her son had been with Morris for hours. She could only imagine how scared her little boy was. The only thing she needed to think about was how quickly she could get to him.

"I really must be going," she said and began to stand up.

"Sit," ordered Sir Orion.

She sat and then scowled at him, blaming him for her immediate obedience. Catryn knew that if she did not leave soon she would be accepting his offer of help. She did not wish to weaken and do so. The problem she faced was hers; it concerned her family, and her son. She should deal with it herself, and she knew this man was about to skillfully show her all the reasons she could not do so.

"There is very little daylight left," she protested. "If you are concerned about your carriage . . ."

"Your father will compensate me," he finished for her. "I am not offering to help you because I am bored or have nothing else to do. I am offering because someone has stolen your child, because the theft has to do with a man wanting everything that child holds a rightful claim to. Those are crimes I cannot ignore. My family is very firm on the need to protect children—primarily our own, but I believe any one of my family would be ready and eager to assist you. As Giles said, it is only honorable and right to do so."

There was such a wry tone to his last words that Catryn had to smile. "And you always do as your son says?"

"Not at all. If I did, we would have an elephant in the back garden."

"Oh dear." She glanced at a grinning Giles and then laughed.

"Quite. No, in this he is utterly correct. A man has stolen your child, a man who covets all that belongs to

the boy, and we both know how dangerous that is."
He nodded when she paled. "There is no proof that he
means the boy harm, but even if he does not, he could
gain guardianship of the boy and bleed your son's inheritance dry."

"He might try, but there are strict rules and . . ."
Her words faded away when he and his son shook
their heads.

"Rules can be circumvented. My cousin Penelope,
now the Viscountess of Radmoor, nearly lost every
penny of her inheritance through the machinations
of her stepfather and then her stepsiblings. Her half
brothers did, too. If this Morris gains control, and he
may be able to do so now that he actually holds the
child, he will steal all he can. Do not doubt that."

She could not. It had been a worry from the first
moment Morris had taken them to court. She knew
that if Morris gained complete control of Alwyn, he
would leave the boy with nothing. What should
have been a blessing, a tidy inheritance so that Alwyn
did not have to worry about his future, had become
a curse.

"No, I do not doubt that," she admitted softly.

"If Giles and I leave you to carry on by yourself, I
foresee only disaster. Even if you caught up with
Morris and could deal with him on your own, I sincerely doubt Morris is alone. Then there are all the
other reasons women do not travel unattended by a
male, family or servant. The least that could happen
to you is that you would have my carriage taken from
you and be left on foot."

"I have a pistol."

"Which means, if you know how to use it with any accuracy, you could take down one man. After that you must depend upon your own strength to fight off the others, and there would be others." He nodded when she scowled at him. "You could be well-versed in fisticuffs, but you are still a small woman who could be, if not easily, at least eventually overpowered."

"This could take days, you realize," she said after a moment of silence that even she recognized as sulking.

Sir Orion shrugged as he packed up the remainder of the food. "I have nothing planned and nowhere to go. I must simply send a note to Penelope to let her know that Giles will arrive later and not today. I can do that when we stop for the night. And we will be stopping for the night," he said firmly when she opened her mouth to argue that plan. "So will Morris. The chances of catching him today are very slim. As you said, this could take a few days." He held out his hand.

With a sigh of resignation she took it and he helped her to her feet. "I should have come home earlier," she muttered.

"Would that have made a difference?"

She sighed. "In truth, I doubt it. Morris stormed into the house and had a hired brute, as my father called him, with him. They fought with my father, knocked him about, and took Alwyn. I suspect they would have just knocked me about as well. Morris must have known it was the servants' day off and that there would be no help from that quarter."

"So you already knew he had hired ruffians with him when you set out after him all on your own."

"He has my child."

"Of course." Sir Orion moved to hitch the team to the carriage.

Catryn was surprised that there was no note of condescension or mockery in his words. The man simply accepted that she had no choice, that the fact that Morris had her child was explanation enough for her risky behavior. It could be that he told the truth when he expressed his whole family's belief in the need to protect children.

Her next thought was that she was about to ride around the countryside with a man who was not her kin, fiancé, or husband. Racing over the roads, driving a carriage, and traveling unattended had been bad enough. Traveling with a very handsome single gentleman would truly cause a lot of gossip. If anyone they knew saw them, her name would be blackened within society in mere days.

She hastily pushed aside that thought as she watched him hitch his mount to the rear of the carriage. If it happened, it happened, and she would accept the consequences of her actions. Alwyn was in danger. Whatever it cost her to get him home and safe again was worth it. The fact that they were trying to save her son would be enough to keep her closest friends at her side, she hoped.

When Sir Orion held out his hand to help her into the carriage, she took it and nearly yanked it back a heartbeat later. Neither of them was wearing gloves, having removed them to eat. The first time their skin had touched as he had helped her stand, her mind had been so preoccupied she had barely noticed the brief brush of his skin against hers. This time her whole body responded to it. That had never happened to her before and it unsettled her, but she forced her mind back to the problem of hunting for Morris and getting her son back.

"Should I not ride up on the box?" she asked, hesitating to get into the carriage.

"If you think the sight of you racing down the road driving a carriage with all that bright hair flying about your face was enough to cause talk, then just consider what talk will ensue if you are seen riding up there with me as we race down the road."

Catryn got into the carriage. He was right. Again. It was very annoying. Giles sat across from her and smiled. *At least someone is enjoying the adventure,* she mused. The boy's insistence that he and his father help her save Alwyn did surprise her a little.

"You truly believe this is what you and your father should do?" she asked as the carriage began to move.

"I do," Giles replied. "Your son is just a wee lad and has not had the rough life I have had. I have skills. Had to learn them, aye? He has none. He is very scared, I am thinking, and it is only right that we men ride to help him."

"It might not be so simple. We have to find Morris first."

"Oh, my father can do that. Finding people and things is one thing he is very, very good at."

There was no point in arguing about that, so Catryn looked out the window. Her whole body was weary and ached right down to the bone. It was nice to have someone else driving the carriage, but she swore she would not allow herself to depend upon Sir Orion too much. She had depended on her husband, only to find out within months that there was little in the man anyone could depend upon. She had depended on her grandfather and father, and that had not turned out well, either, although her father had had the excuse of being lost in his own grief for a while. For now, however, she would savor the rest from driving the carriage and pray that they found her son soon.

Chapter Four

The rapidly encroaching dark settled Orion's uncertainty about stopping or continuing on just a little farther. He comforted himself with the knowledge that the man he was pursuing could not continue for much longer, either. There was no doubt in his mind that he would find the man, no matter where Morris tried to hide, but he would rather not have to leave the country to accomplish it.

Yet again he wondered what would be the right thing to do when he found Morris. The man would have guards, servants, or some hired brutes with him. Orion had just himself, a little redheaded lady, and a boy of eight. That did not make for good odds.

As the carriage crested a small rise, he saw lights and knew they were drawing close to a village. It had been a long time since he had traveled this way, but he was confident that this village had a comfortable inn. A good meal and a clean bed would be welcome. Sharing that bed with a lush little redhead would be even more so, but Orion pushed aside that temptation. Lady Catryn Gryffin de Warrenne was not some adventurous widow. Not only was she trying to get her stolen child back but she reeked of innocence and was most certainly a complete romantic at heart. Giving in to the temptation to bed her, even for one glorious night, could get him entangled in something he had long avoided: a relationship that was not the simple, enjoyable giving and taking of pleasure.

No, Lady Catryn was not a woman a man got sweaty with, kissed on the cheek in the morning, and then walked away from. Since that was the way he planned to live his life, Orion knew he had to keep his hands off her. He just wished his body agreed with his decision. It might be time to reach out to a few of his kin. Not only could they help him find Morris and save the boy, but they would act as a bulwark between him and the woman his body craved so badly.

The innyard was busy but not so busy that Orion feared he would find there was no room available for them. It was a large inn, rooms added as the traffic to and from London had increased over the years. The man who had built it had chosen his spot well, halfway between London and Portsmouth. He leapt from the box as soon as a tall, strapping young man wearing the inn's colors grabbed control of the team. Orion quickly sent a small lad into the inn to make certain he could have two rooms for the night and a private place to enjoy a meal. He hoped he would not have to argue with Lady Catryn about stopping, and reached for the handle on the carriage door.

Catryn blinked, slowly waking up when the carriage stopped. Giles grinned at her and then laughed softly when his stomach loudly protested its emptiness. She leaned toward the carriage door to open it, only to have it opened for her and find herself staring into Sir Orion's face.

He looked like a man who had just spent many an hour on a horse and then more time driving a carriage. Dust coated his fine clothes and his black hair was badly windblown. A few trickles of sweat had left trails through the light coating of dust on his face. Despite all of that, he was still the most handsome man she had ever seen. It annoyed her, for she was certain she looked as if she had been dragged through a hedgerow backward.

"Why have we stopped?" she asked as he helped her out of the carriage.

"If you look about you might notice that night has arrived," he replied, easily catching Giles as the boy flung himself out of the carriage and then setting the boy on his feet.

"But Morris . . ."

"Cannot drive through the night any more than we can. I told you that before we left that clearing."

That was a truth she could not deny, even though she desperately wished she could. Some would travel the road no matter what the conditions, changing horses as they needed them, but she could not see Morris doing that. He liked his comforts far too much. Long hours spent in a carriage were not what anyone would call comfort. He also lacked the coin for such a thing and he certainly would not trust his precious horses into the long-term care of some stable boy at an inn. From what little she had ferreted out concerning Morris's financial state, Catryn was not sure that he had the money needed to spend many nights at an inn, either.

"I am also tired, hungry, and in need of a good wash," he said as he collected her bags, shoved them into her arms, and then got a small one of his own from beneath the carriage seat. "And it does not matter how the man travels or where he goes. I *will* find him."

Before she could argue with that arrogant statement, he was striding toward the inn, Giles at his side. Catryn hurried to keep pace with him. Giles had told her that his father could find anyone and anything, but she had thought that was just a boy's bragging about his sire. It appeared that Sir Orion also believed it. It was an odd thing for a man to boast about.

Once inside the inn, Catryn was impressed by Sir Orion's ability to get people to do his bidding. He gave orders in a way that made them sound more like requests. People obeyed without hesitation or argument, just as she had back at the clearing when he had told her to sit. They were all in their rooms with a hearty meal being readied for them before she even had time to consider what she might want to eat.

She frowned as she quickly shed her travel-worn clothing, washed up, and donned a fresh gown. The man was obviously accustomed to being obeyed. Considering his excellent skills at command, that was no surprise, but Catryn was going to have to remind him that she was a grown woman, a widow, and a mother. She was more than capable of making up her own mind. The first thing she intended to do was request that a bath be readied for her so that she could have a long soak in hot water after her meal.

The second was to make certain Sir Orion understood that she could pay her own way. She might have need of a man to rescue her son, an admission that still irked her, but she did not need one to lead her about like some helpless child.

Her husband had tried that, she thought as she made her way down to the private parlor where she, Sir Orion, and Giles would dine. Old resentments she thought she had conquered rose up and she struggled against the anger they brought with them. Sir Orion did not deserve being stung by that bitterness.

She paused to request her bath, asking that her travel clothes be cleaned as well, and paid for it, which further soothed her rising temper. When she entered the parlor she found Giles and Sir Orion seated at a table before a warm fire, slathering butter on large hunks of bread. They immediately rose and Sir Orion held a chair out for her.

"My apologies," she said as she sat down and they retook their seats. "I tried to be quick."

"You were remarkably quick," said Orion as he served her some bread and nudged a small crock of butter toward her. "I told the maid not to bring the rest of the food in until she saw you come downstairs. Did not wish it to sit there tempting us and getting cold until you arrived."

She started to ask why he would think she would take so long that their meal would grow cold when the maid and two young boys brought in the food and drink. Catryn was tempted to have some of the wine but chose cider instead, for she wanted to be certain she woke in the morning with a clear head. As the scent of roasted chicken and a nice array of potatoes and vegetables hit her nose, it made her all too aware of just how hungry she was. Catryn knew she was about to break one of the rules ladies were all taught to follow. She was not going to eat sparingly.

And was that not a silly thing to be concerned about, she thought and nearly laughed. She was at an inn and was traveling with a man who was no relation to her and not her husband. Even a widow would raise eyebrows by doing so. It did not matter that the man she was with had his son with him, either. Anyone who recognized her, unless they were the closest, dearest of friends, would be utterly scandalized. How much she ate was the least of her concerns.

"I want you to tell me everything you can about your brother-in-law," Orion said.

"What good will that do?" she asked. "You already know what he has done and why."

"Everything can be useful. It will help me judge what route he may take, what decisions he might make along the way, and perhaps even what sort of place he would stop at."

"Well, he is much like a spoiled child, to tell the truth. He wants what he wants when he wants it but has never had the character to even stick to the fight needed to get it. It is why I was so surprised that he would keep at us in the courts. That was very unlike him. It would have been much more like him to try and destroy something that had been left to Alwyn, such as trying to burn the manor house down or the like."

"Despite the fact that he wants it?"

"That would not occur to him until he calmed down. And even then, he would find satisfaction in the fact that, since he could not have it, now neither could Alwyn. As I said, much like a spoiled child."

"Do you think that sort of behavior is why your husband did not name him your son's guardian?"

Catryn grimaced and ate a piece of delicious herb-seasoned chicken as she thought over her answer. "Henry did not like Morris, did not trust him. Morris felt much the same about Henry. I often wondered if Morris disliked his brother just because he was born first, actually faulted him for that. In most other ways, they were very much alike in their habits and vices, so one would have thought they would have been close. Yet, though my husband did love to gamble, he most often won and never approached that cliff where just one more ill-advised bet will beggar you. Morris was never so careful."

Orion nodded and sipped at his wine. "So your husband was certain that all he had clung to would be lost if Morris was in control."

"Yes. Morris cannot seem to resist a bet, a chance to rake in huge winnings. He always thinks he has found the perfect way to fill his purse without working. He is prone to believing anyone who promises him a massive return on an investment. My husband was forever covering his losses, at least covering them enough so that Morris did not end up in prison or worse."

"Did Morris stay with you very often?"

"No. They could not abide each other's company much, and that suited me. I do not like or trust Morris and never have. The fact that Henry felt the same was a relief. I was sad that my son had no fond uncle to turn to from time to time, especially since my husband had so little to do with him, but it was just a brief, occasional sadness caused by watching other uncles with their nieces and nephews. Another man to teach Alwyn how to go on would have been nice. My father does what he can, but he should not be having to raise another child."

"And how does Morris treat you?"

"What do you mean?"

"Does he treat you with courtesy and the respect due his brother's wife, or is he dismissive, scornful, and reveals resentment that you gave his brother a child?"

"Oh, he was always polite as he should be, but no more than that."

Orion had the feeling that was not all, but he did not press her on the matter. "How did your husband die?"

"Stabbed. He had been at one of his clubs, so he said, and was attacked on the way home. Robbed and stabbed several times. The wounds became infected and he died." She smiled faintly when his lovely blue eyes narrowed. "I, too, wondered if Morris had something to do with it, but the men were caught and confessed. They had simply seen a fine gent strolling home and saw a chance for some gain. He fought and they fought back. They won. For the moment. Their victory and new wealth was short-lived. They were hanged a year later, and even when facing that gruesome end, they said nothing about anyone having hired them or even told them where Henry would be. I do think Henry died wondering if his brother had had anything to do with it, for he ranted about his brother while fevered."

Orion turned his attention to finishing his meal as

he thought over all she had told him. Despite what the men who had killed her husband had said, there was always the chance that Morris had had a hand in her husband's death. It was possible to arrange a person's death without actively taking part in the planning. Simply talking loud enough about the person's plans, wealth, and direction within the hearing of known thieves could be enough. It was something to consider. He doubted Morris grieved his loss.

Glancing quickly at Catryn, he thought on how little grief there had been in her telling of the tale. Not a hint of loss or sorrow had been evident in her words. She could have been speaking of someone she had only known in passing. There had been a few other hints that her marriage had not been a happy one, something all too common amongst the *ton*. It was not just his family that suffered from broken or dismal unions, but few of the ones outside of his clan suffered as much desertion as his.

It was too bad she was such a good woman, he mused. She was a widow ripe for seduction. A bad marriage often left a woman yearning for something more, some passion and pleasure. Orion knew he could give her that. He had left behind enough satisfied women to have confidence in his skills in the bedchamber. Unfortunately, Lady Catryn was too good a woman, despite her recklessness in chasing after her child, something he could not help but admire.

"Giles said you worry about how Morris will treat the boy if he hears young Alwyn talking to people who are not there," he said, and almost smiled when she gave Giles an accusatory look and the boy just shrugged.

"It is just a child's game, but yes, I am worried that

Morris will have no patience with it," she replied. "I have tried my best to make Alwyn understand that his little game can upset some people, but he is, after all, only five, and sometimes forgets. I just fear that Morris is one of those who will find it very upsetting. He is a very superstitious fellow."

"Is he now. That will help."

"How so?"

The serving girl entered with some stewed apples, small cakes, and cream, so Catryn had to wait for her question to be answered. She took the time to think about every instance where she had noted Morris's superstitious nature. Although she did not know how such information could help Sir Orion, she wished to give him as much as she had. By the time the maid left and they had each helped themselves to some of the treats set before them, she was a little surprised to discover that her memories revealed that Morris was actually very superstitious, very concerned about all those shadows in the dark that others ignored once they left childhood.

"A superstitious man acts differently than one who is not troubled by such things," Orion said as soon as the door closed behind the maid.

She thought about that for a moment and nodded. "Yes, I suppose he would. I was just realizing that Morris is very superstitious, very worried about ghosts and goblins and things that go bump in the night. It is as if he never matured past the age where he feared what was under the bed."

"There is sometimes good reason to fear what is under the bed, so to speak. A man like that," he continued before she could remark on his words, "will not stay in an inn named, let us say, the Devil's Horseman. He will travel on to one with a less ominous name. He may even do a few things that draw the attention of the people around him, like tossing salt over his shoulder if he spills it or becoming nervous just because a black cat walks by. Most people have a touch of superstition in them, and have limits as to what odd things they will accept with ease, but the worst of such fears have passed except in a few. I suppose he believes in such things as witches."

"Oh yes. There was a fair near us when we were at the country house, and Alwyn wished to go. So did I. But Morris refused to come with us because he said there was a witch there. He meant the gypsy, I suspect, who was doing her readings or whatever they are called. I thought he just used it as an excuse to hurry away from the country, because he left that day; but the more I thought on it, the more I realized he was serious."

"And exactly what does Morris look like? Tall, short, red hair, black hair?"

"He does have dark hair, but it is more of a very dark brown. Hazel eyes. Shorter than you and almost too thin. He prefers to wear his wig when out and about, for his hair is thinning. He also prefers his clothing to be as bright as his carriage. Morris is a bit of a dandy. Otherwise he is not one who would stand out in a crowd. There is nothing about him, aside from his bad taste in clothing, that would make you recall him if you ever met him."

"And your husband had dark brown hair?"

"Not as dark as Morris's, but yes. Why?"

"Because I begin to wonder if we have been following the right carriage, despite my inability to believe there could be two such gaudy carriages on the road. Everyone who has seen it has mentioned the small boy looking out of the window as having black hair, very black hair, rather like Giles's."

Orion noted the faint hint of color that came and went on her smooth cheeks. The boy's hair color had obviously troubled her. He wondered if he had judged her wrong, if she was more daring than he had thought her to be. Had she cuckolded her husband?

"I know." Catryn rubbed her forehead. Even speaking of Alwyn's hair, so different from hers or her husband's, or even her father's, never failed to give her a headache. "My father says that color shows up in our bloodline now and then. It goes back a long way."

"To some distant relative?"

"Yes, but he never told me who. I asked, but he said he would have to search the books he has on the family, and I soon forgot to remind him that I was waiting to know. It would have been nice to have a name to spit out every time someone noted that Alwyn's hair is an odd color for a redhead and brunet to produce. Always remarked upon ever so gently and politely, however."

He was not surprised by the bite in her words. It was easy to imagine just how such a prying inquiry would be made, and the poorly hidden implication behind it. Orion ignored the twinge of disappointment he felt over the fact that she had not cuckolded her husband, thus making her a prime target for seduction, especially since that twinge was overshadowed by how much it pleased him to have her innocence confirmed. What he saw now was more proof that Giles could be right:

Young Alwyn, even Lady Catryn, could be blood kin of the Wherlockes or Vaughns. Thin, watered down, distant though it might be, there was a chance the tie was there, lost in the midst of time and turmoil. It was very hard to vanquish all Wherlocke or Vaughn blood, however, which explained the occasional gift appearing in people who had never realized they were connected to his family.

"Does all this help? I have the feeling that you now believe we have gone from just following the man to, perhaps, having to hunt him down."

Orion pushed his dish aside and refilled his tankard with the last of the wine. "I do. If not immediately, then very soon. He will learn that you are hard at his heels and that he should alter his route to throw you off. It is what I would do."

"Then this is going to take far longer than you may have planned for, and may be far more difficult than I had anticipated. It might be wiser if I went to the authorities or hired someone."

"No, best to keep this all as private as possible. If it is made too public, the man might consider it best to get rid of the evidence of his crime." He nodded when she paled. "Keeping it private could be the best thing for the safety of your child."

"It is what I would prefer, but I also do not want to leave Alwyn in Morris's hands for too long."

"The boy will be freed of the man soon. I am very good at this, Lady Catryn, and that is not an empty boast. Everyone has a particular skill. Mine is finding people and things. The only thing that does trouble me is your opinion that Morris is much akin to a spoiled child. That would mean he is bad at planning, perhaps erratic, but it should only slow me down a little. I will still find him. The thing you must think on now is just what you want done with Morris when we find him and get your son back."

Catryn was still trying to decide about that as she took her bath. Morris had to be stopped, but just how she could do that without actually having him jailed or transported, she did not know. Such a judgment could be made only in the courts, where this whole situation would quickly end up the subject of public gossip and speculation, and she did not wish that either. Nevertheless, the constant court cases, and now this kidnapping of her child, were troubles that could not be allowed to continue.

"Maybe if he goes to a port, I will have a stroke of good fortune and he will fall into the water and drown," she muttered and then felt guilty for wishing death on anyone, even someone like Morris.

She did not need more guilt. She already felt more than enough for not telling Sir Orion the truth about Morris when he asked how the man acted toward her. Catryn simply could not say what she thought and suspected. It not only sounded vain but it was embarrassing. Morris had never actually pushed himself on her, but she had quickly become suspicious that some of his growing anger toward Henry had been because Morris coveted his brother's wife. Shortly after Henry died, Morris had been a little less discreet in his interest, shallow though she had known it to be, but she had soundly rebuffed him and he had then turned to the courts.

"Just thinking it sounds vain," she said to herself

and shook her head as she stood up and reached for a towel. "I should have told Sir Orion though, and let him decide."

Standing before the fire to stay warm as she rubbed her hair dry, she thought about Sir Orion. He was too handsome for any woman's peace of mind, but there was strength within him, a steadiness she had only ever sensed in her father. Despite his privileged position, his good looks and health, she knew without asking that he had known harshness in his life. And despite the fact that he had an illegitimate son, she could not shake the feeling that he was not actually some rake who bounced from woman to woman without any pause. He would understand, when she told him about what she thought Morris felt for her, that she was not just stroking her own vanity.

As she donned her night shift and crawled into bed, she tried to think of exactly how to tell Sir Orion that she thought Morris lusted after her. By the time the maid slipped in and removed the tub with the help of two other young women, Catryn still had no answer. Snuggling down beneath the covers, she decided it could wait. It was probably not important anyway. Morris had gone for her child, not for her, despite once asking her to marry him, and that was what they all had to concentrate on now.

"She is hiding something," Giles said as he crawled into the bed.

Orion looked at the bed and inwardly sighed. He had been planning to spend the night sharing a bed not with his son but with a lush, eager woman. Being

Lady Catryn's gallant knight was costing him. He stripped to his drawers and climbed into the bed. Crossing his hands behind his head, he stared up at the ceiling and considered what Giles had said.

"Yes, I believe she is. Something was there, behind her blithe words when she answered my question about how Morris treated her."

"Since she is a fair lass, I am thinking the man wanted under her skirts."

Orion looked at his son. The boy was frowning as if he would punch Sir Morris de Warrenne in the nose if the man were within reach. Something about Lady Catryn had captivated his son. The boy was on this journey for more reasons than curiosity and the need to help some child. It could be that Giles was experiencing his first infatuation, even if the boy would never recognize it as such.

"True. Crudely spoken, but true," said Orion.

"How are you supposed to say it?"

"That the man is intrigued by her, attracted to her, wants her for himself."

"Oh. Well, he is. Does. It embarrasses her, so that is why she did not say so. Is it important though?"

"Oh yes. It is important. Morris may even have anticipated that she would chase him down if he took her son."

Orion had to admit to himself that he would also like to punch Sir Morris de Warrenne for that. That intrigued him, for he had never before cared who else lusted after a woman he was interested in or even bedding. If she succumbed to any other seduction than his, he simply walked away. He did not share, but not for any deep emotional reason. Since he did not partake of any other woman's favors while he was involved with a lover, he had always expected the very same courtesy. Yet, the idea that Sir Morris may have eyed Lady Catryn with lust annoyed him. More than annoyed him. He wanted to blacken both of the man's eyes.

"So, he really does want everything his brother had, and taking the boy was part of a trap," said Giles.

"It could be, yet I begin to wonder if Sir Morris could actually plan anything as clever as that."

"Because he is like a spoiled child?"

"Exactly. He sounds like a man who has never been through the fire, shall we say. Easy childhood, got all he wanted when he wanted it, maybe did not get something he thought he needed, like the attention of his father or some such thing, and has never fully matured into a man."

"Buys fancy, eye-stinging clothes and carriages and resents a little boy for getting what he had never earned anyway."

Orion nodded. "Exactly right. And eye-stinging was a very good way of describing his taste."

"Thank you."

Turning his head, he shared a grin with his son but quickly grew serious again. "If we are right, and I believe we are, we may need to keep a close watch on her and our backs. As she told us, when Sir Morris wants something, he wants it now and does not take well to being denied. He could feel that she is not falling into his grasp fast enough and turn back to grab her."

"Ha! Just let the bastard try."

Orion had to bite back a laugh. He was continuously astounded by the spirit in his son. Despite what had happened to the boy, he still cared, even enjoyed life to its fullest. He laughed easily and played much as any other child would. One could almost forget that the boy had grown up on the dark, deadly streets of the city with little more care than that offered by his mates, who were not all that much older than he was, and the occasional kind-hearted or avaricious whore. His friends had taken him into their care, and that was why his family had more or less adopted the whole lot. They had more than proved their worth in what they had done for Giles.

"Go to sleep. We will need our rest, as I feel we will be spending a great deal of time rushing about the countryside."

Giles murmured an affirmative and closed his eyes. The boy was asleep in no time at all, and Orion felt his heart clench with strong emotion. Giles could not show him any more clearly how safe he felt with him than by falling asleep so easily and sleeping so deeply. Having had little to do with Paul's or Hector's up-bringing since they had been staying with his cousin Penelope since their own mothers had deserted them, Giles had not realized how easily a child could grab his heart and make it impossible to shake free. He knew it had nothing to do with Paul and Hector being luckier in how life had treated them, either. Once he had all three boys in his home at last, Orion suspected he would be having this trouble with his heart more often. Paul and Hector had just not had the chance to get a firm grip on it yet.

He turned his thoughts to Lady Catryn Gryffin de Warrenne. At the moment when he sensed she was hiding something, he had been annoyed; but the more he thought on it, the more he understood why she had said nothing. Unless Sir Morris had actually tried to seduce or molest her, all she had was her own impression of what the man might feel toward her. Without sufficient evidence, she might worry that she would sound vain or foolish if she spoke of Sir Morris wanting her.

It might be time to send word to some of his kinsmen. The added help in keeping an eye on her would be welcome, probably even wise, yet he still hesitated. Foolish it might be, but he suddenly wanted to do this himself. He could only hope that it did not prove to be a disastrous decision. Cursing softly, he finally admitted to himself that he wanted to be her hero. He had no idea where that urge came from as he had never felt the like before. All he could do was hope that the madness would pass quickly.

Chapter Five

Her heart pounding with fear, Catryn stared up at the first light of dawn streaking across her ceiling. Something bad was coming. She recognized all too well the chill in her blood, the heavy sense of foreboding, and the sour bite of fear in her mouth. In a way that she could never explain well, she always knew when danger approached. Not just danger to herself, either, but sometimes she could sense it approaching others.

Her father had called it instinct and had been rather fascinated by it. He had questioned her extensively and even researched it as much as he was able. Her mother had always found it unsettling, strongly advising her to keep very quiet about it, stressing many times that it was a secret she must hold on to very tightly. Good or bad, it was something she had suffered from for a long time, and she never ignored it.

Scrambling out of bed, she yanked off her nightdress and put on her clothes. Catryn was not sure how she could warn Sir Orion without sounding like a madwoman, but she knew she had to try. She could not hesitate. Whatever was coming, her strange instincts were telling her that it was more than she could deal with alone. It could also reach out and touch Sir Orion, even young Giles, and that was not something she could allow to happen just because she feared a little mockery. Sir Orion and his son were only with her because they wanted to help, and she could not remain quiet about the shadows coming their way.

Creeping across the hall, she opened the door to the room Sir Orion and his son shared, as quietly as she could. Instead of entering a room where two people slept peacefully, unaware of any danger, she found herself facing a man with a pistol. She fleetingly wondered if Sir Orion had the same instincts she did as he pulled her into the room and shut the door. He was certainly well prepared to face a threat. A moment later he lit a lamp and she got a good look at him. Her mind emptied of all rational thought.

Sir Orion stood before her wearing only his drawers and an undone fine linen shirt tossed over his broad shoulders. Catryn stared at his chest, a smooth expanse of taut muscle decorated with a modest triangle of black hair. She had seen a man's naked chest before, as Gryffin Manor was a working farm, and she had even caught a glimpse of her husband's once, but the sight had never left her so breathless and warm. Nor had she ever thought it a beautiful sight, but Sir Orion's chest made her palms itch to touch that faintly golden skin stretched so taut over lean, well-defined muscle. She had to clench her hands into tight fists to resist the urge to reach out and smooth them over all that warm skin.

Despite her efforts not to, she glanced down at his legs, his calves, and his bare feet. Even there the man could rouse any woman's hearty approval. He would need no padding to enhance those well-shaped muscular calves. She nearly shook her head in amazement for his feet were also a pleasant sight, being long and narrow. It seemed ridiculous to her that she would admire a man's feet, yet she could actually see herself enjoying the massaging of them after he was home from a long day. Perhaps even extending that tender administration to his strong calves, she mused, and then quickly banished such thoughts.

Pushing aside her fascination, she said, "Something bad is coming." Silently she cursed and decided the sight of him had certainly disordered her mind, for it was a ridiculous thing to say.

"Bad how?" he asked, hiding his amusement over the way she had nearly gaped at the sight of him and then looked annoyed at him for sparking the interest he had briefly glimpsed in her eyes. "Bad for us?"

It struck her as odd that he was so calmly accepting her statement, but forced her thoughts to remain fixed upon the warning she had come to give him and what they must do next. "It may sound mad, but I have always known when danger is close, and I woke suddenly with all of my alarms clanging. I do not have any idea what is coming, what the exact danger is, but it *is* coming and it is coming for us. I think we need to leave here now."

"No more than that? No hint of a vision of armed men, or Morris?"

"You need not make jest of me. I am quite serious."
She was surprised at how deeply it hurt to have this
man mock her.

"Oh, I do not jest. I but wished to be certain you
were not holding secret any more information because you feared I would mock how you said you came
by it. You did not get this sense of danger when your
son was taken?"

It was a shock to discover that he was not teasing
her but actually heeding what she said. "No. I do not
understand why, except to think that perhaps he was
not, at that time, in any real danger. What Morris was
going to do would be wrong and mightily troublesome but not dangerous. True, he hurt my father, but
not as seriously as I had feared, so even that might not
have been enough to make me sense a true danger."

"True. Get your things and bring them in here. I
will await whatever is coming in your bedchamber.
I suspect you are the one they are after."

She was entering her room before she really
thought about what he had just said. The man had believed her warning with no hesitation, no doubt, and
that still shocked yet warmed her. Even stranger, he
had inquired whether or not she had also had some
kind of vision. No one had ever done that before,
aside from her father, and even he had ceased doing
so when he saw how it upset her mother. Her warnings had only ever invoked doubt and fear in everyone else. That was why she had found it so easy to
follow her mother's advice to remain silent about
them.

That had not always been easy advice to follow,
either. The greater the danger, the stronger that un-

settling sense of doom. At times she had withheld her words of caution, resulting in harm to a person she could have warned, and she had always been left feeling intensely guilty. Her mother's assurances that the person would never have heeded her warnings anyway had done little to ease that guilt.

Catryn intended to ask Sir Orion why he had accepted her warning so blithely when she returned to his room after gathering all her things, but he was already dressed and checking his pistols. "You mean to face whatever is coming all on your own?"

"No," he replied. "While we waited for you in the private parlor last evening, I had a quick word with the innkeeper. I believed it might be wise to know if there was someone close at hand whom we could call on if we needed assistance. He said he had a man or two ready to help if needed, for a small fee. Giles has already gone down and said we have need of them, paid the fee, and come back."

"I should be paying for such things."

"I will make certain to keep a tally."

She ignored the sarcasm that dripped from his every word. "How will you explain how it is you know you have need of those men?"

"Simple," he said as he started out the door. "I will tell them you are a witch."

The door shut behind him on the last word of that outrageous statement. Catryn was tempted to run after him and hit him over the head with something heavy. These forebodings she suffered from were not something to make jests about. It was wonderful that he actually listened to her, but she would not tolerate him teasing her about it. When she returned she would also tell him how important it was to keep silent about her odd gift, just as she had done for most of her life. She had to make him understand how dangerous it could be for her if people became aware of how different she was.

Then she thought on how he was walking into danger, and nearly ran out to drag him back. She looked at Giles, who was sprawled on the bed calmly eating an apple. The boy did not seem very concerned about his father. She did not think it was because Giles had no understanding of what danger his father could be facing, because the boy had had a hard enough life to understand such things better than she might. Yet, he could also be suffering from a boy's absolute confidence in his father, even if it was not warranted. Sir Orion certainly looked fit, but he was a gentleman born and raised, not a man who lived a very hard life fighting for every scrap of food or a few coins to pay for his lodging. Having recalled a little of the gossip she had heard about the Wherlockes, she knew he did not live in some hovel near the stench of the river but in a fine town house in an area that was rapidly becoming fashionable, even though it was rumored to be inhabited mostly by Wherlockes and Vaughns.

"He does not even know what he might be facing," she said as she sat down on the edge of the bed.

"He is a king's man, m'lady. He knows what he is about."

"What do you mean by a king's man? What does he do for the king?"

Giles frowned. "I am not sure, but it is something important. Men come to visit and there is a lot of talking softly behind closed doors. That is always a sure sign that something important and secretive is about. At times he is gone for a few days and not because he found himself a woman, either. Though he does like the women and they like him. Cody said I was not to speak of it for it was important, secret things done for king and country. I think he finds things or people for the king or hunts bad people who need a quick hanging."

"And that is why he is so very certain he can find Morris and my son?"

"Aye." Giles threw his apple core into the fireplace. "That is what he does. That is his gift."

"I am not certain Morris is leaving us very much of a trail to follow."

"He is driving a fine blue carriage pulled by four speckled gray mares."

"Ah, true enough. That is certainly something people notice. I am so accustomed to the sight of it that I sometimes forget how it stands out even in the crowded streets of London." She nodded. "I discovered all anew how it catches the eye when I was chasing him. Everyone he passed noticed it and not always in a flattering way."

"And do not forget that my father found us easily enough."

That was a truth she could not argue with. Catryn sighed and settled her pistol on her lap. Since she was facing the door to the room, she would not have to worry about being caught by surprise. A glance over her shoulder at Giles revealed that the boy was keeping a close eye on the window even though it was rather small for any man to get through. Although it made her sad to think on why Giles would know how to be on guard for any danger, at the moment she was heartily glad of his skills, for it meant she did not have to worry about constantly watching out for him. Giles might be only eight, but he had survived all of those eight years living on the harsh streets of an unforgiving city. He had told her himself that he was very good at running and hiding. Now all she had to do was guard the door and hope that Sir Orion did not suffer any severe injuries during his kind attempt to help her.

Then something he had said blazed across her mind. He had said he wanted to be sure she was not keeping secret any more information just because she feared he would mock her. There was only one thing she had not told him, and for that very reason. Somehow she had given herself away and he knew she had not told him about how Morris might be lusting after her.

She inwardly cursed. That was not a conversation she wanted to have yet knew it was coming. If he had figured it out then he would demand some answers. A part of her wanted to tell him it was none of his business, but she knew that was wrong. It was his business. He was helping her find her son and deal with the idiot who had kidnapped him. He had a right to know everything about Morris, even if it was something that would embarrass her.

Sighing, she shook all concern about that out of her head. There was trouble headed their way and now was not the time to fret over what she had or had not told Orion or what he would ask her when he returned. And he would return, she thought, her body tensing with resolve. Catryn would not have it any other way. Nor would she allow anyone to come in and threaten Giles. That was all she had to keep her mind on now. Everything else could wait until the threat to them all was gone.

Orion nodded to the two men with him and they each moved to the sides of the door while he went and sat on the bed. The sound of men coming up the stairway was easy to hear. If he had not caught sight through the window of the two ruffians slipping inside the inn, he would have thought they were guests. The men Morris had hired had absolutely no gift of stealth. Obviously, Sir Morris was not paying well enough to get truly skilled thugs.

He hoped the innkeeper had not suffered any harm. Orion had told the man to give the men the information they requested, reluctantly but not too reluctantly. Since he was prepared for these men there was no reason for the innkeeper to guard a guest too avidly and suffer a hard beating for it.

For a moment he wondered if he was wrong to think Morris was behind this, but he inwardly shook his head. If this was an attack by enemies he had made, those people would never have hired such incompetent men. Orion knew, despite a lack of any proof, that this was an attempt by Morris to get his hands on Lady Catryn. She may have neglected to tell him about the man's interest in her, but he had planned with it in mind, so this attack came as no real surprise.

The footsteps stopped just outside the door and, to Orion's disgust, one of the men spoke with no attempt to keep his voice low. "Are ye sure it be this room?" he asked his companion.

A quick glance at his compatriots showed both men shaking their heads in disbelief at the idiocy of the men they were about to take down. He reminded himself that without Lady Catryn's warning, even these fools could have been a threat. He would have been back in his bed after relieving himself and possibly half-asleep, a state that slowed down any man's reactions. Lady Catryn would have been asleep in her own bed and helpless. His anger at Morris grew sharper as he thought on that.

"This is the one that fool downstairs told us to go to," answered the other.

"Hope she be no screamer. I hate screaming."

That the man would even mention such a thing told Orion that he had knowledge of how a terrified woman might act. He was sorry he would probably not have a chance to beat the fool. The man would not get his hands on Lady Catryn, but he deserved a beating for whatever he had done to know that he hated a woman's screams. A man using his greater strength and bulk against a woman was something he had never been able to tolerate. It had happened occasionally while working for the king, as spies and criminals came in all sizes, shapes, and were of both sexes, but those women were usually trying to kill someone.

The door slowly opened, creaking loudly with every careful inch, bringing Orion's attention fully back to the men. By now a smart man would realize all attempts at stealth were useless and rush the bed where their victim was supposed to be peacefully sleeping.

Orion was almost embarrassed by having the two men, Thomas and John, waiting on each side of the door with him. Anyone with just a little skill and wit could defeat these two idiots and he did not think it too vain to acknowledge that he had both. Now the only advantage to not being alone was that the whole capture-and-interrogate plan he had devised would proceed with much more ease and little bruising.

The moment the men stepped inside and started toward the bed, Orion's companions shut the door behind them and stood with their pistols aimed at the men's backs. Orion lit the lamp by the bed before the men could think of the possibility of there being a hostage they could use and then aimed his pistol at them.

"Might we assist you, sirs?" he asked and was pleased to see both men pale. "Disarm them," Orion ordered his two men, and then he shook his head when both of the intruders fumbled with their coat pockets a heartbeat before Thomas and John relieved them of their weapons. "Slow. Too slow. Too loud. Too stupid."

"Hey!" the bigger of the two cried, looking outraged despite standing there in the bedchamber of a woman he intended to kidnap, unarmed, and with three pistols pointed at him.

Orion ignored them as Thomas and John set two chairs behind the men. "Sit down," he ordered Morris's men and nodded at his own men when the two fools obeyed.

As Thomas and John tied the two failed kidnappers to the chairs, something Orion decided was probably unnecessary, he thought on what he wanted to know.

It was possible that these two thugs knew no more than where to find Lady Catryn and where to take her, but there was a slim chance they had been with Sir Morris long enough to have some useful information. Before he dragged the men to the magistrate to be dealt with, he intended to get them to tell him everything they knew.

"Who are you?" asked the big one.

"That really isn't your concern," said Orion. "Who are you and who sent you?"

"I be Jed and this fellow is Robbie. We got sent here by some fancy fellow named de Warrenne to get his woman back. Suspect you be the one who took her."

"She is not Sir de Warrenne's woman."

"But he has her brat."

"He kidnapped her son and now obviously wishes to add the mother to his collection."

Robbie frowned. "But the brat and the woman be named de Warrenne, too."

This was going to be very slow work, Orion thought and sighed. "It is a common enough name in France. Rather like Jones in Wales." He ignored the sound of choked-back laughter from his men. "So de Warrenne wanted Lady Catryn and sent you to get her. Where were you supposed to take her?"

"We were to take her to the Downs to a sheep shed and wait for him to come and collect her," replied Jed.

"Nay," said Robbie. "We would find word on where else to go first. Remember, Jed? Weren't seeing him then but at the next place, and do not know where that is."

Jed nodded. "Robbie has it right. De Warrenne

said there we get word where to go next and to be careful dragging the woman around with us. He told us she was his and so not to bruise her much. You sure she—"

"Very sure," Orion replied through tightly gritted teeth as he fought the urge to pistol-whip both men for the ease with which they spoke of not bruising Lady Catryn too much.

"Huh. Ne'er thought the man would be lying. Women run a lot." Jed shrugged his big shoulders. "Thought that was what she did. Saw she was following him, too, and was thinking she done changed her mind."

"She wants her son back."

"Not his son then. Thought so. Said that, aye, Robbie?"

"You did that, Jed. Brat calls him uncle, too. Should have thought on that more."

Orion suspected it would have been a painful process if they had tried. "How long have you been with de Warrenne?"

"Just long enough for him to give us some money and tell us what he wanted us to do. Found us in the pub, he did," answered Jed. "Came in with a couple of big fellows and sat down and said he had a job for us to do. We needed some coin. Ain't worked in a while. So, here we be."

"What pub?"

"The Hanging Tree in the next village."

"How apt," Orion murmured, pleased with the way both men paled as they abruptly realized the possible consequences of their actions. "Did de Warrenne say anything about what he planned to do with Lady Catryn when he had her in his grasp?"

Jed shrugged again. "Said he had to take her home, that she needed to be with her family and all. The little lad was with him. One of those men had a good hold on the boy. Boy said his mother would never be family with de Warrenne and she was going to come and get him and leave de Warrenne coughing up her dust or maybe just shoot him in his big, fat head. Thought that a fine threat, I did, but he got a good slapping for it."

Robbie nodded. "Got another for telling the man he would pay for that first slap because someone was going to tear out his innards and tie them around his neck in a bow. That was a fine, fine threat, that was. Better than the first. Got the lad knocked to the ground though."

That was not something he would tell Lady Catryn, Orion decided, even as he wondered how a five-year-old child could think of such a gruesome threat, one that sounded oddly familiar to him. She was worried enough and, wrong though it was for de Warrenne to touch the boy, a slap would not kill Alwyn. Orion would make the man pay for it though.

He looked at his men. "Get them on their feet. We will take them to the magistrate."

Jed and Robbie protested, but Orion ignored them as they all left the inn. The magistrate's home was not a long walk away and he was impressed by the speed with which the man answered their early morning rap at his door. He also appreciated how the man had neither protested nor admonished him when Orion had punched both men, something he could no longer resist doing as the two had babbled on about how they had not intended to hurt the lady too much. The magistrate had summoned two men to come and drag both unconscious fools off to a cell.

Orion told the man all that had happened and was given a date to return to tell his tale to a judge, since an attempted kidnapping was a crime beyond the magistrate's powers to judge and sentence. That was an inconvenience he was not looking forward to, but Jed and Robbie needed to be dealt with. Any man who saw nothing wrong with kidnapping women needed to be transported or hanged. There was no doubt in his mind that both men had a long history of petty and brutal crimes for which they had somehow escaped punishment.

As they returned to the inn, they met up with three more men sent by Morris. Morris may have seen the limitations of the first two men and sent more in case they were needed to get the job done. Orion and his men quickly beat them unconscious although not without gaining a few bruises themselves. He stood staring down at the men sprawled on the ground.

"Jed and Robbie did not mention bringing others with them," he murmured.

"Might be because these were sent to keep a watch on the two idjits," said Thomas, the larger of his two men. "Might also be because they are so witless they think these fools will be out to save them."

Orion nodded. "I thought the same. Their mistake." When one of the men groaned and partly opened his eyes, Orion bent down, gripped him by his filthy hair and asked, "Who hired you?"

"Fellow named de Warrenne," the man answered and then turned his head to spit out a tooth.

"To do what?"

"Watch those fools Jed and Robbie and finish the job if they mucked it up. If they did it right we was to make certain you could not come rushing to the lady's rescue. Man was not happy when he discovered you had joined with her."

Orion silently cursed, for that meant de Warrenne now knew for certain that Lady Catryn was not alone. "And where were you to meet to turn over the woman or collect your coin?"

"On the Downs in a wee sheep shed he would leave word telling us where to go next. So, nay having gone to the sheep shed, have no idea where that is."

At least Jed and Robbie had told the truth, Orion thought. "Morris find you in a pub?"

"Aye. How'd you know that?"

Dropping the man's head so abruptly it hit the ground hard and caused the man to curse, Orion watched as Thomas and his brother John tied up the three men. "Can you take them to the magistrate and tell the man what happened? I should not leave Lady Catryn and my son alone any longer. Who knows how many more of these twits de Warrenne has sent after us? Also, is it possible for you to go to this sheep shed on the Downs to see what message may have been left?"

Both men nodded and Orion paid them well before slowly making his way back to his bedchamber. One thing Jed had said had confirmed a growing suspicion in Orion's mind. De Warrenne wanted Lady Catryn, and she knew it. His anger over her keeping such a secret grew a little with each step he took. He had asked her to tell him everything, and she had not done so. A part of him understood. There were a lot of good reasons for a woman to keep silent about a man other than her husband lusting after her. Yet this situation called for complete honesty. Knowing every fact, no matter how trivial it might seem, was how one achieved success in a mission, a lesson he had learned early in the dangerous game he played for king and country.

Still angry, Orion leaned against the wall outside his bedchamber and attempted to calm himself. It was easy enough to forget the two men he had just handed over to the magistrate. Just as easy to forget the three that had just been taken to the magistrate to join their friends. He had been expecting Morris to try and get him out of the way simply because he was helping Lady Catryn. That would have happened even if there were not a few facts she had neglected to tell him. It was a little harder to not consider all he would like to do to Morris for hiring thugs and thinking he could kidnap Lady Catryn and make her bend to his will.

Suddenly, he grinned. Morris would be in for a large comeuppance if he actually believed he could make that woman bend to his will. Lady Catryn had spirit, and she also had a temper when provoked. Her marriage had been a failure, judging from all she had said about it, which was not too much; but he suspected she was not a woman to silently accept her husband's acting the bachelor after the marriage vows were said. No, Morris would never be able to get Lady Catryn under his thumb even if he somehow got her in his hands. He never had the ghost of a chance, and even if he had, stealing her son had ended that forever.

Orion had no intention of letting the man get his hands on her. He had guessed that Morris was motivated partly by lust for Catryn, but she should have told him. He should have been planning to protect her from that from the very beginning. The only reason he had men on hand to call to his side and help was because he and Giles had known she was hiding something.

What struck him as odd was that it was more than a need to protect a woman from a man she did not want that was brewing his anger at Morris, and at her for not telling him the truth. There was a thread of sharp possessiveness running through all the emotion he was having so much trouble subduing. That was something he had never felt for any woman. When his affairs ended, either by his choice or because the woman strayed, he always walked away without another thought and never felt a twinge of any emotion upon seeing that woman with another man. He knew he would feel more than a twinge if he saw Morris even try to put his hands on Lady Catryn. Orion was also concerned about how even the thought of walking away from her bothered him.

Shaking off such thoughts as they accomplished nothing, he decided it was time to confront Lady Catryn. He had not stilled all of his anger over what she had neglected to tell him, but now he could talk to her about it without a lot of yelling or sharp words. That would have to do. He opened the door, planning his first words, and found himself facing a pistol aimed straight and unwavering at his heart.

Chapter Six

"I believe there is a part of this tale you have neglected to tell me."

Orion was impressed by how quickly she hid her shock over his statement, but he had seen it. That glimpse of emotion had also revealed a hint of guilt. She was definitely hiding something. He and Giles had known it, but seeing the proof of it in her eyes still stung a little.

He was also impressed by how she had aimed the gun at his heart when he had entered the room, her small hand so admirably steady and her face set in cold, determined lines. The way she had so quickly shifted her body to put herself between him and the boy won his hearty approval. Giles grinned at him over her shoulder and Orion suspected his son found Lady Catryn's attempt to protect him amusing and a little too endearing. When he got the full truth out of her, Orion intended to have a talk with Giles about his growing attachment to Lady Catryn. There was a chance Giles was thinking he would play the matchmaker, and that was something Orion wanted to put a swift stop to. If he ever decided that the life of a bachelor no longer held an appeal for him, and he would like to think that was still a very big *if*, he would do his own courting without direction from an eight-year-old boy.

"You can put the pistol down now," he said as he stepped into the room and shut the door.

"Oh." Catryn quickly set her pistol down on the small table near the bed. "My apologies."

"No apology necessary about that. You did not know who was coming through the door. Next time I will announce myself before entering." He moved to the washbowl to clean off his hands, the now cold water soothing the slight sting in his knuckles.

Catryn watched him. He did not look wounded, aside from some scrapes on his hands, just mussed. It could be that Giles's confidence in his father's skills might not be born of nothing more than a boy's blind belief in his sire.

"Did you find out what the danger was?" she asked when he dried off his hands and moved to stand in front of her, crossing his arms over his chest.

"Morris sent five men after you," he replied.

"Five? After me?"

Her heart sank as she realized that her fleeting thought that Morris may have taken Alwyn to get to her should not have been shrugged aside. Marrying her would put Morris in reach of all he coveted. The moment they were married, his chance of becoming Alwyn's guardian would become a certainty. When he had turned to the courts after her resounding *no* to his proposal, she had foolishly believed that he had given up the idea of marrying her.

"They were not after kidnapping me or Giles," Orion said. "The two we caught sneaking into your bedchamber even had the good sense to confess that they were after you. The three we met outside were to kidnap you if the first two failed or, if their friends succeeded, to make certain I would not be able to set out after you immediately."

"They were here to hurt you and Giles?" Guilt washed over so strongly she felt ill with it.

"Which means that Morris not only knows you are on his trail but that you are not alone."

"He has been watching for me," she whispered, shocked by such foresight on Morris's part.

"It would appear he has, and there is no way we can be sure who is doing the watching and reporting, so we must go on with the knowledge that Morris is fully aware of the fact that you are chasing him."

"And just what were they supposed to do with me?" she asked.

"Take you to Morris. Unfortunately, none of them knew where he was. The man had devised a rather clever and convoluted way for them to get word to him if they were successful in capturing you. A message left in a sheep shed on the Downs would be only the first step. I have men going to see if they can find it. Once they finished following whatever trail Morris set out for them, only then would Morris come to collect you and pay off his hired ruffians. Or send someone else to do so."

"He thinks he can use Alwyn to make me do what he wants."

"And what does he want aside from all your son's holdings as his father's heir?"

Catryn inwardly cursed, knowing that she was cornered and could not hide the truth from Sir Orion any longer. It had been wrong to hold back anything when the man was so willing to help her. The fact that the truth embarrassed her, even made her worry she might sound vain, did not justify her actions. In truth, none of the reasons Morris had for wanting her were the sort worthy of stroking a woman's vanity.

"When Henry was barely cold in the ground, Morris suddenly decided that marrying me would be a good idea. He obviously believed it was the easiest way to get his hands on all that Henry's will had denied him. It was after I said no that he started trying to get everything through the courts. Not only did I refuse him quite vigorously but I told him I was certain it was actually illegal for a man to marry his brother's widow."

"Under ecclesiastical law, yes; it is illegal. But he could take you to Scotland or to some other country where they do not demand by law that you be wed in a church as they do here The only legal way to end such a marriage is if a close relative protests it, takes it before the courts."

It took only a moment for Catryn to understand the ramifications of that. "Then my father could be in danger, for he would protest very loudly and Morris knows it."

"Not until you are actually married to Morris. And I have come to believe that he is rather consumed by his plans of the moment. Those plans now appear to be getting his hands on your son, which he has done, and then you, which he just failed miserably at."

He frowned. "That could mean he is not willing to leave the country until he has both of you, which could definitely complicate matters."

"I believe matters are quite complicated enough now."

"For you, yes. I was speaking of myself."

It was an effort, but Catryn stopped herself from rolling her eyes. "I do so beg your pardon." She silently cursed when he grinned at her, revealing that he had heard that touch of sarcasm she had not been able to fully repress, and found it amusing.

Orion quickly grew serious again. "It makes plotting his course of action a little more difficult. I thought his plan would be to go straight to a port, catch a berth on a ship, and try to become your son's guardian from a safe distance, all the while holding Alwyn as the weapon to force full cooperation from you and your father."

"Which brings us back to the chance that my father is in danger?"

Her voice was calm but her fear was clear to see in her eyes and the paleness of her face. Orion knew her father was important to her. It had been apparent even in the few times she had spoken of the man. He hoped the possibility of two people she deeply cared about being in danger did not make her reckless. Then he remembered that they were together because she had stolen his carriage to chase Morris down, and inwardly grimaced. For once in his life he might have to be the one with the calm, steady hands on the reins. His family would laugh uproariously at the thought.

"As I said, your father is safe as long as you remain unwed to Morris."

"That has always been my plan. I was wed to one de Warrenne. I have no wish to repeat the experience." Not unless it would save her family, she thought, and suspected Sir Orion knew exactly what she had left unsaid.

"We will have something to break our fast now and then I will leave you and Giles here whilst I go a-hunting."

Before she could say a word, he opened the door and waved her and Giles toward it. Sir Orion really was far too accustomed to giving orders, but she was not accustomed to blindly obeying them. Rebellion was difficult, however, when the orders were so rational and he was just telling her to do what she had planned to do anyway. But, she thought as she walked down the steps with Giles, it would not hurt Sir Orion if he made an attempt to just ask instead of command.

It was not until the morning meal was winnowed down to a few scraps on the plates that Catryn finally thought of what to say to Sir Orion. "Why are Giles and I to stay here? Would it not be better for all of us to go after Morris? If you do find the man's trail, you will only have to return to collect us anyway."

"I can hunt better alone and on horseback," Orion replied and watched her as he sipped his coffee.

Lady Catryn de Warrenne did not take orders well. He knew she was struggling to be cooperative only because he was going to help her find her son. That temper he could see flash in her beautiful sea-green eyes would break free soon. Although he was tempted to see it do so, he knew they did not have the time to play that game. Nor would it be fair. Neither of them spoke of it, but despite Giles's presence, she was risking her good name by traveling with him, no matter how good and righteous the reason might be.

He set his cup down. "At first I thought as you did. Morris was either going to his home in Easebourne or some other house he considered safe, or to a port to flee the country. Now that we know he seeks to grab you as well, the port is the only possible place, for he is heading in the wrong direction to go to Scotland. It is the safest. What I am no longer certain of is whether Morris will take that route."

"Is it truly that difficult to guess what plan he may have made?" she asked.

"It is proving to be so. The man is either brilliant beyond anyone I have dealt with before—"

"No, I do not think that could be the reason."

"Neither do I, considering who he hires to carry out his little plans. So, he is not brilliant, but so erratic, so without a hard, clear plan that it is difficult to sort out what path he will take next."

"Spoiled child," said Giles as he grabbed a sharp knife to cut up an apple.

Catryn almost reached out to take the dangerous knife away from the child, only to nearly gape. The way Giles wielded that knife as he cut and cored the apple was smooth and fast. Far more efficient than she had ever been with a knife. She had to try harder to recall that Giles was not your normal eight-year-old son of the gentry.

"We know that," said Orion. "It is but a part of the puzzle though. Why do you think it important to remind me?"

"Suspect you have had little to do with a spoiled child," said Giles. "I watched the gentry a lot. Naught much else to do and always best to keep an eye on the ones who might think you need jailing, or transporting, or some other less-than-kind reformation. Seen some spoiled children. Easy to say what they are like, but if you never dealt with one or watched one, suspect you cannot really know one. He will never do as you think he should. Can change his mind in a heartbeat. Can get so furious you can never guess which way he will jump. Blind furious. 'I want, I will, I can and you cannot stop me.' Bounce all about, they do."

"'And if you try to stop me you will suffer for it.'"

Giles nodded his head. "Seen one lad throw himself such a fit he had trouble breathing and all, but he did not stop until his nurse gave him what he wanted, mostly because she was terrified he would harm himself. Then, when he caught his breath, he kicked her and called her a stupid bitch and he was going to see her tossed out on the street. Next minute he is smiling and laughing and playing with some other boys."

"That sounds like Morris," Catryn murmured. "I can easily imagine him doing the same as a child, if the opportunity arose. Did the poor nurse end up out on the street?"

"Aye," Giles replied. "She did, but I got into the house and had a word with the father, who was a reasonable man and he made sure she had a good recommendation. Next I saw the lad, he had a big ugly brute of a fellow watching over him." Giles grinned.

"So there is a problem in using my usual skills with this man," murmured Orion. "Yet I have dealt with a few like him, or nearly so, before. It remains a bit of a puzzle. I will keep it in mind while I go do a little hunting today. You two are to stay here, and I will hire John and Thomas again to stay close and keep watch."

"We are not to go with you?" Catryn asked. "It is good weather for following Morris. If you find him, I should be there to help Alwyn. He has to be terribly frightened."

"We now know that Morris is fond of hiring men who probably should have been hanged long ago to deal with anything bothering him. It could be very dangerous to continue to chase him. A little spying-out of the situation is called for. Once I gain some useful information on where he is, perhaps what direction he is now headed in, since his plan to grab you failed, and how many men he has riding with him, it will be safer to follow him. We can then better plan the inevitable confrontation in a way that will keep us and your son safe."

Catryn wanted to argue with him but could not. Everything he said made perfect sense. They were but one man, one boy, and one small woman against Morris and whoever he had hired to do his dirty work. Blindly approaching him would be foolish. Accepting that fact did not ease her worry over her child, however. It was not going to be easy to sit at the inn and just wait, not knowing how Alwyn fared or what might be happening to Sir Orion.

"You will send word if there is any trouble?" she asked, unable to hide her concern for him.

"I will. And the two of you are to stay here and yell for John or Thomas if there is even the smallest sign of a threat."

"Agreed."

"Then I shall set off now."

Catryn watched him go back to his room to gather his things, tried to keep her mind on drinking the last of her tea, and then gave up. She hastily excused herself, leaving a smirking Giles behind, and went outside to wait for Orion by his mount. John nodded a greeting to her and walked away, but she could see him settle down on a bench just past the door to the inn. He was already taking up his guard post. She wanted to ask if he had discovered anything at the sheep shed but decided to wait and ask Orion.

When Orion walked out, he looked surprised to find her there waiting for him but smiled as he settled his packs on his horse. "Going to plead to go along again?" he asked.

"No, there may be a large part of me begging to do so, but I understand that it would be unwise. I just came out to again ask you to be very careful. I begin to think I have long underestimated the threat Morris can pose. Did John and Thomas find anything?"

"No. There must have been yet another man watching what happened. There was no note and no trail."

Orion gave in to the urge to touch her hair when she sighed in disappointment, and lightly stroked the thick braid hanging down her back. It was as soft as he had imagined. He ached to see it loose and falling in waves around her shoulders. Since such thoughts made his blood stir, he quieted them before it put him in such a roused state that riding would be uncomfortable.

"He was no true threat before now. Not really. He had little chance of winning in the courts, if only because he did not have the money to bribe enough judges." He grinned when she frowned. "Too cynical?"

"A touch, yet, sadly, probably deserved." She rose up on her tiptoes and kissed his cheek. "Be safe."

Watching her hurry back inside the inn, Orion touched his cheek. The spot she had kissed was no warmer than the rest of his skin, yet he had felt the heat of her lips seep straight into his blood. He glanced to the window of the private parlor they had booked and saw his son in the window grinning at him. There was definitely a long, serious talk due with that boy.

Mounting his horse, he ignored the urge to go back inside the inn and see if Catryn was interested in a little more serious kissing. At the moment he had quite a few places on his body that would welcome the touch of those soft, warm lips. Shaking aside that salacious thought, he waved at Giles and rode away in the direction he was certain Morris had gone.

There was another talk that was long overdue as well. Catryn had to be told of the possibility that she may be a far distant relation to his family, either Wherlocke or Vaughn. If Giles was right and Alwyn was talking to spirits, he would need training to deal with such a gift. Although the child could be one of those rare people outside of his clan who were born with a gift, Orion doubted it. The way Catryn could sense danger made it highly likely that there would be a Wherlocke or Vaughn lurking on the family tree. It was not unusual for families to have hidden the connection as deeply as they could; in the past, many of them had paid a high price for their gifts.

That was not going to be an easy discussion to have. He would have to tell her some truths about his family that could have her running for the hills. Orion had to trust that she would not be afraid. She had accepted his assurances that he had a skill beyond understanding for finding anyone and anything, and she clearly accepted Giles's assurances that he "just knew things." Then there was how she dealt with her own son and her own gift, one she had confessed to him already.

He had to carefully plan his argument, for he expected she would immediately deny any such connection, not out of distaste for his family but because such a connection would mean that her father or mother, or both, had hidden it from her. Orion did not need Giles's gift to know that would sting, and sting deeply.

Hours later, he was still sorting out the best approach to his coming talk with Catryn when he came across several big men standing around a very recognizable carriage. The man with the calf had been right the other day. It was a foolish color to paint a carriage one used to travel on these roads. The blue and gold was barely visible beneath all the filth that covered it halfway up. One of the wheels was broken and the carriage listed badly at the side of the road.

After making certain his pistol was close at hand, Orion rode closer. To present no appearance of a threat, he kept the horse at an easy pace but also kept a close watch on the area until he was certain Morris was not around. The absence of the man did not mean it was safe to approach, as the men studying the carriage could be some of his hirelings.

"There is a sad end for such a vehicle," he said when all four men standing around Morris's gaudy vehicle turned to look at him.

"Just a broken wheel," said a man with thick, graying hair. "All else is fine. You know this carriage?"

"And the gent who drives it," replied Orion, sensing that all he had here were men hired to fix Morris's carriage. "Assume he and his precious horses have gone on to some inn."

"The Bald Nun." The man grinned when Orion could not fully stifle a laugh. "Aye, fool name. If the one who named it meant to honor the woman, he could have just called it Sister Anne's, but I suspect men would hesitate to have a pint at such a place."

"I think I would be counted among them. So you were sent out to fix this?"

"We were, but I am wondering why ye are so interested."

"Sir Morris de Warrenne and I are at odds at the moment. He thinks he should have all his nephew has inherited and I think he should not, as does the boy's mother."

"Wee lad with black curls and what can have a foul mouth from time to time?"

"Well, I know about the black curls and big blue eyes, but had not been warned about the foul mouth."

The man laughed. "It can be foul indeed, but only for Sir de Warrenne. Lad was all sweet and polite to me until de Warrenne ordered him to get walking to the inn. Then the wee lad looked like he was thinking hard and said he would walk, but he would walk behind and stick his sword right up the bastard's fat arse." He grinned when the other men laughed but quickly grew serious again. "Lad had no sword, but fair wished I did when de Warrenne knocked him to the ground and kicked him. Poor wee lad. He sore wanted to cry. Could see it, but he stood up, brushed himself off, and started walking. Have to admire that."

"Good thing he did though, for that wind what whipped across the road there would have sent such a small boy sailing off into the fields," said a stocky, dark-haired man.

"Wind?" Orion looked around. "This was a while ago, was it?"

"Only came up when de Warrenne was here," said the gray-haired man. "Came up, knocked de Warrenne on his arse, and then was gone. Oddest thing."

Not so odd if you happen to have a spirit as your close friend. Whatever spirit was attached to young Alwyn was clearly enraged with its inability to truly protect the child. Orion needed no more proof that little Lord Alwyn de Warrenne was the possessor of a very strong gift, one much like Penelope's. Such things had occasionally happened to his cousin when a particularly strong spirit formed a deep attachment to her. The fact that the boy was obviously carrying on sensible conversations with the spirit told him that this was a very strong relationship. Peppered with profanity, but sensible.

"How long do you think it will take for you to fix the wheel?" he asked.

The gray-haired man narrowed his eyes, and Orion could almost hear the man calculating how much payment he could ask for to not do the work he was already being paid for, without sounding greedy. When he then turned to face the other three men, Orion pretended to not notice the almost silent consultation, only a few whispers passing among the men. Orion idly wondered if he should try to bargain for a lower price than whatever they asked. He needed them to delay Morris as long as possible so that he and Catryn could get closer to their quarry but did not want these men to know just how badly he needed it.

Abruptly the gray-haired man turned to face him and stated a price that Orion had no intention of arguing with. He suspected it was the same as what they had told de Warrenne it would cost to replace his wheel. "Just how long do you think you can delay?" he asked the man as he counted out the payment and put it in the man's big calloused hand.

"Well now, we were just talking of sending Abe here to get a new wheel. That would only take but a few hours, as there is one in the stable at the inn. But, if we say he has to go farther to find the right one, or if I have to make a new one, well, that could take a day or two. "

"A day would suit me fine. Two days would be even better."

"We will lag about as much as we can. De Warrenne gets too heated, though, and we will have to complete the job."

"Agreed. He promised to pay you the same amount I just did, did he not?"

"He did. I decided that this way at least we will get what we earned as well as the pleasure of irritating him."

"Believe he will cheat you?"

"Without hesitation. Has that look about him. In the way he talks, too. Man is too fond of himself."

"And he will be staying at The Bald Nun?"

"He will. Funny that, he was quite pleased with the name. Most folk laugh as you did. He said that finally he would be resting at an inn with a good name and mayhap his luck has changed, or something similar. No idea what the fool was on about."

"Superstitious," Orion said. "Must like the word *nun*. Probably weary of all the devils and hangings in the names of the inns he has passed or stayed in. Any chance you heard anything about where he plans to go once he has his carriage back?"

"To the coast. Portsmouth. They were all talking about ships and the cost of sailing, and the men with him were not even sure they wanted to go as they have no interest in being in a foreign place. One was saying he had heard some tales about France and all, and was thinking it might be a place to stay far away from."

"Ah, at least one of them appears to have some wit. And now I will leave you to your work, or lack thereof. One last question, how many men does he have with him?"

"Four, and one appears to be the manacle for the boy."

"Thank you kindly and forgive me if I send up a prayer or two for some rain."

"Tsk, that would be a shame. No work done when it be raining."

He left the men laughing behind him and turned to go back to Catryn and Giles. It was several miles before he realized he had stopped calling her Lady Catryn. He was growing inordinately comfortable with her company. That was also a change for him. Orion knew it was shallow, but he chose women who would give him sex and be a pretty bauble on his arm for a while. In return he gave them pleasure, a companion to take them to various events, and a shiny gift when he moved on. If he thought about companionship at all, it was just to hope that they did not bore him into a stupor or set his teeth on edge. Then he moved on a little more quickly than he might have otherwise.

Catryn was the first woman outside of his relations that he had ever simply enjoyed being with, talking to, arguing with. She held his interest even though she was not sharing his bed. Orion recognized the danger in that but experienced no panic. That was something he should give some careful consideration to. They were bound together until they settled this trouble with Morris. Orion was not a man to leave a job half done.

Orion touched his cheek and could not stop himself from smiling. She had told him to stay safe, and sent him off with a kiss. It was the first time in a very long time since anyone had done so. He also knew she was worrying about him and could not banish the good feeling that gave him. Complications lay ahead of him concerning little Lady Catryn, but he almost looked forward to them.

Chapter Seven

Orion leaned against a tree and took a deep drink of ale while he watched his son with the woman they were both so determined to help. He had been surprised when Thomas had told him Catryn had taken the boy to the green next to the inn for it was no garden, simply a place where the innkeeper let some of his livestock graze. Lady Catryn sat on the grass, toy soldiers spread out on the ground in front of her, the setting sun bathing her in a warm golden light. Giles sat by her side, listening intently as she spoke of the Battle of Worcester in 1651 with a keen knowledge of not only the people involved but tactics used, and what gave one side the victory over the other. Orion found that surprising because most women knew no more about the military than what uniform they appreciated most on a man, or the name of a battle if an ancestor had gained his title for fighting in it.

She fascinated him. That both thrilled and disturbed him. It had been a very long time since he had been fascinated by a woman. Lustful, pleasured, and sated, but not fascinated. Most of his interest in a woman had centered in his groin for more years than he cared to think about. It was true that he only pursued women he knew he had a good chance of bedding, but outside of the bed he had never found them more than passingly pleasant company, his interest in them fleeting.

His body ached to seduce Lady Catryn but, for the first time in years, he was doing his best to ignore its demand. Instinct continued to warn him that Lady Catryn was not a woman a man easily walked away from. That was what he did; he walked away. That is what he planned to continue to do until he was too old to be interested in bed sport, or dead. Or it had been. He was beginning to think something was changing within him and did not know whether to be glad or scared.

It must be the ale making him think so much and so deeply about a woman, he decided as he took another drink. That was the only explanation for why he stood there watching the pair, why he wanted to join them. In his mind's eye he could see the three of them spending time on a rare sunny day like the happy family in a portrait. Wherlockes were not known for having happy families. And it would include four children: three boys he had bred on other women, plus her son. The portrait did not appear quite so calm and pastoral now but was still oddly tempting.

Giles sat up a little straighter, cocked his head as if listening for something, and then sneaked a glance over his shoulder. Orion raised his tankard in a silent salute. As a result of his hard years living on the streets of London, Giles was far more keenly alert to his surroundings than most children. He was surprised that the boy had not noticed him sooner. He welcomed the disruption of his thoughts, however, as he walked toward Giles and Catryn, for they had begun to make him think on all the promising marriages that had recently occurred amongst the Wherlockes. That was certainly a dangerous path for a confirmed bachelor to meander down.

Catryn hastily sat up straighter, a little disturbed at being found scrambling about in the grass like a child. It was not just the tankard of ale that told her Sir Orion had stopped in the inn for a while before he had come looking for them. He was far too clean and tidy for a man who had spent most of the day hunting someone. He also appeared to have suffered no wounds, and the tight ball of worry she had carried in her stomach all day loosened.

"You are well?" she asked.

"I am, and I found out a great deal about Morris the kidnapper," he replied.

She scrambled to her feet. "Did you get any news of how Alwyn fares?"

"Alwyn is still alive, but we can talk about all I learned over the meal I have ordered. It is ready in the parlor by now." He moved to help her pick up the toy soldiers. "Some of these are wooden." He studied the fine detail on the Roundhead soldier he held. "The carving is exquisite."

"My da does them for Alwyn. He makes the leaders and the horses, the cannons, and a few other items but buys the rest. He said if he tried to make the whole army, Alwyn would be a grandfather himself before it was done. I thought they would help comfort Alwyn after his ordeal."

He looked at the box she held open for him to put the soldier in, studying the dragons carved on the sides as he carefully placed the figurine in with the others. It did not surprise him to see a griffin carved on the lid when she closed the box. The work was some of the best he had ever seen.

"An unusual skill for a baron," he murmured, taking her by the arm and starting to walk back to the inn.

"Da says it calms him and helps him think things out. He started as a boy, soon outpacing the man who taught him." She smiled. "There are a lot of his works at our country house. There are a few at the house where I lived with my husband, as well."

Orion coaxed her to speak more of her father as they made their way to the small private parlor where the maid was just finishing setting out a hearty meal. He could hear the love she had for the man in every word. What he did not hear was any hint that her father had any special gift aside from the one he had for carving.

The meal was cleared away and the sweet placed out before he gained the courage to talk about the possibility that her family had crossed with his sometime in the past.

"So your father does not know when danger approaches nor speaks to people no one else can see?" he finally asked, deciding the blunt approach was needed.

"No. Why should he?" she asked.

"Because both you and Alwyn have a rather special

gift. It is not strange to think that your sire might have one, too."

"Gift? You call such things *gifts*? One does not have to hide a gift, sir."

"Oh, but you do. You most certainly do," said Giles before stuffing his mouth full of stewed apple and clotted cream.

Catryn stared at Orion. "Do you have one of these gifts? Does Giles?"

"Giles is too young for his gift to be evident, although I begin to think I know what his gift is, and that it is very strong. It appears he knows what a person is feeling. I can find anyone and anything, as I have said. I even know a plot's twists and turns with but a tiny fragment of a clue. Few will gamble with me, as I can tell what their next move will be and what the next card will be. I can draw a loud groan from my relatives if I even suggest a game of chess. All the Wherlockes and Vaughns have gifts, some strong and some weak. It is why I am so curious about the ones you and Alwyn appear to have, because the name Gryffin is unknown to me."

For a moment she stared at him and wondered what he was trying to tell her. All of this talk about gifts was confusing. Then her eyes widened so much they stung as her mind filled with scraps of knowledge, whispered tales, and gossip about his family that had been buried beneath her fears for Alwyn.

"Oh. Oh dear. You are one of *those* Wherlockes. I *have* heard of you."

"By the look upon your face I must conclude that you have heard very little that was complimentary," he drawled.

The hot sting of a blush swept over her cheeks as she realized how rude she had been. "What I heard was that your family is large, distressingly handsome or beautiful, and rather odd. Also that it appears to be very good at producing sons even though there appeared to be only a rather angry envy of that as if the blessing was wasted on you. A few spoke of darker things, but I refused to listen to such tales. That might be why it took me so long to recall any of them. Then, too, I have ne'er believed it right to mark someone evil or wrong for being different in some way." She smiled a little. "Or an entire family, and one that rarely appears in the society that so many of their number were born into."

He returned her smile. "We visit with that horde when it pleases us."

"How politely condescending." She was not surprised when he laughed, for there had been no bite to her words. "Yet none of you make any attempt to silence the whispers?"

"People have been whispering about us from the moment the first of my ancestors revealed that he was different in a way people did not understand or trust. Mayhap now we simply do not care what society thinks for they are no longer allowed by law to condemn us, jail us, or murder us for our differences. And mayhap we are too aware of how many of our ancestors died at the hands of persecutors like them. I can, in a small way, excuse the peasantry for their actions, for most are uneducated, but those of my class should have had more sense."

Catryn thought that over for a moment and then nodded. "I believe I would feel the same."

"Do you know if any one of your own ancestors was killed or jailed for being different?"

"Killed or jailed? That would be some clue, would it?"

"Yes. In the past it happened quite often. It is why our family became such a reclusive one and has only recently fully come out into society." He smiled faintly. "Well, what we consider fully. It is why we even pick our servants with the utmost care, the majority of them coming from the Pugh or Jones families."

"But would you not know your own family lines and history? Would you not know if the name Gryffin appeared somewhere along the way?"

"Oh, we have our histories and our inheritance charts and family lines, but they are not always complete. In the old days when there were bad times, when the witch cry grew loud and people were either dragged to a stake or hanged, some of our ancestors hid or even burned their family ledgers to prevent other family members from being identified. We all learn the story of the entire family that was slaughtered for being decried as witches, the parents and eldest daughter burned at the stake, and the young children tossed into the flames to join them." He nodded when she paled and placed a hand over her mouth. "Ancestors of the Duke of Elderwood. If there had not been one brother who was out to sea at the time, that line would have been completely wiped out that night. He stayed away for a long time, too, and raised his family elsewhere until that period of turmoil passed. What better way to ensure that all of your family does not get slaughtered than to rid yourself of all the writings and histories detailing marriages and births and all of that?"

"It was that bad?"

"It could be from time to time. It eased some after the Church of England was founded, but then when Bloody Mary sat on the throne there were the witch-hunters for a while. Even now, though the law allowing people to torture and kill a proven or confessed witch has been repealed, it is not wise to be too open about one's differences. We learned to keep few records and hide them well."

"Which leaves you with a lot of, well, holes."

"Exactly. Several of my family have made it their business to hunt down as much information as they can, try to find records that were hidden away, but many records are lost forever."

Catryn frowned. "So you truly think the Gryffins may have joined with your family for a while?"

"We are all Welsh originally. It would hardly be a surprise if they had."

"There is that to consider. Yet, why would my father not tell me?"

"He may not know. Your lines may have a few unexplained breaks and lost information as well."

"Why would you believe Alwyn has a gift?" she asked, even though she was frightened to hear his answer. "He is just a little boy who speaks to people of his own creation."

"I think you know it is more than that," Orion said, recognizing the fear in her eyes, the deep desire to utterly and firmly deny what he was about to say. "He speaks with the spirits of the dead, Catryn."

She slowly shook her head. "No. No, he does not.

He is just a little boy, only just turned five years of age. He does not even truly understand what dead is."

"He might not, especially if the loss of someone has not yet darkened his world."

"His father died."

"You said they were not close."

"That is true, but Alwyn was there in the house when he died, and he attended all the services."

"With his friend?"

"How could you possibly know my son speaks to the dead? You cannot see his friends any more than I can."

He reached across the table and placed his hands over hers, stilling their agitated movement. "Answer me this: Would your son know how to threaten someone? Know enough to tell a man that he was going to rip out his innards and tie them around his neck in a bow?" He nodded when she paled. "Does he know the sorts of words that would have him saying he was going to stick his sword up a man's arse? He has said these things and more, and one man said he pauses as if he is thinking hard before saying it. Just as if he is listening, then repeating someone else's words. Another man, who paused near Alwyn when he was in the carriage, swears he saw a light behind the boy, even though Morris was blocking any light that might have come in through the carriage window. And, as your son walked away from a very angry Morris, a strange wind swept across the road at just that point and knocked Morris down."

Although her hands had stilled beneath his, she was rocking slightly, back and forth, in her seat. Orion feared he had given her far too much to deal with.

She dearly loved her child and she was smart enough to understand what this particular gift could mean for his future.

"I shall write to my father and demand he find out if there are Wherlockes or Vaughns in my family. You shall see there are none, and that means Alwyn is just a boy so in need of friends he makes them up in his mind." She leapt to her feet and hurried out of the room.

Orion cursed, took a deep drink of wine, and slumped in his chair. "That did not go well."

"She loves her boy," said Giles, "and she is afraid, very afraid, that he really is different. It is not a fear for herself or anything like that, but fear for him. Why would she fear for him?"

"Because this is going to make his life difficult. Perhaps not as difficult as she fears, but it will not be easy for him."

"Oh. That is true enough. I am thinking it is not easy for any of us, is it?"

"Not really, no. Some have it far worse than others."

"Such as the young duke who has to hide in his castle?"

Orion looked at his son and frowned. "I did not think I had told you about him yet."

"No, Cody did. I think he thought I knew." Giles stared down at the apple core he tossed back and forth in his hands. "That is what you think will happen to me, aye?"

"Not completely, but it is certainly not going to be easy for you. We will wait, and if your gift is what I think it is and grows stronger, I will send you to train with Modred. Our aunt Dob is the one who helps him, and he can rejoin the world a little more every day. She has a true skill at helping a person build walls in his mind to keep out all the noise."

"It helps to know that. Maybe Lady Catryn needs to meet someone who has grown up with the ability to see and speak to spirits. Penelope could help her understand that her son will do well, that he just needs to learn a few things and how to keep it all a secret."

Orion clapped his son on the back. "A very good idea. Penelope could help Catryn. Once we have her son, we will go to Radmoor. We will stay a little while and, if we have not yet ended Morris's games, we will leave you and the boy there and go hunt the fool down. While we do so, young Alwyn can meet others like him and learn from them."

Walking to the window that overlooked the attractive little garden at the side of the inn, Orion sipped his wine and wondered if he should go and try to comfort Catryn. She sat on a bench and stared out over the small garden that the light of the moon cast in shadows. He had grown up with the knowledge of the things he had just told her, accepted them from the time he could first understand what was being said around him. He had also had to accept at a very early age that many people, even ones who should love you, saw what his family doggedly called gifts as a curse, something evil and frightful. Catryn accepted but obviously would much rather her child was not so gifted, and he could not blame her for that.

It did not help that the boy had the gift of speaking to the dead, which even members of his own family could find discomforting. The dead were supposed to stay dead and silent. He was glad he had not been given such a gift, or the one that he feared Giles had been given.

Shaking his head, he set down his tankard and decided to go and see if she was willing to hear any more. Orion discovered that he could not abide her being sad or upset. He felt a deep need to try and make her smile again. He paused by the table to look at his son.

"Do you think she is ready to hear any more?" Giles asked, and briefly frowned toward the window.

"I have no idea, but I cannot leave her out there, afraid for her son and sad."

"Ah, I see."

"And just what does that mean?"

"'Tis hard to care at times," he said and returned to cutting and coring another apple.

Orion decided to ignore that, and headed out to the garden, taking her shawl with him. Now that the sun had set, it was growing cool. Glancing up at the full moon as he approached her, he grimaced. A nice romantic night and he had to talk about gifts and ghosts and calm her fears.

"Have you come to give me more bad news?" she asked as she took the shawl he held out to her and wrapped it around her shoulders.

Orion sat on the bench next to her and bit back a smile. She sounded more cross than sad. Even a little sulky. That he could deal with. It was the possibility of tears, heartbreak, and sorrow he had not wished to confront.

"That was all of it, I believe," he said.

"Can people really speak with the dead?" she asked in a soft voice.

"They can. My cousin Penelope does. She can also tell you where the bodies are buried, even if their spirit has already gone."

"Gone where?"

"The question of the ages. She is not sure. None come back to tell her. She says the good just go away; sometimes there is a light and sometimes they just smile and fade away. The bad are the worst, she said. They looked terrified for a moment and then are pulled down into the dark."

"And she sees this?"

"She does. Fortunately, the few bad she has seen were so bad she was little troubled by what happened to them. The spirit with your son," he said, ignoring the way she tensed, "is a little different from what Penelope has spoken of. It is apparent that he can converse with the spirit. She says that is not usually the way of it, that spirits usually just say cryptic things and 'beware.'"

Catryn could not help it. The way he said the word *beware*, with deep, dramatic tones, made her smile. It was a short-lived smile, however. The mere thought that her sweet little boy was conversing with dead people was enough to banish it.

She stared up at the moon and wondered how Alwyn was doing right now. Her heart ached to hold him. She knew he trusted her to find him, but it was taking a lot longer than she had anticipated. Now she had the added concern that he was conversing with a foul-mouthed spirit. At least he has one of his friends with him to comfort him, she thought, and then shook her head. This matter of gifts and talk of ghosts was obviously disordering her mind.

Coming out into the garden had been intended to calm her enough to compose a sensible letter to her father. It was not working as well as she had hoped. All she could do was try—and fail—to deny what Orion said, and worry about her little boy.

"He will be fine, Catryn," Orion said and slowly put his arm around her slim shoulders. "He is young, and the young accept so many things better than adults do. From what you say, he has always been able to see and speak to the dead, so it must seem quite normal and ordinary to him."

That was true, she thought. Alwyn did not understand that he was doing anything unusual. Probably thought all children had friends no one else could see or hear. He might even understand that the friends he spoke to were dead, for he had never asked that they go and find one or put out food for them. Yet, to think of such a young child being so close to, so familiar with the dead, was a little chilling.

Suddenly she was aware that she was seated very close to Orion and he had his arm around her. It was nice, the warmth of his body keeping away the encroaching chill of the night. It was also highly improper, but then she was already doing a lot that was improper, such as riding around the countryside with an unmarried man who was not related to her. She looked up at him to find him looking down at her.

His face was so close and so very handsome. She could see concern for her in his beautiful blue eyes. His mouth was almost as pretty, the bottom lip a little fuller than the top. Catryn could not recall the last time she had been kissed by a man, and she suddenly craved a kiss.

Orion knew it was a mistake as he lowered his mouth to hers, but the way she had looked at him had been a temptation he could not resist. There had been the glint of want and curiosity in her sea-green eyes, and his body strongly encouraged him to respond. It took but one brush of his mouth over her full, soft lips to tell him that he could be risking a lot just to steal that little taste, but he ignored the warning.

Catryn curled her arms around his shoulders as he kissed her. When he nipped at her bottom lip, she opened her mouth so that he could deepen the kiss. Her body trembled from the strength of the desire that flooded her. He tasted so good, his body pressed against her was a delight, and he even smelled wonderful. She wanted to sit there in his arms and keep on kissing him until the sun rose.

That thought was enough to make a warning bell sound in her mind and she gently pulled free of his hold. "I believe I need to write a message and send it to my father, for we must try to learn if there is Wherlocke blood in my family," she said as she stood up and brushed down her skirts with shaking hands, knowing it was a ridiculously abrupt change of subject but desperate to get away from the man.

"Have him send an answer to Radmoor, the Earl of Radmoor's country home, as we will stop there soon."

"Good night, Sir Orion."

"Sleep well, Cat," he said, and smiled at the way her shoulders stiffened as she hurried away.

It had been an abrupt ending to a sweet moment, but he was not surprised. She had not shied away from his kiss but had not shown any great experience,

either. It was yet more proof that he should stay far
away from her, but he knew he would not be able to.
Already he wanted to hunt her down and kiss her
again. Licking his lips, he deemed hers the sweetest
mouth he had ever tasted.

"There is trouble for you there, fool," he muttered
to himself as he headed back inside, but a part of him
refused to heed any advice, actually anticipated running
right after that trouble until it was caught.

Catryn sealed the letter to her father and stared at
it for a moment. It had not been easy to write. How
did one ask one's father if he had hidden some dark
truth from her? She had thought she knew all that was
truly necessary about her family but it was evident she
had not; her father had to have hidden information
from her. He was a scholar, a man driven to find
answers, and he would never have ignored any gaps
in the family history. Any place where the lines or histories did not connect, he would have noticed and
pursued all avenues for an answer until he found one.

After what she had learned of the Wherlockes and
Vaughns, she supposed she could understand the
secrecy, but not when it concerned his own family.
When she revealed her gift—she still had some difficulty seeing it as such—her father should have told
her about any connection to the Wherlockes or
Vaughns; he would have known just where those odd
talents had come from. Likewise when he learned of
Alwyn's gift. He knew that Alwyn's black hair was
something that showed up in the family now and

then, so she could not help but think he also knew just where it came from.

A twinge of hurt was hastily banished. She would wait until she heard from him. Her father had never lied to her, and she had no doubt that he dearly loved her and Alwyn. If he had been keeping secrets, he had to have a very good reason. Since he was a scholar, she doubted it was because of some superstitious fear such as what her mother had suffered from.

She sat up straight and frowned at the thought of her mother: There was the reason that he would keep any connection to the Wherlockes or Vaughns secret. Her mother had loved being out and about in London society, and would have known all about those families. She had probably believed everything said about them as well. Catryn had loved her mother dearly, but the woman had been a very superstitious person, and had believed all manner of strange things that had never made any sense to Catryn. Even knowing what she did now, her mother's beliefs still appeared to be based more on fear and rumor than fact.

"And now I sound just like my father," she muttered and went to find someone who could see that her letter was posted as soon as possible.

She kept a close eye out for Orion as she accomplished that little chore and hurried back to her bedchamber. It was a bit childish, but she did not want to face him just yet. She was no experienced flirt and she needed time to adjust to the fact that she had just kissed a man she had known for such a short time. Not only kissed him but wanted to kiss him again.

That was something she needed to think on before she confronted him again.

Back in her bedchamber, she stood before the tiny mirror on the small dressing table and touched her mouth. It was far too easy to recall the feel of his lips on hers, of his tongue in her mouth. It had been the most powerful thing she had ever experienced outside of the first time she had felt her child move. There had not been one part of her body that had not reacted to Orion's kiss.

That was passion, she realized. Henry had never shown her that. A brief fumbling in the dark, and discomfort, were all her late husband had ever given her, and those memories were blissfully hazy. He had not even made up for the lack of passion with companionship, rarely being home and, when he was, rarely interested in even sharing a meal with her. It had been a miserable marriage and, although she would never have wished for his death, she could not say she was sad he was gone.

Now she was faced with Orion, a handsome man she doubted any woman could hold on to. A man who had given her a taste of true passion, of what all the happily married women, or widows with daring enough to take lovers, talked about. The talks, whispers, and laughter had always made her feel envious as well as ignorant. She had not fully understood what they were talking about, but she had also wished she could have known what they had.

Here was her chance to discover what those women had sighed over. Orion was attracted to her and she knew it was not vanity that made her think so. No man could kiss a woman like that unless he wanted her, and she had the feeling that she wanted him, too. All she had to do was decide whether or not she wished to take a lover. It sounded so simple, and yet Catryn suspected she was going to lose a lot of sleep before she could decide.

Chapter Eight

"I shall ride up with you, Sir Orion," said Catryn as she followed him out of the inn.

"No, you shall not," he replied without even glancing her way.

She scowled at him as he secured their bags on the carriage. The lack of any stiffness or awkwardness during their morning meal had cheered her, allowing her to simply enjoy his company without worrying that they would have to discuss their loss of composure last night. She needed time to privately consider all that he made her feel, all that heat and need, and what to do about it. Stepping out to meet a beautiful day, the sun shining and the air more warm than cool, had only added to her pleasure. Sir Orion's cold refusal to allow her to ride up on the box with him put an abrupt end to her sense of contentment.

"Why not?" she demanded. "'Tis a fine, sunny day."

"So it is." He turned to look at her. "Clear skies and all. A truly rare day in this country. You would be easily seen and perhaps recognized by anyone we might pass upon the road under such clear, bright skies. Now, that would prove to be a lovely piece of gossip for someone to spread far and wide."

Catryn realized he referred to her reputation, or, more specifically, the utter ruination of whatever good name she had. She felt foolish for not giving more consideration to the risk she was taking, but that embarrassment faded quickly. Her every thought had been about rescuing her son. The few times she had faltered in that single-mindedness had been when the strong attraction she felt for Sir Orion had intruded. The rest of the time she was so caught up in chasing down Morris that she never thought about such things as trying not to be seen. And, in the end, her reputation was not, and never would be, worth more than her child and his safety.

"I am not well-known within society," she said, knowing it for the weak argument that it was.

"You *are* recognizable as a lady of some standing, and I suspect you are better known than you think you are. A description of you would be enough to shake free a memory or two." He opened the door to the carriage and held out his hand to help her inside. "Anyone seeing you brazenly riding on the box with me, that red hair blowing in the wind, would make it their business to find out exactly who you are. That is especially true since I am not quite the stranger to society that you believe you are."

She was seated in the carriage with Giles and the door shut before she had time to think over all he had said. "Brazenly?" she muttered. "I would never do anything brazenly. The man has a lot of gall to speak to me like that."

Giles shrugged as the carriage started to move. "A lady sitting up on the box of a gent's carriage would be a bit brazen." He grinned when she glared at him. "And that hair of yours would catch all eyes and be remembered. It is a shame your boy does not have that color hair, for then he would be easily noticed and we would have an easier time tracking him down."

"No, he has dark hair like his father. Well, darker than Henry's was, actually."

"No, you said he has black hair. That sometimes one of your kin is born with it and your father thinks it comes from some ancestor. I was sitting right there when you told my father."

"Fine then, it is black. Alwyn has black hair."

"Like mine."

"Somewhat."

A lot like Giles's hair, she silently admitted, right down to those beautiful waves. Her son had the same deep black hair that, when it caught the light just right, one could swear one saw hints of blue in its depths. Just like Giles had and just like Orion had. Catryn was not sure why she was so reluctant to admit to that, since she had already had to accept the fact that her son might be talking to ghosts. Yet it was getting harder and harder to even think of denying that somewhere, back in the history of her family, one of her ancestors had joined their line with one of Orion's.

"And you are certain there is no Vaughn or Wherlocke in your blood?" he asked.

"I have never heard it mentioned. Just as I told your father. There would be no point in lying about such a thing."

"I know, although some folk still do, because of what we can do and how it frightens them. But it puzzles me that you do not know, because I thought all your sort knew your bloodlines well."

"My sort is interested in the line of succession, the one that leads to inheritances of titles and entailed properties. Other little branches are noted if someone did something heroic. Cowards, criminals, scandals, and lunatics are most often just hidden away in the family lore. Most families keep a precise record of their lineage, but I doubt you will find many who can readily speak knowledgably about it for, as I said, the line to the title and lands is all that is seen as important. I know that line for my family very well, but little else except for the occasional tale of some ancestor who could not inherit. However, I have sent a missive to my father asking him to clarify whether or not there could be some connection between our families."

"That line being important because your boy can inherit?"

"Ah no, he cannot. He is not in a direct line from the one holding the title because I am not a male. My uncle Garrick has four children, and his eldest son, Michael, will inherit from my father. My uncle also has two other sons, so that leaves little chance for Alwyn. Unlike many another title, the Baron of Gryffin Manor title could fall to a daughter, but only if she is all that is left in the direct line. The man who gained the title for the family pushed for that because he had six daughters; but then he ended up with three sons before he died and passed on the title. There has always been at least one son to inherit through the direct line ever since."

"So this Morris fellow would have to kill four people to make it happen." He frowned. "No, it would be five. Or maybe six."

"Sweet mercy," she whispered, "that cannot be part of his plan. Morris is not a pleasant man, but I cannot believe he would kill so many. I have never sensed that sort of bloodthirstiness in the man, not even when he was having one of his temper fits. And then it would still come down to Alwyn, not any of Morris's progeny. Morris is not connected by blood to my family, not by one tiny drop." She shook her head. "How could it work?" *And why am I asking a boy of eight?* she asked herself.

Giles folded his arms over his chest in a way that made Catryn think of Sir Orion. "Morris wants to marry you. We know that now that you finally told us everything, as you should. That would put any child he bred on you in that line for gaining the title and all it brings, aye?"

Catryn ignored the fact that she had just been chastised by an eight-year-old boy. "He would have to kill my father, my uncle, my three little cousins, and Alwyn."

"Children die. Children disappear. Old men get sick and die. Fevers have been known to take down whole families."

The calm, almost cold way the boy spoke those

hard truths made Catryn shiver. It was not only that such a young boy could even think of such things but that Giles accepted them as simply a part of life. She could hear that acceptance in his voice. She wanted to weep for the loss of so much of his childhood. The urge to also shake him for putting such horrible thoughts in her head was strong, but she pushed it aside. It was not the boy's fault and it was also something she should consider, no matter how much she might want to reject it, push it right out of her mind, and never think of it again.

"You had a hard life before you met your father, and that might be why you can even think of such a dark plot. I, on the other hand, have led a very sheltered life in comparison. I fear everything within me is denying that such a crime could ever be committed."

"It can be, but I am thinking Morris does not have the spine for it. Beginning to think he does not have the wit to plan it out well, either. It was just a thought." He pulled a book from the bag at his feet and suddenly smiled, as if he had not just been discussing the murder of nearly an entire family. "You could pass the time by reading to me, aye?"

She took the book from him and saw that it was one her father had praised, calling it a well-written account of the Battle of Taunton. "You are very interested in military matters." So was she, but she did not tell too many people, for it was considered an odd thing for a lady to be interested in.

"Some, aye. Not enough to be a soldier though, I am

thinking. Too hard, too dangerous, and too dirty. I am done with being dirty. You talking on that battle the other day made me remember I had this book and was planning to read it. I could read it myself, but it would be slow work." He blushed. "I am still learning the skill. I had a bit of skill before meeting my father, seeing as Katie did teach us boys some, but it would be a hard slog through a book like that."

"Katie? Was she one of the women you said occasionally had the care of you?"

"Different women, different times. Katie was the last. She had a little learning and was teaching us, but she mostly wanted us to bring her things we stole. We thought it was needed, that the men she had round did not pay much for the pleasuring she gave them, and since she was letting us bed down in her little room when she did not have a man in, we felt we owed her." He grunted. "More fool us. She did not need the pittances we brought her and risked our necks for."

"She had some other scheme?"

"That she did. She was carrying, and had stopped seeing as many men as was usual. It was why we thought she needed the help. Then, after the babe was born, she left the rooms we shared one day and I followed her." He blushed. "I was afraid she was going to leave the babe, like I was left."

"But she did not."

He shook his head. "She went to a tavern, one of the better ones, and met a man and woman in one of those private rooms. Had the babe stuffed in a bag so no one could see him. I could see they were of a better kind than us, and I had seen her with the man from time to time, but not as one of the ones she pleasured. She gave them that little boy babe and they gave her a heavy sack of coin. Did it all as sly as possible so no one but me noticed she had come in with a bag and left without one. That was when I understood why she had let herself get caught when she never had before. It was her plan all along to sell a babe. It also explained how she had herself a true gent for a while, when she never had before—not of a rank like my father's or yours, but not some dockworker or the like, if you understand."

"A younger son. Perhaps a banker or solicitor."

"Just like that. Think that couple chose the fellow to get her with child. I could see the woman with the man was real pleased by the babe, so I did not try to get the babe back. Also saw that the woman was looking as if she was about to have a babe herself. Thinking that was all for show. Did go to see where they took him, though. Nice house. They slipped inside all quiet like, with the babe still in the bag, and when I went round the next day they were greeting all kind of folk who were happy and congratulating him on being a father now. Saw them a fortnight past in the park. The lady and a young maid were with the boy and he was all plump and laughing, so I let it be. He is better off where he is. The woman still had that look on her face, too."

"What look?"

"That look that said she was still happy with her bought babe, that she wanted that little boy to be all hers. I could feel it inside her."

"Then he is much, much better off where he is."
She frowned. "What happened to Katie?"

"Fool woman started to flash her new riches about,
buying some pretty baubles and all. Got her throat cut."

Catryn swallowed her gasp of shock. It was a life she
had no understanding of. Whores, baby sellers,
women getting their throats cut. Thinking of Giles
growing up in such a world made her want to sweep
him up into her arms and hold him tightly, but she resisted the urge. He needed no comforting. He had
come out of that world hardened but not ruined by it,
and she had to respect that. Even while living that
rough life, he had cared about what happened to
others, such as that baby, so that goodness was deep
inside his soul and no longer at risk of being lost to
the world.

"And you and your mates have ended up in a much
better place as well," she finally said.

"We have. Lady Olympia helped us for a while, and
then I met my father. He took us all in and Lady Pen
is teaching us all how to be gents. It is a fine life."

"Then let us put all that aside and learn more
about the Battle of Taunton."

The stopping of the carriage pulled Catryn out of
a light sleep. As she sat up, she noticed that Giles was
also rubbing his eyes and yawning. Both turned to
look at Orion when he opened the door to the carriage. A brief look beyond him revealed that they were

not near the docks, and yet she could swear she smelled that distinct fish and filth odor of a port.

"Where are we?" she asked as he helped her down from the carriage.

"Portsmouth. Just down the road from one of the docks," Orion replied.

"Have you seen Morris?" she asked.

"I saw his carriage and team at an inn we just passed. This is the first place where I could put the carriage out of sight yet ready to make a fast escape. It is a short, easy run from the docks to here. Someone could see the carriage unguarded and ride off with it, so I have already hired a lad to watch it and have given him a whistle to blow to warn us. I have not yet caught sight of Morris or your son, so thought it best if you come along to help me look for them."

"You had thought to leave me behind?"

"I did. This is no game, and these men may be stupid, but they are dangerous. At times, stupid and dangerous is worse than smart and dangerous. Smart at least considers their own skin in all they do. Now, we need to hide that hair or at least stay within the shadows."

Catryn turned and reached inside the carriage for her bag. She got a scarf out of it, and with a few twists and turns had it tied securely over her hair. She then tucked the rest of her long braid beneath her coat. It was not very fashionable and she probably looked like some aging crone hiding her thin hair, but her bright red hair was now covered.

"That will do," Orion said. "Now we shall hunt the man down."

She glanced at the boy who sat under a tree watching them, and nodded in greeting before she hooked her arm through his and they began to walk through the town with Giles, keeping to the shadows and blending in with the crowd to shield them as much as possible. "You do not think Morris will recognize you?"

"If you had not noticed, I am not dressed in my usual finery."

"Oh." She looked over his attire, clothes more suited to a prosperous businessman than a knight from a large family riddled with titles. "I just thought that you wished to save your good clothes from becoming too travel worn."

"There is that advantage, but this is a clever mask for the most part. Everything is of good quality but not too fine. Dull in color so not apt to catch the eye. Even the hat"—he touched his tricorn hat—"is good, but not a single thread of embellishment to make it fashionable. The same with my coat."

He was right. If one came up to him and really studied his clothing, they might perhaps notice that it was made by an excellent tailor, one not many men could afford, but people rarely looked that closely at someone just strolling down the street. For once she, dressed in the rather plain serviceable gowns she had packed for this journey, did not feel dowdy standing near him.

She began to look around as subtly as she could. There were a lot of people wandering the streets, taking advantage of such a fine day. It would not be easy to see the unremarkable Morris in such a crowd.

Catryn knew she would see her son, however, if Morris did not have him hidden away somewhere.

They had turned and were idly strolling back in the direction of the carriage before she finally saw Morris. Alwyn stood next to him, and she actually took a step in his direction. Orion's grip on her arm immediately tightened and Giles stepped up so that he walked on her other side. It was hard not to push them both aside and run to her child, grab him up, and then flee with him. As her companions walked her across the road and into a shadowy alley between a dress shop and a hat shop, she fought to get a firm grip on her common sense. To run after her child would be idiocy, for Morris had four big men with him. All she would do was allow him to capture her as well.

"We need to make a plan," Orion said as he lightly pinned Catryn between him and the wall of the hat shop. "Morris and his men outnumber us and out-weigh at least two of us."

"I know. I *know*," she repeated with a little more force as she nudged Orion aside and moved so that she could look at Alwyn across the street. "I have been repeating that to myself since I first saw him and took a step toward him."

"The boy looks hale," Orion said as he moved to stand beside her.

"Yes, he does. That makes it easier to be cautious. It appears Morris is having some difficulty arranging a berth on a ship."

Orion looked at the almost too thin man dressed in bright finery arguing with a burly, hairy sailor. The little boy stood by his side, a big man on guard on his other side, and appeared to be watching the boats. Then the boy said something and Morris glared at him. From the way the man was waving his hand in the child's face it was obvious he was scolding Alwyn. The sailor just frowned at the boy, the look on his bearded face one of confusion.

"I gather he has given up on the idea of getting his hands on me as well," Catryn said. "After all, he is obviously planning to leave the country."

"That would depend on when he wants to sail," replied Orion. "The carriage is a quick run from here through those trees, but I'm not sure what would be the best way to separate the boy from Morris so that we can grab him and have even the smallest chance of escape."

"I can get him," said Giles.

Orion turned to look at his son. "You may be a few years older than he, but he looks a healthy lad. Not sure you could catch him and run very far with his weight in your arms."

"I will not have to." Giles looked at Catryn. "The boy can run, aye?"

"He can," she answered. "He can actually run very fast for someone with such short legs, and it is something he dearly loves to do."

"Then all I need to do is to lure him away from Morris and his men, and get him just far enough away that he and I can run for it."

"That could work." Orion looked at the pub near the docks where Morris stood. "Wait here a moment."

"What is he doing?" Catryn wondered, watching Orion stride away and disappear into the pub.

"My guess is he is seeing if there is anyone he can hire to step between me and your son and Morris and his bully boys," said Giles. "Would not have to be a big delay or even a fight. Just enough time gained for me to get Alwyn to you and all of us to get to the carriage. That would be what I would do."

"It would?"

"Aye. Used that trick on the streets a lot to stop the one we just lifted a purse off of from catching the one who did the lifting."

"Oh." Catryn could not stop herself from reaching out to smooth her hand over his hair, as if she could smooth away the memories of that hard life he had lived.

"I just need to think of a way to catch your boy's attention," Giles said, moving a little closer to her and tilting his head slightly so that she could stroke his hair more easily.

"You just have to get near to him," Catryn said, pretending not to notice his silent bid for more affection, continuing the idle stroking of his hair as she spoke.

"What do you mean?"

Catryn sighed. "Alwyn is so drawn to be with other children that just seeing one is enough to have him moving closer. At the house in the country I let him play with the servants' children when I can, although his father did not like that so we had to be circumspect about it when he was alive. In the city it is much harder to find him other children to play with, although I can get lucky on some days in the park. Alwyn wants to be with other children very badly, so smile at him, maybe wink, but act welcoming and he will do all he can to slip away and get closer to you."

"He is that lonely for boys his age?"

"Think how you would feel if you did not have your mates."

"Oh. Nay, would not like that at all. Bad enough we are living in different places now, but at least I know where they are and can go there most times I want to. And they are in London during that season you rich folk have."

"Careful how you speak of us, my lad, for you have joined our ranks."

"Damn. Keep forgetting that, but I have."

Catryn decided not to scold the boy for his language this time and, with Giles at her side, watched Morris and her son. Her arms ached to catch Alwyn up and hold him tight, to check him for any bruises. She had never been parted from him, she realized. From the day he was born, he had been with her, in London and in the country, with only a maid to assist her in the care of him. Or her father and one of the other servants. There would be someone else now, she decided. Even if she believed the threat Morris posed was ended, she would never leave her child without a proper, trained guard again.

Although she knew time passed slowly when one was eager to get something done, she found waiting for Orion to return very difficult. The fear that Morris would get whatever he was arguing for and leave grew with each passing moment. She was actually considering going to find Orion when Giles tensed at her side.

"Here comes my father," he said and stopped leaning against her to stand straight as a guard at her side.

She watched Orion walk over to them. "Did you find what you went looking for?"

"I did." He glanced toward the docks as half a dozen burly, somewhat rough-looking men began to wander out of the pub and congregate near where Morris continued to argue with the sailor. "Now, Giles, how do you plan to get young Alwyn to come to you?"

"Our lady already told me how to do it," Giles replied. "The boy wants to be with other boys. So I will just catch his eye and let him see that I am a friendly sort." He looked toward Alwyn. "It does not look as if he is being all that closely watched at the moment. The men are too busy arguing with that sailor. Best I get to it."

"If you sense that Morris or his men guess the threat you pose, get out of there as fast as you can. Disappear and make your way around to the carriage."

"I will, and getting away fast is something I am good at. But I will get the boy. So the plan is, get boy, run here, and then run for the carriage. That it?"

"That is it. I have also made certain that Morris will not find it easy to get his carriage on the road to come after us."

"What did you do?"

"Broke one of his wheels. Paid the stable hand to look the other way while I did it. Morris does not endear himself to the workers and servants. He obviously does not see how valuable it can be to treat such people with respect and kindness. Or pay them decently, if at all."

"A man like that one never will. I will get your son

for you, m'lady," Giles told Catryn before starting toward the docks.

Orion watched his son wander off and wondered if he was putting too much faith in the boy. "This is madness. Giles is only eight."

"Easy to forget that at times," said Catryn. "He is also, despite how his life is better now, a boy of the London streets. I do not believe he is given to empty boasting either."

"No, true enough. Then, too, with his gift he will have ample warning if things turn dangerous for him. This will work."

She suspected he was working to convince himself, but she prayed he was right.

Chapter Nine

Her stomach was so knotted up with fear and expectation, Catryn was amazed that she was not hunched over like some ancient crone. It was bad enough seeing her son so close yet unable to grab him, but watching Giles walk toward Morris and his men only made it worse. She had grown very fond of the boy and hated watching him put himself in danger for her sake.

"As you reminded me not a moment ago, he grew up on the streets, Cat," Orion said quietly and kissed the top of her head before moving to stand in a spot that gave him a better line of sight. "He is skilled in the game."

Startled by the softly spoken pet name he had just used, it took Catryn a moment to realize he not only stood between her and the docks but he had placed her completely in the shadows. Leaning to the side a little, she could see that his gaze was fixed unwaveringly on Morris, his men, and Alwyn. He held his

pistol at his side. Catryn was pleased that this Sir
Orion was on her side. There was a strong air of
danger around him now and she knew it ought to
frighten her. Instead, it made her more certain that
this was the man who would help her save her son.

"I cannot see Alwyn with you standing there," she
said, although she knew her soft protest would not
make him move. "Or Giles."

"I can."

"Were you born with this arrogance?"

He did not chance glancing her way but briefly
grinned at the false sweetness of her tone. "I believe
I was."

"How lovely for you."

With a twist of her body and a little bending,
Catryn was finally able to see past him. Giles used a
stick to bat pebbles around on the road while he sang
a rhyme he should have scrubbed from his tongue. A
couple of men unloading fish from a battered boat
laughed heartily when they drew close enough to hear
him, as did the men Orion had hired. Giles showed
no sign of concern, no fear at all. There was a lot of
his father in that boy, she decided.

Then she saw Alwyn standing next to Morris, who
was still arguing fiercely with the sailor. Alwyn looked
so sad, her arms ached with the need to hold him.
Then he caught sight of Giles showing off his skill at
dancing a jig in front of the men who had laughed at
his song. Now he had Alwyn laughing. Catryn promised herself she would give Giles a big hug and kiss as
soon as they were safe and riding far away from this

place, simply for making her boy smile when he had to have been so scared for too long.

She tensed when she saw Alwyn begin to shuffle ever so slowly away from Morris and his men. It was as she watched her son take tiny steps toward Giles that she noticed something else. The men who were finding Giles's antics so enjoyable were also subtly moving, cautiously making themselves a barrier between Morris, his men, and the two boys. Catryn scowled up at Orion.

"I think there was a little more to this plan than I was told," she whispered.

Never taking his gaze from the boys, the men he had hired, and the enemy, he replied in an equally soft voice, "I could not be certain the men from the pub would do as I asked. There was the small chance that they would just pocket my coin and run. Or simply stand about and not risk putting themselves between the boys and Morris."

"That is what Giles said you had gone to do, hire men to slow any pursuit."

"Clever boy, my son. There. Giles has him. Be ready."

Catryn stepped back to give Orion room, hitched her skirts up so that she could run with more ease and speed, and waited. Morris and his men remained completely involved in their argument with what she now believed was the captain of a ship that Morris clearly wished to sail away on. Giles had Alwyn's hand in his and was inching his way backward toward them. She took a deep breath to try and remain calm, praying that Giles was as clever as she thought he was and would know just the right moment to run.

Giles knew the boy whose hand he now held trusted him completely. He could feel it. It made no sense, and that made him falter for a moment. Then he stiffened his backbone before fear could weaken him. This boy had put his faith in him and he would not fail him. It was what his mates had done for him and he would do the same for this child.

"Your mother is near," he told the boy.

"I know. My father told me." Alwyn smiled at Giles. "He told me you would take me to her."

"That is the plan."

"Good, because I do not like Morris. My father says he is a filthy bastard."

Moving a little more quickly, Giles kept his gaze fixed on Morris and his men. "So your father is with you now?"

"My mother and Grand-da tell me I should not say so."

"You can tell me."

"Yes, I can, and Papa just said that we had better start running our wee legs off right now."

Giles did not question or hesitate. He tightened his grip on the boy's hand and started to run toward the narrow alley where his father and Alwyn's mother waited. The speed of the smaller boy impressed him, but he was wise enough in the ways of small children to know it would not last long. Giles hoped one of the adults was ready to catch up Alwyn and run with him.

Catryn was just holding her arms out to catch her son when one of Morris's men let out a cry of alarm. She grabbed Alwyn and started to run for the carriage even as Morris's furious bellow rang out. A quick glance behind her revealed that the men Orion had hired were doing an admirable job of impeding Morris and his men, but she knew that tactic would only work for a little while. She doubted Orion had paid the men enough for them to be willing to die for him.

Orion loped past her as they neared the carriage, tossed several coins at the boy who had been watching it, yanked open the door for her and the boys, and then leapt up into the driver's perch. Giles was next, passing her and hurling himself inside. She tossed Alwyn in, leapt in, and was just shutting the door when the carriage started to move. Orion was not sparing the horses, either. Catryn wrapped an arm around each boy and tried to protect them from the worst of a rough ride.

"Hello, Mama," said Alwyn, grinning at her. "I knew you would come. So did Papa." He saw her glance at Giles and said, "He knows, Mama, and he understands."

Catryn sighed. "I suspect he does."

"Papa says Giles is one of us."

"Well, he is certainly a good man to have on your side." She felt Giles sit up straighter beneath her arm. "Did Morris hurt you, sweetheart?"

"He slapped me sometimes, but that is all. I did not like it and Papa wanted to gut him, but it is fine. I just wanted to come home, and waited for you to come and fetch me."

"I do not recall Henry being so, um, blunt in his manner of speaking," she murmured.

"Papa is not Henry."

"Of course he is. Your father was named Henry, Henry Joseph Louis de Warrenne, Baron of Cutler Broadhurst."

"No, my papa is called A-E-D-D-O-N. Aeddon. That is what he says. He says Henry was a bastard who deserved that knife in the belly."

Catryn did not know what to say. She was ready to accept that her son could speak to spirits, and unusually talkative, cursing ones as well, but that the spirit he spoke to would pretend to be his father was a shock. A look at Giles revealed that the boy was watching Alwyn with interest.

"Whatever this Aeddon says, I would like you to not repeat the bad words, if you please," she finally said and ignored Giles's snort of laughter.

Alwyn nodded and then they hit a particularly bad stretch of road and had to concentrate on bracing themselves. Catryn did wonder why Orion was racing away so fast and for so long, since he had crippled Morris's carriage. Even if Morris hired a carriage or some horses, he had lost a lot of time. Then again, she thought as she propped her feet up against the other seat in an attempt to steady them all, Orion was undoubtedly more accustomed to solving such problems than she was. If he thought they needed to get as far away as possible as fast as possible, she would not argue, just hang on to herself and the boys so that they did not arrive at their destination covered in bruises.

* * *

Orion eased up on the reins, allowing his team to slow to a less strenuous pace. He had run them hard, but they did not look too worn. After another mile, he found a good place to pull off the road and let the animals rest for just a little while. He was a little cautious about opening the door to the carriage, for he knew his passengers could not have had a pleasant ride.

He peeked inside, met three sets of eyes, the blue eyes curious and amused and the sea-green eyes not so amused. Catryn had clearly protected both boys as best she could, for neither one looked as if he had gained any bruises. She looked beautifully tousled. He held out his hand to her.

"We will have a short rest here before continuing on," he said as he helped her down from the carriage and then turned to catch each boy as he jumped out.

"We have lost Morris?" she asked as he began to gather some grass to wipe down his horses and she moved to help him.

"We will find some water, Father," said Giles as he grabbed a small bucket from the back of the carriage and, taking Alwyn by the hand, wandered off to find a source of water.

"Yes, we have lost Morris," Orion finally replied as they wiped down the horses. "I wanted to put as many miles as I could between him and us during the time it would take him to fix or hire a carriage, maybe even to hire a few horses. Even took a detour or two to throw him off our trail."

"And where are we going?" She tossed away the grass and looked around for Giles and Alwyn.

"To my cousin's. Radmoor. The seat of the Viscount of Radmoor. Penelope married the viscount and cares for a lot of the children her—and I quote her here—'randy kinsmen' keep breeding. And it might be best to tell you now that I have two other sons at Radmoor. Paul and Hector."

Before she could recover from her shock enough to question him, Alwyn and Giles returned with a bucket of water and helped Orion water the horses. Catryn watched her son with his new friend and Orion, and nearly smiled. Alwyn was at ease with both the boy and the man. In fact, the way Alwyn stared at Giles made her suspect her son considered his new friend the hero of the day. Considering all the work she and Orion had done to get him back, it was a little lowering, but she could be magnanimous. Giles had done a very good job as well.

Catryn fetched the basket of food from the carriage, pleased to see that it had been packed firmly enough not to have suffered much from their rough ride. Grabbing a blanket, she spread it on the ground and began to set out all the food. It did not surprise her when Orion and the boys soon appeared. Nothing brought males out of the woodwork like the smell of food.

"This Penelope," she said as everyone helped themselves to some of the bread, cheese, and cold meat, "is someone you know very well?"

"Oh yes," said Orion. "She has been taking care of my sons Paul and Hector for several years now, ever since their mothers left them at the Warren."

"The Warren?" She frowned and felt a trickle of alarm as she wondered just where the other two boys had come from. "You were married once?"

"No." He grimaced, knowing he was about to tarnish his armor in a way. "Paul was born to a mistress I had for a while. Hector came from a truly senseless frolic about town when I first arrived in the city. Both women were supposed to have the care of the boys, for which I paid well, but they gave them up. At times, and I fear it is happening with greater frequency, children show what their gift is early. Paul's mother did not like it. Paul is a bit like you, Catryn. He can sense danger, sense a threat as it approaches. He warned his mother or someone she knew just one too many times, and she did not want him near her any longer. Hector has, well, visions of what might happen and draws them out in some very skillful pictures. I gather he drew a fate for someone his mother knew and she could not be rid of him fast enough."

Catryn shook her head. "I do not understand that. I truly do not." She looked at Alwyn, who was eating with a lack of delicacy she probably should have scolded him for but she was too happy to see him acting normally to care. "I appear to have a child who speaks to the dead, which means spirits must be wandering about near him, thus me, all the time," she said quietly, leaning closer to Orion so that her son, busily chatting with Giles, did not overhear, "but I would never, never give him up. He is my child, my blood, my heart."

Unable to resist, Orion kissed her on the cheek and then grimaced when he heard one of the boys gasp. Glancing their way, he saw his little rogue of a son grinning like a fool while young Alwyn stared at him with wide eyes. He could not stop from wondering if that look of shock was because a man who was not her husband had kissed her, or because the boy had never even seen his father do that.

"Your mother is a very good woman and said something that demanded a reward," he told the boy, ignoring the way Catryn was blushing.

Alwyn stared at him for a moment more and then smiled. Orion was stunned. When the boy smiled like that he could see so many of his family in that youthful face. Even if Catryn's father had found no written proof of a connection between her family and his, Orion knew he was looking right at all the proof anyone else in his clan would ever need. The tie was there, and he would have to decide what to do about it, for Alwyn's gift was so strong that the boy would need some training.

"Yes, Mama is very good," agreed Alwyn, and then he rushed over to fling himself into her arms and kiss her. "And I should reward you for coming and getting me so quickly."

"Oh, love, it was not as quickly as I would have wished," she said.

"Fast enough. Morris did not get me on that boat."

"Very true. Did he happen to say where he was thinking of taking you?"

"Prussia. Can Giles and me run about some? I have not had a run-about for days. It was all sit, be quiet, stand there, and do not move a step."

"If Giles does not mind—and it is Giles and I, dear."

"You want to run about, too?"

She could see by the way his eyes almost danced

with laughter that he had not misunderstood at all. "Go on. Silly fellow. Run about but stay in sight, please. I need to be able to see where you are. I was frightened when you were taken and it will be a while before I can be at ease when I cannot see you."

Alwyn patted her on the cheek. "There was no need to be frightened. Papa was with me the whole way. I was scared at first, but he made me brave again." He ran off and Giles joined him in dashing round amongst the trees.

"So it is your husband haunting him then," said Orion.

"No, it is some fellow named A-E-D-D-O-N. Aeddon. That is exactly how Alwyn said it. I have no idea why he calls him Papa. I am certain I have never even met a man with that name. It might be something as simple as the fact that my husband was such a poor father that Alwyn has dubbed this spirit as his sire instead. Although that does not explain why a man whose name I have never heard should be haunting my son."

Orion was very glad that Catryn was watching her son and not looking at him, for he suspected he had gone pale. Aeddon was not a common name, but he had heard it before. Aeddon Vaughn, a rogue who was not much trusted even by his own family yet had also been dubbed a likeable fellow. Likeable but not one to be left alone with the family silver, a cousin had once told Orion. Last he had heard, the man had been found in the Thames with his throat cut about four or so years back, which had surprised no one in the family who had known him, although he had been grieved for by some. He had not heard if anyone had found out who did it, although he knew the family would do their best to try and discover the truth.

For one brief moment he struggled with anger and jealousy. If Aeddon was truly Alwyn's father, that meant Catryn was not quite the innocent she appeared. It was a ridiculous thought. How would Aeddon have ever met Catryn, let alone left her with a child in her belly?

This was something he was going to have to look into. He would have to be very careful about it as well, for the only one he could really find out much from was a boy of five. If it truly was Aeddon Vaughn haunting the boy, then that was where he needed to go to find out the full truth. Aeddon was speaking through the boy and he would get the truth out of the rogue at his first opportunity.

"It is beginning to alarm me that you do not have an answer for that puzzle," Catryn murmured even as she smiled at the way Giles chased a laughing Alwyn through the trees, roaring like some huge beast.

"Perhaps the spirit was near your home when he died or near someplace you went to," Orion said. "I could look into the matter if you like. There cannot be many people named Aeddon. Might even ask Alwyn, if the ghost has said anything about who he might be or where he met his fate. Whoever it is, he was a man who did not temper his speech much."

Catryn was surprised that she could laugh about such a thing as a foul-mouthed spirit that had attached itself to her child, but she did. "No, it is a spirit with the speech of a dockworker. And ask Alwyn if you like. He would probably enjoy talking about his spirit, as I fear we mostly shush him when he tries."

"Penelope is the one to talk to. She grew up speaking with the dead. She will understand and may even have some ideas for how you can help him learn how to hide his gift when needed or explain why it is that he has to."

"That is going to be the hardest thing to do. I do not wish him to think he is so different that he is somehow, well, wrong, yet he has to come to understand that this is something he simply cannot share with the world." She grimaced. "And I wish to do it in a better way than my mother did with me and my foretelling the presence of danger."

"It is something my family has been dealing with for generations, so trust Penelope to have a few answers for you."

"I will consider it. So, are your other sons going to be at Radmoor?"

It shocked him but Orion could actually feel the tickle of heat from a faint blush on his cheeks. "They are. They have been with Penelope so long, since each was very small, that she is their mother in both mind and heart. My sons also see the rest of the boys as their brothers. Juno is their sister. They all have families and a few have joined their fathers, as mine have joined me, but they always go back to Penelope and the rest, and do so regularly. As I said, it appears Paul has some foresight, as you do, and Hector has even more."

"Has Giles met them?"

"Yes, and Paul and Giles deal together well. Hector

is being a little slow to accept another brother, but there is no true animosity there. One thing Penelope's boys do is welcome more children. They welcomed a lot when they lived at the Warren, including little Juno."

"Why would they not have welcomed Juno if she was left behind as they were?"

"She is a girl. All of the rest are boys. One can never tell at that age how they will feel about a little girl entering their boys' world. But they did not care, and even saw to it that she had her own room. Penelope said that when the mother brought Juno to the Warren, the boys put themselves between her and the child and even told her to leave. They proclaimed that Juno belonged to them now." He frowned when he noticed how her eyes shone with moisture. "That makes you wish to cry?" he asked as he put an arm around her shoulders and held her close.

"It is touching, that is all." She felt his mouth press against her hair and wondered how such a kiss could stir her blood as fast as it was doing. "I am pleased they have all made themselves a family. Odd as that family may be, it sounds a very strong one," she said as she slowly pulled away from him.

"And no more kissing me in front of the boys," she whispered.

He quickly kissed her on her cheek. "I am not sure I can promise that."

She was not sure she could promise not to welcome such kisses either. Catryn shook aside the thought. She and her son were together now, and she was not sure what her next step would be. A treacherous voice in her mind told her that she should step right into

Sir Orion's arms and finally discover what a man could give her that would have her smiling in sweet memory like so many other women did. Catryn was not sure how long she would be able to shut up that insidious little whisper of temptation.

"Best call the boys," said Orion as he began to pack up what few scraps of food were left. "We cannot linger long. I do not see how Morris would be able to follow us, but nothing has been going as I thought it would, or should, since this little adventure began. I want to get to Radmoor as quickly as we can."

Catryn called the boys, pleased when they responded quickly, and then slipped off into the wood to relieve herself. She hated the need to see to her private business outside, but there was no choice in the matter. Worse, she was going to have to tell the boys to do the same and she knew they would think it a lot of fun. Hearing the faint trickle of water, she moved toward it and found a small brook running through the wood. She decided the males could just wait a little longer because she was going to wash some of the travel dust off herself before they moved on to Radmoor.

Orion frowned when Catryn did not return quickly. He was just about to go and search for her when Giles looked at him, cocked his head in the direction Catryn had gone, and raised one brow. Seeing a good chance to have a few private words with Alwyn, Orion nodded and signaled his son to go and see what the woman was doing. The moment Giles slipped away, Orion looked at Alwyn.

"The spirit you speak to is named Aeddon?" he

asked the boy, and waited until Alwyn stopped staring after Giles and turned to face him.

"A.E.D.D.O.N. Aeddon. Aeddon Vaughn. He is my papa," replied Alwyn.

"And he tells you that he is your father?"

Alwyn nodded and glanced toward the woods. "Will Mama and Giles come back?"

"Oh yes. They did not work so hard to find you just to walk away now."

"That is what Papa said. He knew when I was scared and he would tell me to be calm, that my mother was on her way. He knew about you, too."

"Did he now? But I am curious about why he thinks he is your father."

"Because he is, although he said my mother might not know and he has to think on how to tell me the why of it. Says he does not know the right words yet, only ones a little boy should not say." His eyes widened. "Oh, I was supposed to keep it a secret."

"Do not fear. I will not tell anyone. Do you know what happened to Aeddon?"

"He got his throat cut and the bad men threw him in the river."

"What bad men?"

"He will not tell me yet. Says it is a long tale and a bad one. He says he has not got the right way to say it when it has to come out of my mouth, but he is thinking on it."

Orion sighed and lightly stroked the boy's hair. "I will wait then." He saw Giles leading Catryn out of the woods. "Here they come. Into the carriage with you, lad."

Catryn hurried over and smiled guiltily. "Sorry,

Orion. I heard some water and all I could think of was washing some of the travel dust off."

"Not to worry," he said as he helped her into the carriage after Giles leapt inside. "I do not believe Morris is hot on our heels. I will, however, travel as fast as I can without wearying the horses." Just as he moved to shut the door, she put her hand on it.

"Might I ride up with you?" she asked quietly and then glanced back at the two yawning boys. "I believe the boys might like to lie down on the seats since the ride should not be too rough."

Orion hesitated only a moment. "Have your pistol?"

She patted the side of her skirt where the weapon was tucked into a hidden pocket. "Still with me."

"Come along then. There is little chance of you being seen on the route I will be taking." He looked in at the boys. "Behave yourselves."

As soon as they were on their way, Orion glanced at Catryn and considered what he had learned from Alwyn. The spirit clinging to the boy was the one he had thought it was, and he had obviously died hard. Yet, there was little chance Catryn or her son would have been in the area where Aeddon died. That still left the puzzle about why Aeddon's spirit had attached itself to the child and why they had such a strong connection that they could carry on whole conversations. From what his relatives with similar gifts had told him, that was very rare.

The thing that troubled him the most, however, was why his late cousin would tell the child that he was his father. That made no sense at all. Orion knew Catryn had been faithful to her husband. He had absolutely no doubt about that. The fact that Aeddon said he could not say how it could be yet, because he did not have the words a young child should say, bothered him even more. It implied that something bad may have happened to Catryn. Orion had never heard that Aeddon was a man who abused women, however.

He glanced at Catryn one more time and savored the sight of her sitting beside him, her hair slowly coming undone as the wind tore through it. She smiled faintly as she watched the countryside go by. There was nothing about Catryn that made him think she had been forced by a man. Left unsatisfied, most certainly, and used for no more than breeding an heir, but not abused.

Orion decided to set the puzzle aside for now. He concentrated on getting them to Radmoor as quickly as he could without endangering the team. Once Alwyn was safe with his cousins, he could work hard to catch Morris and just maybe find a few answers to all the puzzles that surrounded Catryn and her son.

Chapter Ten

"Are you certain we will be welcome?" Catryn asked when Orion helped her down from the driver's perch, and she gasped at the sight of the huge manor house.

"Of course we will." Orion idly assisted her in tidying her windblown hair. "Once you have met them you will understand my confidence. Penelope has more heart than is wise sometimes." He smiled at Alwyn when they reached the ornate oak doors and he knocked. "I think you shall quite enjoy staying here, young man, and talking with our Penelope. She is like you."

Before Catryn could ask what he meant by *staying here*, they were being let into the house by a tall, thin butler. The next few moments were chaotic as they were led into a large parlor filled with boys. She struggled to recall each name spoken as she was introduced but was heartily glad when the introductions were over. She was seated next to her hostess and sipping at a cup of tea served to her by a smiling maid while Orion explained all they had been through, idly rubbing the heads of the two young boys who clung to his legs.

The array of delicacies that was set before her was so tempting, she allowed Orion to tell his cousins her story while she filled a surprisingly large hole in her stomach and fought to conquer a large twinge of jealousy over how he had given three different women some almost beautiful boys. She studied Lady Penelope and Lord Ashton Radmoor. The Viscount of Radmoor was a tall, lean, handsome man with his golden hair and bluish gray eyes. The viscountess was a good match for him. Small, and lithe despite the rounding stomach that revealed she was with child, she had thick brown hair that gleamed with hints of red and gold and eyes that reminded Catryn of the sea. Rather like her own, she mused, or so Orion had claimed as they had driven here. Catryn thought Penelope's were a much more dramatic color than her own.

They made a beautiful couple, she decided, and looked around the large, crowded room. They were also well matched in the goodness of their hearts. She was humbled and fascinated by this couple who opened their luxurious home to children whom so many of the gentry had tossed aside. Ones of their class usually cared only for their legitimate children, giving barely a thought to any others they bred so carelessly. A man was considered quite a good fellow if he gave the woman who bore his illegitimate child some money to raise him or her. They certainly cared little for the urchins scratching out a life on the streets of the city.

The fact that Orion obviously cared for his sons was probably why she was no longer shocked and a little disgusted by his profligacy. The boys were healthy, dressed warmly, accepted fully despite the irregularity of their birth, and Orion supported them very well. He may have been heedless in one way, but he was a good father in every other.

"You must have been terrified," Lady Penelope said, breaking into Catryn's thoughts as she patted her arm.

"I was always trying very hard not to envision the worst, my lady," Catryn replied honestly.

"Please, call me Penelope, and with your permission I shall call you Catryn." She waved a small hand to indicate the room crowded with children. "As you can see, we are a bit lax on the formalities, especially here, away from the critical eyes of society."

"Sir Orion was right about you."

"Oh dear, what did he say?"

"That I should not worry about meeting you for you have a very big heart." She smiled when Penelope blushed. "You do, as does your husband. To care for so many even when you are starting a family of your own"—she nodded at the rounding stomach Penelope's gown could not quite hide—"requires a very big heart indeed. Especially when some are not even of your blood."

"Ah, well, those boys helped Giles when he needed it, and we do have our suspicions about two of the little devils, that they may be kin, but we are not certain yet."

"No one would take them in? Mother or father?"

"The mothers did not want any of them. The fathers have not cast them aside but most are single gentlemen. I set up a house to care for my brothers when, after our father died, they were cast aside by my mother. Soon, one by one, they will all leave us, for if my uncle Argus is any indication, the men will take their child or children into their new household once they are wed and settled."

Penelope smiled at Catryn. "And do not think that they do not help support or care for their children, the rogues. In some ways we are akin to a boarding school here, keeping the boys civilized and seeing to their learning while their fathers do whatever it is they do. But even though we can well afford the care, every father who leaves a child with us pays for that child's upkeep. Wherlockes and Vaughns are taught to care for and support their children, legitimate or not, and few ever break that rule."

There was a touch of ferocity behind those last words that roused Catryn's curiosity, but Giles and Alwyn ran up to her before she gave in to the urge to ask any impertinent and far too personal questions. She noted yet again that Giles was staying very close to Alwyn, much like an appointed guard. The boy had that protective, watchful stance of a dutiful guard as well. He was far too young for such an important task, but Catryn would never tell him that. Not only could she never sting his boyish pride in such a manner, but she strongly suspected her son would get quite cross if she tried to separate him from Giles in any way. It was clear for anyone to see that Alwyn already adored Giles despite having known the boy for only a few hours.

"May I go outside with the other children?" Alwyn asked.

Catryn abruptly discovered that having Alwyn back

had not diminished her fear. Before Morris had taken her son, she would not have hesitated to say yes to him. She hastily smothered the fear that had her aching to say no. They had left Morris far behind. They were now safe behind the walls of a viscount's well-manned house in the country and surrounded by people. Alwyn would also be surrounded by boys, some of whom had been hardened by a life on the streets and others who had gifts that could also help keep him safe. It was just as she was struggling to say yes that Penelope patted her hand and she realized she had clenched them together tightly in her lap.

"He will be fine," Penelope said. "He will be very well protected at all times."

The face Alwyn turned toward Lady Penelope held a wary look, but then he suddenly smiled. "Yes, I am, and I will have Giles with me, too. He will keep me safe. He saved me from Morris."

Watching the way Lady Penelope studied the empty space behind Alwyn and then smiled, Catryn wanted to ask the woman what she was looking at. Then she saw how Giles stood straighter at Alwyn's words, his thin chest puffing out, and knew that getting some answers from Lady Penelope would have to wait. The uneasiness she felt crawling through her veins over the way the woman acted would have to be ignored for a while.

"Yes, you do have Giles and I know well that he will watch over you like a hawk," she told her son. "So go. Go and play." She could see that her words pleased Giles far more than the kiss and hug she had given him before climbing up on the driver's perch for the second leg of their journey here.

In only a moment Catryn found herself alone in the room with Penelope. Orion and Lord Ashton had left the room just before the boys to go and study some maps, although Orion had not explained why. Catryn ate one of the small ginger cakes and struggled not to ask Penelope what she had been looking at, what she had seen, behind Alwyn. Sipping tea to wash down the last of the cake, she decided she could not just ignore it. It was something that concerned her child and she had a need, a right, to know.

"What did you see behind Alwyn?" she asked as she placed her cup and dish back on the table. "You were not looking at him but at something else. Was it something dark? Something evil?" Her voice grew softer, became nearly a whisper as she put her greatest fear into words.

"No, most certainly not. I saw a protector. Your son has a gift . . . ," began Penelope.

"Sweet Mary, not a *gift*," Catryn muttered and then saw Penelope frown. "I am sorry. I mean no insult. I am trying, truly trying, to understand these matters, but it is not easy. My baby talks to spirits. And how can my son have a gift? We are not Wherlockes or Vaughns. Although my father has yet to respond to my message in which I questioned him about it, I cannot see why any such connection would have been kept a secret."

"Oh, any connection to us has long been kept secret by many. Families buried that connection as deeply as they could," Penelope said. "We have a long history of being rejected, reviled, hunted, killed, tortured, and ignored. Once the laws changed and people were no longer allowed to hunt, torture, and kill us for what we can do, we began to step out of the shadows more. We were never fully hidden and we are not showing our secrets to the whole world now, but some of the fear of us remains. That is why we keep our distance from the rest of society, for the most part."

"And that would be why any family that had some connection to yours would hide it from the world if it could." She nodded, understanding that. "I told Alwyn not to let anyone know that he talks to people no one else can see. My mother told me not to tell anyone that I could sense danger, threats. Do you think you will ever know how many are still hiding their ties to your family or have actually lost all knowledge of that connection?"

"Well, there is that little something about us that cannot be hidden, and it can lead us to lost family members."

"Oh." Catryn sighed. "That."

Penelope laughed. "Yes, that. You know, have always known, that what Alwyn does is more than a child's game, have you not?"

"Yes, despite trying very hard not to acknowledge that. I doubt any mother would welcome something that will make her child so different, something that could cause him untold trouble later in his life. I am not very pleased about the idea that there are spirits in my house, either."

"True enough. Does your father have any gift? Anything he does that is, well, unusual?"

"He is very good at investments but that is all. The only time our family suffered from a bad investment was when my mother's father decided my father did not know best and put the money into something else. It nearly ruined us. My father had specifically told him not to place the funds there, but . . ." Catryn shrugged.

"Older man too prideful to follow the advice of a much younger man. Always a ripe brew for trouble. Your grandfather would, of course, not want to always follow such a younger man's advice, being that he surely knew more about the world than that boy." Penelope shook her head. "A problem as old as mankind itself."

"But that can hardly be termed a gift. My father just understands such things better, has a sharper eye for what would pay and what would not. When my grandfather told him what he wanted to put our money into, my father studied it, listened to what he had to say, and said that it would fail, that we could lose everything. The only reason we did not was because my grandfather obviously felt a little guilty about going behind my father's back and investing our funds anyway, so he secured some funds out of the reach of any creditors that might follow a failure." She sighed. "In a way, I believe that mistake and the shame he suffered from it were what killed my grandfather."

"Sad to say, that is possible. Or perhaps it simply exacerbated something that was already within him."

Catryn nodded. "You said Alwyn has a protector?"

Penelope nodded. "That is what clings to him. It is the spirit of someone who feels he must watch over the boy, must make up for something he did, but he is not inclined to tell me what, despite the fact that he is the most talkative ghost I have met in a very long time."

"I think you need to tell me a few things about

spirits. Perhaps if I know more, understand more, I will calm myself and know how to go on with my son."

Catryn's mind was still reeling when she wandered out into the moonlit garden Penelope had urged her to visit. Not only had she learned more than she could fully comprehend about what her son was doing when he spoke to the spirit, but over dinner they had discussed what she and Orion would do next concerning Morris. Now that Ashton and Penelope had retired, she needed to sit in the garden, let the quiet of the night surround her, and just think.

There had been too many changes in her life since Morris had taken Alwyn. Not only was she suddenly plunged into a rescue of her son, risking her reputation, and more, to get him back, but she had met a man who stirred something inside, a very hungry something, that was both exciting and frightening. Now she had to accept that her son truly was speaking to the dead and always would, as well as the fact that this trouble with Morris was not at an end.

She supposed it had been foolish to think getting Alwyn back would end it, that she could then just return home to her quiet life. Morris could not be allowed to lurk out there unpunished for what he had done, free to try again. Recalling how doggedly he had fought her in the courts, she knew she should have thought about that more. Her mind had been set on getting her son back and she had not allowed much else to concern her. But she had to agree with Orion. Morris had to be punished in a way that made him leave her and her son alone from now on. If not, she would spend the rest of her life, or his, always fearing the worst.

And then there was the too handsome Sir Orion Wherlocke. He had thought to leave her behind and, with a few of his relatives, go find Morris and settle the matter. She had made her disapproval of that idea plain enough. It had been a long argument, finally settled by Penelope. The woman had pointed out that it was Catryn's fight, Catryn's family, and Catryn had a right to join the battle. It was clear to see that Orion had not liked that, but he had conceded.

Now Catryn wondered if that was the right thing to do. Despite all she had just been through, she was no warrior, nor skilled in hunting someone down and threatening them. All she had to aid the search for Morris was knowledge of the man and where he might try to hide. The compromise had been that she and Orion would leave Giles and Alwyn at Radmoor, search for Morris, and then send for help when they found him.

That compromise meant that she had just agreed to spend more time with Orion, alone, traveling around the countryside. Catryn knew she also had to decide what to do about that desire he could so easily stir within her. Her choices were simple. She buried it deep and remained no more than a traveling companion or she set it free and became a daring widow who could take a lover for a while and walk away when the journey was done.

Catryn was surprised at how tempted she was to do the latter. Daring was not something she had ever thought herself to be. Orion and the attraction she knew without doubt was mutual made her that way.

For once in her life she wanted to reach out and take what she wanted and not worry about consequences. The only thing that held her back was that she knew there was a good chance one of those consequences could be a broken heart.

The soft sound of someone approaching nearly made her sigh with irritation, but that changed when she caught the gently enticing scent of Orion. It was odd how she could scent him in the air like a dog scented its master. The man wore no strong perfumes and he was a very clean man as well. Yet he had, to her, a very distinct and attractive scent that drew her attention the moment he was anywhere near her.

"I still believe you should stay here, safe with Alwyn," Orion said as he sat down on the bench next to Catryn.

"You lost that argument," she said as she bit back a smile, for he sounded almost sulky.

"I know. If I was not having so much trouble finding this cursed man before we can do no more than run from him I would have fought harder. But there is that shield around him which hides him from my gift, and Penelope agrees that the man must have one. That leaves me with the need to have someone who knows him well, or at least better than I do, at my side to help decide where to look next."

"You believe he is in hiding now that we have taken Alwyn back."

"I sense by your tone that you do not," he said as he studied her, thinking how well the moonlight suited her.

"No, I do not. It would make sense to stop now. We know what he did, and might think to bring charges against him. The correct thing for him to do now is to flee the country, let this all fade away."

"That is certainly what I would do."

"And I. But I would also have given up after I lost the first court case to gain guardianship over Alwyn. Such things are very costly and I would never want to throw good money after bad."

He put his arm around her shoulders and tugged her up against his side, ignoring her frown. She did not tense or pull away and, silent though she was, he knew that was acceptance of his touch. A part of him was pleased that they would continue on together, while a larger part wanted her to stay at Radmoor, safe and out of Morris's reach. Since that was not going to happen, he was beginning to think he might just reach out for what else he wanted. The women in his family would give him an ear-burning lecture if he tried to seduce someone like Catryn, but he was thinking it might be worth it.

"Money Morris does not have," he said as he slyly rubbed his nose against her sweet-smelling hair.

"I did not believe he had it. All that I was able to learn about his finances implied that he was in debt, perhaps even the depth and kind of debt that will get you beaten severely if you do not pay it off in time. Then again, he may not have paid his solicitor yet, either."

"Solicitors are usually very good at judging who will or will not pay their bills. He probably had to pay a fair amount before they took him on as a client. They would not be spending time unless he was paying. But that could be one reason he is so in debt."

"Ah, of course. Our solicitor has been with the

family for years and trusts my father to pay his debts. Even so, our purse was definitely being pinched. It is that doggedness he revealed with the court cases that makes me think he has not given up yet."

"I agree. And what do you do if it becomes clear that he will never give up?"

She lifted her head to look at him. It was a question she had often asked herself, but she still had no answer. The best thing would be if Morris died, but she was appalled every time such a thought entered her mind. Nevertheless, if Morris promised to be a continuous threat to Alwyn, she suspected she would overcome her distaste of such a violent solution to the problems he presented.

"I hate to even say it, for it makes something within me curl up in horror, but if Morris will not cease and accept defeat, then he will probably have to be ended. That could mean prison, which would cause the whole lot of us to be a ripe piece of gossip for a while; but I fear the only true solution, since he is of the gentry and it is not easy to get one of them jailed, is for him to die."

He brushed a kiss over her forehead. Her voice had dimmed to a whisper at the end and she looked distressed by that judgment. It was a rational one for the safety of her child, but a hard one. He realized he wanted Morris to pay simply for putting Catryn in the position where she had to consider such things.

"There is always a chance he will listen to reason once we find him and speak with him," he said as he stroked her cheek.

She smiled faintly. "Morris is not one who responds well to reason, but yes, I will hope for that."

Unable to resist, Orion lightly kissed her. The soft warmth of her lips, the way she leaned into him, quickly turned the kiss into a deeper one. He wanted her but tried to remember that she was not the sort of woman he usually dealt with. He needed to move slowly, to rein in his hunger until she was ready and willing to feed it.

When she wrapped her arms around his neck and pressed her body even closer to his, he decided it would not hurt to let her have a taste of his need. He slid his hands up her sides until they rested at the very edge of the curves of her breasts. A soft sound of pleasure escaped her as he stroked those curves with his thumbs. Orion moved his kisses to her throat, savoring the way she tilted her head back to allow him better access to the silken skin there.

It was just as he slid his hands over the fullness of her breasts, felt the invitingly hard tips of them rub his palms, that a sound cut through the fog of his growing desire. Orion was pulling away from her even as she tensed and yanked away from him. He nearly cursed when Killer, the ugly dog Penelope and her boys insisted on keeping, came running up to them.

"That is a very odd-looking dog," murmured Catryn, her voice low and husky with a faint tremor, as she scratched behind the dog's ragged ears.

"Most do not recognize it as a dog," said Orion, inwardly sighing, for the moment of passion was definitely ended. "He saved Penelope, in a way, by attacking the man who shot her. Yet another fool who felt he had a right to take an inheritance that was not his. The boys had already asked to keep him anyway. She finds it difficult to refuse them much but said she never would have been able to anyway, for she knew, as they did, that the dog had been thrown away."

"As they had been," she whispered.

"Exactly."

A soft whistle came from the direction of the house and the dog raced toward it. Orion looked at Catryn, who was busy brushing dog hair off her skirts. Her skin was still a little flushed, but he suspected at least some of that came from embarrassment, a reaction to desire that marked her as the innocent he knew her to be.

"You need not be ashamed of what you feel when I kiss you," he said as he brushed his fingers over her cheek.

"I am not ashamed," she said firmly as she stood up and looked at him. "I do believe, however, that you ask for more than I may be able to give, even if I wished to do so, and that is something I need to think about."

Orion cursed under his breath as he watched her return to the house. The last thing he wanted her to do was think too much about what flared between them. She had had an empty marriage, and if she thought on what could be shared between them too much, comparisons would be made and past wounds revived. That could easily end all chance he had of tasting the passion her kisses promised him.

Shaking his head, he decided he would seek his lonely bed. They needed to hunt down Morris and put an end to the threat he presented. That would be work enough to warrant a good night's sleep. It appeared he would also need the strength to resist the temptation of a lush little redhead.

Catryn crawled into bed, turned onto her back, and stared up at the ceiling. Her body still carried the memory of his hands and her mouth the memory of his kiss. If that dog had not come crashing through the bushes, she suspected the lovemaking they had begun would have gone much further. Instead of being embarrassed by the idea that she might have given herself to Orion in his cousin's garden, a little thrill of excitement went through her. The man was turning her into a wanton.

The question she had to answer was, did she want to be one, just for him, just for a little while? Her body had a growing need for him, a hunger it was aching to have fed. She could not allow that to make her decision for her, however. Actions had consequences. In a society that thrived on gossip and had a very long memory for such things, her actions could easily haunt Alwyn almost as consistently as his spirits. Catryn shivered at the thought of being an embarrassment to her son, a source of pain as he suffered the whispers about his mother.

A knock sounded at the door and she hurried to don her robe. She opened the door and was surprised to see Penelope. "Is something wrong?"

"No, but this came while you were out in the garden with Orion," she said and held out a letter. "I meant to catch you before you went to your bed, but the babies distracted me. I hope it is not news that will upset you."

"I hope so, too," Catryn whispered and forced herself to smile at Penelope. "Sleep well and thank you."

After shutting the door, Catryn went back to the bed, turned up the lamp, and stared at the letter from her father. She found that she did not wish to read it, which she knew was foolish. Yet, she suspected that he was about to confess that he had hidden some truth about their family and she knew that would hurt.

"You are a grown woman," she scolded herself, then broke the seal on the letter. "Act like one."

She read her father's words in growing disbelief. There was indeed a connection to the Wherlockes, although hers was actually with the other half of the family, the Vaughns. Her great-great-grandfather had married a Vaughn woman who was a gifted healer. One night the mob had come for her, claiming she was responsible for all manner of horrible, impossible crimes. There had been no way for him to save her, so he had done as she had begged him to and saved their children. After that, all mention of the Vaughn name had been stricken from the family records; only the heir in each successive generation was told the truth.

Catryn carefully put the letter away in her bag, shed her robe, turned down the lamp, and climbed back into bed. She was not sure how she felt. Her father had explained that he had never even told her mother, a woman he had truly loved, especially once he saw how she acted when her child showed a hint of a gift that he knew had come from the Vaughn side of the family. His reasons made sense to her, but there was still a part of her that was hurt. If he had told her she might not have spent her life being afraid that she was somehow marred or that her child was.

"At least I have an explanation now," she told herself and then thought of the large family of Wherlockes and Vaughns. "I also appear to have more kin to help me and Alwyn than anyone could ever hope for."

"Even better," she murmured as she closed her eyes and fought to clear her mind so that she could sleep, "the relation to Orion is too distant to be of any concern. So, if I decide that I do wish to become a wanton widow, at least I will not be doing so with my cousin." For reasons she did not care to examine, the thought comforted her enough to allow her to fall asleep.

Chapter Eleven

Catryn read her father's letter for the fifth time as she sat at a table and waited for Orion to finish speaking with the innkeeper. She was delighted that her father had suffered no lasting injury from the attack, was simply sore and bruised, and she was touched by how eager he was for her and Alwyn to come home. Despite that, she was still furious that he had kept secrets about their family. That anger had been there when she had awakened the morning after getting the letter, two long days ago, and she had not been able to shake free of it. Yet again, she had to take several slow, deep breaths before that anger faded.

It was foolish to feel so betrayed. Her father was an honest man, a good man, and he loved her. There had been a very good reason why he had said nothing about that distant familial connection to the Wherlockes, not even when she had shown signs of having a gift and then when Alwyn had. The thing that nagged at her was that that reason had died with her mother, the person who had demanded such strict secrecy about her child's gift, before Catryn had gotten married and had a child with a gift.

"Are you still fretting over what your father wrote?" asked Orion as he sat down across the table from her.

She waited to respond to his query until a serving girl had set the light meal of bread, cheese, and cold meat on the table. It was difficult to ignore the way the buxom young woman flirted so brazenly with Orion as she poured them each a tankard of cider. Catryn was very close to giving in to the urge to kick the woman when a bellow from the innkeeper had the woman hurrying away.

Jealousy, she mused. That was jealousy that had burned in her heart when the woman flirted with Orion. It was something she had never experienced before, not even when her husband had spent so many nights away from home and her bed that she had been certain he had a mistress. It had stung her pride but little else. It was then that she realized that she no longer loved Henry and now wondered if she ever had.

A part of her was troubled by her jealousy. It indicated that she was feeling far more than a liking for Orion and a natural womanly attraction for a strong, handsome man. Sir Orion Wherlocke was not a man a woman should give her heart to, and not just because he had three illegitimate sons who were proof of his rakish ways. Catryn needed no special gift to know that the man enjoyed women, a lot of women. She did not want to be just one of many. If she did give in to her lusts and became his lover, she wanted to be sure she did so with that understanding firmly in her mind and heart.

Another part of her, however, was utterly fascinated by the angry surge of possessiveness that had gripped her when that serving maid had touched Orion, displaying her ample bosom in a way that had been one breath away from being indecent. It was not a soft, ladylike feeling. Not genteel at all. It had been rough, fierce, and raw. The man roused strong emotion within her, good and bad. There was a hunger inside of her to reach out for all of it and revel in it, for it was something that had been sadly lacking in her life.

"Did you learn anything from the innkeeper?" she asked in a desperate attempt to quiet her thoughts, not at all eager to discuss what was in her father's letter, even though she had shown it to Orion.

"Just that Morris passed this way." He began to slice the cheese. "I have never had such difficulty hunting someone. Never."

His frustration was so clear to hear in his voice that she felt compelled to try and soothe it. "Perhaps it truly is just because Morris is not actually planning out what he is doing." She took one of the pieces of cheese and nibbled on it as she gathered her thoughts. "He just does it. The man might begin with a plan of some sort, but he rarely sticks to it. It was something Henry often decried about his brother, now that I recall. As I told you, I was surprised by how doggedly Morris worked to try and get the guardianship rights over Alwyn. It was very unlike him."

"That may well be the problem. Everyone makes some sort of plan when they want to do something, legal or not, and most stay with it in some form or another. I can usually see it as if it had been drawn out for me. I can usually even see how the plan might change, and why. It is not so clear with Morris. It is as if I see what he should be doing, because I know what he wants, but there are"—he frowned as he struggled to think of some way to explain his difficulty to her— "no straight lines."

"That makes sense, for I do not believe Morris thinks in that precise a way. I often thought he was like a small child, his thoughts and his desires quickly flitting from one thing to another. That is why his battle to gain control of Alwyn and all that is his was quite a surprise, but he may have actually hired a very clever solicitor and had the wit to leave the business of it all to that man. When Morris wants something, he wants it immediately, and if he cannot get it, he will soon become bored and turn his eyes on something else. This, however—what he is doing now—is madness."

"You think the man is insane?"

"No, not insane, but not quite sane either. It is as if he can only plan one step at a time. If the man ever thought beyond getting ahold of Alwyn, then getting hold of me, I would be most surprised. Anyone taking the next step after that, even if just in their mind, would quickly begin to see all the problems that could arise. Maybe he simply thought all would go as he wished once he kidnapped us."

Orion leaned back in his chair, drank a little of his cider as he thought on her words, and then nodded. "There are a lot of problems he has not considered, and most who would devise such a plot would consider the ending of it, the consequences."

"I should have seen it."

"That Morris may decide to kill the son of his only brother just to gain a title? Or, as my bloodthirsty son thought possible, kill the entire direct line to your father's baronetcy, save for you, so that he could gain even more by breeding a son with you?"

"I just cannot believe he would go that far." She could tell by the look on his face that he knew she was trying very hard to convince herself of that, that the fear of such a possibility was still lurking in her mind and heart. "I knew he believed the title should have been his. He even believed it would be, as if he truly believed his brother would never breed an heir. I often got the feeling that he knew something I did not. Morris was enraged when I got with child. He tried to hide his fury, but I saw it."

"Did he try to hurt you?"

"No, although he did make me uneasy and I did my best never to be alone with him or alone when he was near at hand. Then Alwyn was born, and I still felt no sense of imminent threat from Morris. No foreboding. And, considering what has occurred, that is a bit odd, is it not? I know I said it was probably because Alwyn was not actually in any true danger, yet I keep thinking that I should have felt something. He hurt my father and stole my baby. There should have been something, some alarm sounded in my mind, if only a sudden urge to get right back home, but there was not even that."

"Just as I see no clear pattern, no map I can easily follow. You have no warning and I see no plan. For both of our gifts to falter is very unusual. And the same man was at the heart of both failings. I become more certain that Morris has a shield."

"A shield? You mentioned that before but I am not certain I understand what you mean by that."

"There are some people who cannot be read, who are immune to nearly all of my family's gifts, even the strongest ones." Orion shook his head, disgusted with himself for taking so long to consider such a possibility. "It is not just Morris's scattered thoughts and errant behavior that are making this difficult for me. There is something about the man that simply stops me from seeing his plan, knowing his next move. The same thing, I would wager, that stopped you from seeing the danger he presented even when he attacked your father and took Alwyn. Others in my family have met such people, but Morris is the first for me."

"He has some wall around him that blocks you? And me?"

"In some ways, yes. For some of us, that is actually a blessing."

There was a shadow in his eyes, the blue darkening with worry. Catryn knew what troubled him now. He was thinking of Giles. Although she did not fully understand all the talk about gifts, how they came to be, or even how they worked, she was able to clearly see what the future might hold for Giles. The boy knew what emotion rested in a person's heart. If that particular gift strengthened as Giles aged, the child could easily be tormented by all he could see and feel. There were some very dark emotions out in the world and some very black hearts no one would willingly look into.

She reached out and Orion smiled faintly as he clasped her hand in his. He idly brushed his thumb over her knuckles and Catryn wondered how such a simple touch could stir her blood so. It was both a delight and a curse. When the serving girl interrupted them again, the woman's intentions were still clear to see. Catryn watched as the woman rubbed her breasts against Orion's arm as she refilled his tankard and then had to be reminded that there was another guest at the table who might wish more to drink.

Before Catryn could embarrass herself by saying the sharp words already burning on her tongue, Orion spoke quietly to the woman. The serving woman blushed but nodded. When she turned to leave, however, she gave Catryn a look of such anger that she was tempted to quickly hide the knives on the table.

"What did you say to her?" she asked Orion when the woman was gone.

"That she should take more careful notice when a man is not alone nor wishes to be," he replied, and smiled at her even as he filled his plate with food.

"Oh. Well, if this is how she behaves with the men who come here, I wonder why the innkeeper allows her to continue to work here." She frowned. "Did I just sound as pious as I think I did?"

Orion laughed. "It was a little pious sounding. You have not traveled much, have you?"

"I have been places with my father and a few times with my husband. I have stayed at an inn or two before this adventure."

She frowned as she thought back over those times. Women had flirted with Henry and even with her father, but she had paid little heed. Her father had been oblivious, at least until he became a widower, and what Henry did had quickly become of little importance to her. Now, however, she could recall a

few exchanged smiles and looks, after which there
would be no visit in the night. He would not even bed
down in the room to sleep. And suddenly Catryn
knew exactly what had been happening right beneath
her nose.

"That bastard," she hissed. She stabbed a piece of
cheese and shoved it into her mouth.

"Henry has returned, has he?"

She sighed and then laughed briefly as she saw his
grin. "So I am naïve. There was no need of him taking
advantage of that. I knew quite soon after we married
that he did not hold to his vows, but to break them
while I was traveling with him seems an even more
egregious sin. Why, 'tis rude."

The scowl she tried to give him when he laughed
was weak, and she had to smile. It was foolish to get
angry now, when the man had been dead for almost
two years and their marriage had been dead for far
longer than that. It stung her pride that he would
sneak away with a serving maid while she was in the
same inn, but she suspected he had just been behaving as he always had, never giving her a passing
thought. She could not continue to let that anger her.
Henry was gone and she needed to be completely free
of him. Now that she understood that some of the
maids at the inns served up far more than meals, at
least her father had behaved himself. The moment
she thought that, she knew differently, could recall
times during a trip to or from London when he had
undoubtedly answered an invitation from one of the
maids. She was horrified.

"Oh, dear heaven, my father, too?" When Orion

burst out laughing, she had no trouble managing a scowl for him this time. "This is not funny."

"Not to you, I can see that." Still struggling with the urge to laugh, he reached across the table and took her hand in his. "Did he, let us say, indulge while your mother was alive?"

"Of course not." She thought on that for a moment and then nodded, certain she had a right to that conviction. "He loved my mother."

"Then why so shocked? The man did not die with her."

"But he is not a young man."

"My father was still chasing women when he was three score and ten. Last one was one too many and his heart gave out. So long as a man is healthy enough and all his parts still work, he will be wanting a woman." He shrugged. "'Tis just the way of it. Probably has something to do with the need to reproduce, go forth and multiply and all that."

"Oh." She thought on how lonely her father must have been after her mother was gone, and sighed. "I believe I do not wish to think on it any more, at least as concerns Papa."

"That is what most children prefer to do, no matter how old they get." Having eaten all he cared to, he sat back and drank his wine. "I need to go out now. I want to do a little hunting before all the light fades."

"But if Morris has this shield you mentioned, how can you do that?"

"The way all other men do. I rely on my gift, true enough, but I learned all the other ways to hunt a man down. Although I was arrogant enough to believe I would never have to use them, I learned them all the same. The man I work for in the government insisted."

"He knows about your particular skill?"

"There are ones in the government who know a lot about the Wherlockes and the Vaughns and have no qualms about calling upon our particular gifts when they need them. I begin to think the man also knew that there are times when our gifts might fail us. So, I learned. I will put those skills to use now."

"And if you find Morris?"

"We will keep close on his trail and I will send for some of my kin. Your kin, too, now."

"But very distant."

"Yes, and is that not a good thing," he murmured as he stood up.

Catryn could not think what to say to that. He kissed her on the forehead and left her. She stared at the food, decided she could eat a little more before seeking out her bed, and reached for some of the bread. Perhaps before he returned, she could make up her mind about him. Would she cling to propriety or would she become a daring widow and explore that desire he so easily stirred within her?

Orion sighed as he left the alehouse he had traveled to in the hope of gaining some useful information and got his horse. Morris had been sighted by everyone but him, it seemed. He was always just one step behind the man as well. If the man had been known as some sort of brilliant criminal, Orion could more easily accept his inability to find and stop him from ever being a threat to Catryn and Alwyn again. Yet, the man was a fool and still managed to slip through his fingers.

"Sir?"

Orion turned to find a stableboy behind him. "I can manage my own mount," he said even as he dug in his pocket for a coin to give the boy, who looked to be on the cusp of manhood.

"I heard you be looking for that fellow in the hideous carriage."

"Yes." He idly wondered where such a boy learned the word *hideous* but knew it would be insulting to ask. "You had dealings with the man?"

"I did, and he is a right bastard, he is. Tight with his coin, too."

And that was why he was about to hear something that could be useful, Orion thought. It always amazed him how so many of his class did not understand what servants were worth. Or what making a servant angry with you could cost you. Servants knew everything, saw everything, and often overheard things you would wish they had not. Treat them badly enough and a few coins could be enough to loosen their tongues. Treat them really badly and, as this boy was about to do, they would go looking for someone to tell.

"Did he still have four big men with him? The men in the alehouse were not certain."

"Aye, he did. Dumb oxen they were, but quick with their fists and enjoyed using them. My brother will be a long time healing."

"What did your brother do that drew their attention?" Orion asked even as he tried to think of any of his family's healers who might be in the area, even one who just had a gift with potions and salves.

"Tried to help the kitchen lass one of them was bothering. She is a good lass with a man wanting to wed with her, so she were not looking to make any coin on her back. Not that that bastard would pay anyway. Could see he was the sort to just take it and not even leave behind a ha'pence. But he would not leave her be, though she was saying no clear as a bell. So me brother tried to get him to leave her. She got away, but my brother got beat on quite a bit before others came and stopped the pig. Toddy, he be the owner, told the whole lot of them to get out."

That was news he had not been given. Could be the owner did not let anyone aside from those involved know, he decided. The man might have thought it bad for business or he could even have thought to protect the maid.

"Do you know which way the hideous carriage went when they left?"

"Headed out north, toward London, I am thinking. Headed back from where they came, aye? They looked and sounded like London folk."

Orion inwardly cursed. Somehow Morris had gotten around them. The man was becoming a true thorn in his side. Yet, it could prove to be a good thing, for he had a lot of family in the city.

"Do you know a Mistress Lonee Tantum? She resides in the next village, I believe."

"I do. Her husband owns an inn there and Toddy sells him his ale. Best ale in the county, it is." He sighed. "I did hear once that she has a gift for the healing, but she costs and is reluctant to do it often, though she will sell some salves and the like."

"Take your brother to her." Orion gave the boy

more than enough money to pay Lonee for her work. "If you cannot move him safely, ask her to come here to see to his care. This should cover even that. Tell her that her cousin Sir Orion Wherlocke asks this favor of her. That should ease any hesitation she might have."

"I always thought she was gentry," the boy muttered as he finally tore his wide-eyed gaze from the money in his hand and looked at Orion. "She speaks real fine, she does. I listen real careful when I am round her so I can learn the better way of talking and all. You planning on dealing with that bastard in the hideous carriage?"

"If by *dealing with* you mean making him pay for a few wrongs, then yes, I am."

"Good. Maybe you could add my brother's hurts in amongst all them wrongs."

Orion promised he would and then mounted his horse. As he headed back to the inn where he had left Catryn, he cursed his luck. It was lowering enough to accept that he had failed to find the man as he had promised. To now know that the man had somehow managed to get past him and start back toward the city was somewhat humiliating.

Despite his personal embarrassment, he was also pleased by the news that Morris might be headed back to London. There were a lot of people there he could call upon to give him some help. Not everyone could be hampered by whatever shielded Morris from his and Catryn's gifts. He had a few true trackers in his family who might be able to help. He also knew every place where a man like Morris could hide if he did not foolishly return to his own town house. And if the man was as superstitious as Catryn believed him to be,

Orion knew a few of his kin who could scare the man so badly he would never get within miles of Catryn and Alwyn again.

It was going to be difficult to tell Catryn, however. She was as tired of this hunt as he was, and he knew she had been hoping the confrontation with Morris, one that was long overdue, would soon be behind her. Orion could only hope that she saw that there were advantages to Morris returning to the city as clearly as he did.

Patting the horse on the neck, he decided he did not need to race back to the inn and kept the horse at an easy pace. He had a lot to think about and he did not get much of that done when he was around Catryn. Even when he retired for the night, his thoughts rarely stayed fixed on the problem of Morris. He wanted Catryn, more than he had ever wanted another woman in his life. Orion was not sure what to make of that.

Lust was an old companion to him, arriving right along with the hair on his body. Restraint was something he had taught himself, however, as his father had had none and his mother had had too much. In the end, his mother had deserted him just as too many parents in the Wherlocke clan did their own children; those parents who came from outside the clan, anyway. The ones who came from within the Wherlocke and Vaughn clans were better at seeing to their children's needs, but were not necessarily the best of parents. Some because their gifts consumed them, and some because they themselves had had such miserable childhoods they were trapped into repeating it with their own children. It was one reason so many of his family avoided marriage, or tried to.

Lady Catryn Gryffin de Warrenne was a woman a man married. Orion knew that, yet it was not enough to cool his desire for her. Before he gave in to that need, which he suspected he would if she gave him even the smallest sign of welcome, he should decide if he was ready to toss aside his plan to remain unwed for his whole life. The odd thing was, that no longer looked like such a good plan.

"I believe I have been infected with Morris's confusion of the mind," he muttered and almost smiled when the horse tossed its head and snorted.

He took a few minutes to consider the recent marriages amongst his clan. Penelope was a good choice to study, for she had a gift too many were terrified by. Yet he had absolutely no doubt in his mind that Ashton adored her, and could not see any chance that the man would ever hurt her or the children they were so busily breeding. The man had taken in all the children who had lived with Penelope, and their gifts were wide-ranging. Even his powerful, arrogant cousin Argus, a frightening man even to his own family, had found a wife who accepted him as he was, and all of his family. It was enough to raise the hopes of many of the clan who had survived the miserable unions of their own parents.

Catryn was one of them, distant though the connection was. She had a child who spoke to spirits, his current ghostly companion a rogue of a Vaughn, so she understood them in a way few others outside of the family did. Nor had she turned cold and judgmental when she discovered he had three sons. She had been utterly appalled that the children's own mothers had deserted them. There was, he realized, a lot to appreciate about Catryn aside from the passion that flared between them. It could be that he should not be quite as concerned over a possible future with her as he was. The thought of it did not inspire any urge to run for the hills.

Every instinct he had told him that if he crawled into Catryn's bed, and she warmed it as he thought she would, it would be the end of his carefree bachelor days. He wanted to say that would be because he loved her, but he had little understanding of that emotion. He liked her, enjoyed her company, appreciated the way she accepted who he was and those gifts that cursed everyone in his family in one way or another, and he lusted after her. Even more important, he realized that he trusted her, completely, and he trusted few outside of his own family. Being as inexperienced as he knew she was, there was a good chance his need to hide his back from sight would not rouse her curiosity. He could even see her accepting his scars. Yet, there lingered the faintest touch of that unwillingness to give up his freedom.

"Perhaps," he mused aloud, "it is time I grew up."

Chapter Twelve

A sharp rap at the bedchamber door yanked Catryn from her thoughts. She was just reaching for her pistol when Orion announced himself. Catryn grabbed up her robe, hesitated, and then tossed it on the end of the bed. Wrapping herself up in a heavy woolen robe would not help her succeed in the seduction she planned, she decided, and hurried to open the door.

He barely gave her a glance before going to stand in front of the fire, and that stung. Either the man was far too accustomed to seeing women in a state of undress or she simply did not warrant a second look. Trying not to take that to heart, she shut and latched the door before walking over and standing right in front of him.

A touch of damp on his hair told her that he had paused to wash up. It hung past his broad shoulders in thick waves that she ached to run her fingers through. Catryn was both intrigued and a little frightened by how just standing near him could make her desperate to put her hands on him. The indication that, despite the heated embraces they had shared, he did not suffer from the same need, hurt more than she cared to think about.

"Did you discover anything new?" she asked, becoming unsettled by the silence between them.

"Merely confirmed my original supposition," he replied. "I have difficulty grasping what his plans are and he has been seen in this area. It appears he may be headed back to London. That was the direction the stableboy said the carriage turned in."

She could hear the deep frustration in his voice. For a man with Orion's skills, ones he was rightfully arrogant about, it had to be galling to be thwarted by someone as foolish as Morris. Catryn patted him on the arm and was startled when he suddenly covered hers with his own, holding it in place.

"We did not pass him on the road," she said.

"No, and that puzzles me, but I am no longer surprised. It may be a good thing, however."

"How so?"

"Not only do I have a vast amount of family in the city but we can trap him within, find him more easily for he is a man who would never dirty himself even if he is trying to hide. Hiding successfully requires getting a little dirty and accepting a lack of comforts. The man must realize that you have allies now and he no longer has Alwyn as a bargaining chip to save himself from prosecution. So we can watch the docks, for it is possible he may be thinking of fleeing the country. I will have a lot of help in doing those things, too."

She thought about that for a moment and then nodded. "Then that is our new plan."

"You need to put your robe on," he said.

The words were so unexpected that it took Catryn a full minute to understand what he had just said, for it had nothing to do with what they had just been talking about. Then, despite the blush she could feel stinging her cheeks, she began to get annoyed. It was scandalous to stand dressed in only her linen nightdress before a man who was not her husband, but *he* was the one who had come to *her* bedchamber. It was also an extremely modest night shift. Her own maid had called it the spinster aunt night shift.

"I beg your pardon, but I believe *you* are the one who came to *my* bedchamber," she snapped. "This is the customary attire for a woman in her bedchamber so late at night. I also suspect it is far more modest than any you have become accustomed to seeing." Just thinking of all he had seen and how many bedchambers he might have seen it in irritated her.

"True, it is very modest." He reached out and took a thick lock of her hair in his hand. "Until you add the allure of this hair. And the fact that I can see how your nipples have hardened and it tempts me, very strongly, to lick them."

Catryn was stunned speechless. She was also intensely aroused. At least she thought arousal was what made her clench her thighs in reaction to a sudden rush of heat in her nether regions. His voice was deep and rougher than usual and it moved over her skin like a lover's hands.

"Perhaps I would not object," she said, and a soft voice in her mind gasped in shock over her brazen words. She ruthlessly ignored it.

Orion studied her face as he idly stroked her hair.

Her cheeks were flushed but he could not be certain if it was from arousal or simply a blush. She made no attempt to hide the hard, inviting tips of her breasts. They still shaped the front of her girlishly modest night shift. With any other woman he would have already been carrying her to the bed, but this was Catryn. Despite being a mother and a widow, he knew she was no well-practiced lover or confident seductress.

"Do you understand what you are inviting me to do, Cat? All of it?" he asked.

"I am no virgin, Orion."

He almost smiled. She was no virgin but she was still very innocent. Orion suspected she had never truly been made love to, not even on her wedding night. She had been used to breed an heir and little else. Everything she had told him about Henry confirmed that opinion. The man had not even tried to please her. It would be wise to begin slowly with her, but he was not sure he would be able to be so wise. Despite all his bachelor-loving instincts telling him to stay far away from her, he wanted her too badly to heed them. That could well mean he wanted her too badly to gently introduce her to the pleasure a man and woman could share.

"You have until I remove my boots to change your mind," he said as he sat down and began to tug off his boots. "It is not much but it is all I am inclined to grant."

"I will not change my mind."

A nervous part of her badly wanted to, but Catryn ignored that voice. That cowardly part did not have the strength to conquer the need that had been

growing inside her since the first time she had seen
Orion. It did not matter that she could be inviting
pain into her heart because he was not the sort of
man who had any intention of settling for just one
woman. It did not matter that she was certain she
knew she was not the sort of woman, being neither
daring nor sensuous, who could hold the interest of
such a man for long. She would take what she could
get and remember it well.

That conviction wavered a little when he tossed his
second boot aside and stood up. He took a step
toward her and she was strongly reminded of what a
big man he was. Catryn stiffened her spine and did
not give in to the urge to take a step back. She had
been failed by her husband in so many ways, slighted
by him again and again, but now she had a chance to
mend one of those slights. Now she had a chance to
discover exactly what pleasure a man and a woman
could share. This man would not fail her in that. She
would not allow herself to retreat from the promise in
his eyes.

She stood like a soldier ready to be given her
orders, Orion thought, as he stepped up to her and
brushed his lips over hers. Soft, warm, and sweet, the
taste of her lips only added to the craving he had
finally stopped fighting. He would have her and deal
with the consequences, if and when there were any.
A man could suffer many a worse fate than having to
spend a lifetime with Catryn.

He picked her up in his arms and took her to the
bed. Her soft gasp of surprise pleased him. Orion
gently set her down on the bed then sprawled on top
of her, resting on his forearms so that he did not put

all of his weight on her slender body. As he bent his head to kiss her, he noticed that she had begun to frown.

"You have not darkened the room yet," she said.

"Why would I have you in a darkened room?" he asked as he undid the front of her night rail and kissed the space between her breasts. "Then I would not be able to see your beauty."

"But that is the way it is done, is it not?"

Catryn fought hard to hold on to the warmth his light kisses and gentle touch stirred within her, but it was difficult. She was far too aware of all the light in the room. It was a soft light, thrown out by a low fire and a small lantern, but she could see him easily. That meant he could see her with the same ease. Even her late husband had never seen her unclothed body in the light, any light, soft or bright.

"Did you not know that?" she asked.

A heartbeat later she silently cursed her stupidity. This man was neither inexperienced nor saintly. She knew he had had more experience with women, bedded more women, than Henry probably ever had or ever could have hoped to have done. Willing women, pleased to climb into his bed, who did not have to be drugged. It was not something she wanted to think about, either, especially as it clarified in her mind the idiocy of her question. So did the sting of a blush upon her cheeks. The faint smile he was giving her revealed both kindness and a touch of amusement. She supposed she was fortunate he was not laughing outright. Loudly.

"Your husband preferred the dark?" Orion continued

to undo her nightdress. "Such a foolish man. Perhaps he did not wish you to view his many faults."

"Henry was handsome and quite fashionable."

Orion slipped his hands inside her nightdress, gently clasping her full breasts. She had known Orion would give her an experience she had never had before, could show her that a woman could actually enjoy the bedding, but she now wondered if she had the courage to let it happen. With each stroke of his hands he was stirring a wildness within her she did not recognize and a craving she feared would linger long after he left her.

And he would leave, she thought, shivering with pleasure when he lightly nipped the side of her neck. This affair she had daringly embarked on would not last. She had known that from the first moment she had begun to wonder what his lovemaking would be like. It was foolish to give in to cowardice now, just because of a little light. Instead of worrying over what he was about to see, she would savor all that she was about to see. A smile curving her mouth, she began to undo his shirt.

Just as she bared his chest and slowly moved her hands from his taut stomach up to his broad shoulders, he kissed her. This was what she wanted, what she needed. The weight of his body on hers, the warmth of his skin, even the scent of him. It all fed the pleasure that was rushing through her body.

That pleasure dimmed ever so slightly when he removed her nightdress and tossed it aside. She had never been naked with a man, and it was not as easy to allow it in the heat of passion as she had thought it would be. Suddenly she was far too aware of her vulnerability, of the exposure of all her physical faults, of those faint scars left by childbirth. The fact that Orion was still more dressed than undressed did nothing to still her growing unease. Nor did it please her, for she had a need to see him, to freely touch his skin.

"You have not yet shed your own clothing," she whispered against his mouth.

"Oh, I will shed all that is necessary. Soon." He nipped at her bottom lip.

"Do you have a large, hairy wart you are trying to hide?"

His warm breath flowed over her lips as he laughed. He did not answer her jest, however, just kissed her. Catryn knew she ought to press for a reason why only one of them was naked, but her determination faded with each stroke of his tongue within her mouth. He tasted so good, made her feel so good, that she did not want all the pleasure she was enjoying to be disrupted by questions.

Orion savored the way she softened beneath him, the last of her inconvenient curiosity fading. He had not considered the possibility that she would question him about how slow he was to shed his own clothing. The women he bedded usually believed it was their beauty and the lust they stirred in him that made him too eager to remove all of his clothes. He let them believe it, even encouraged the idea that he was in such great need of them that he simply did not wish to waste a single moment. Catryn had so little vanity he doubted she even considered that possibility.

Since he was not sure he could stop her from catching a glimpse of his back if they remained lovers for any length of time, Orion decided this one night would be all they would share. Then he looked down at her lush body, ran his fingers over the warm, soft skin of her breast, and kissed her. He knew that plan would never work. He had known it from the first time he had kissed her. She tasted too sweet to turn away from. All he could do was ply all his usual tricks to keep anyone from getting a good look at his back and pray they continued to work. Orion realized that seeing that look of distaste or horror on Catryn's face would cut him far deeper than the whip that had scarred him ever had. His mind told him she would not react in such a way, but the rest of him cringed at the thought of running the risk that he was wrong.

Catryn held Orion close as he kissed her, stroking the inside of her mouth with his tongue as he stroked her body with his clever hands. Everywhere he touched her, her skin came alive, growing warm and sending that warmth into her veins to reach each and every part of her. When he did as he had threatened and licked at the aching tips of her breasts, her breath caught in her throat. For a moment she forgot how to breathe. The ability returned when he drew her nipple deep into his mouth and sucked, her captured breath escaping her in a long, soft moan of delight.

This was what those happily married women and daring widows whispered and smiled about. Catryn had both disbelieved and envied them. Now she knew those smiles and whispers had been born of sweet memories, and envy pushed aside disbelief.

Lightly calloused fingers slipped between her legs and Catryn's thoughts scattered. The only time she had ever been touched there was just before the joining had begun. She struggled to cling to the pleasure

Orion had filled her with and push aside the cloudy memories of discomfort.

"You have become a little tense all of a sudden, Catryn," Orion said, his breath warming the hollow of her throat. "Have you changed your mind?" He lifted his head to look at her.

"No," she replied in as firm a tone as she could manage. "It was but the unwanted intrusion of an old, bad memory." She wrapped her arms around him and held him close again.

"Ah." Orion realized her husband had not only cared nothing for her pleasure, he had cared nothing for her comfort either. "I am not him."

Before she could reply, he moved his long fingers in a way that made her gasp and arch into his touch. She rubbed her body against his as he continued to intimately caress her, her desire growing so swiftly and fiercely that she could not remain still. With every skillful caress, every kiss, and every brush of his warm skin against hers, Catryn felt an ache deep inside her belly grow tighter and more demanding. She whispered his name against his mouth and, even lost in desire's madness as she was, Catryn could hear the demand in her voice.

Then he was there. Inside her in one clean, hard stroke. Surprise over how perfectly he filled her was nearly swept away when he began to move. Catryn wrapped her body around his, arching into his every thrust. The soft growl that escaped him was enough to tell her she was returning the pleasure he was giving her. Then the tightness in her belly bloomed, spreading throughout her body and she cried out with the joy of it. A heartbeat later she felt him thrust deeply and shudder in her arms as he groaned out her name.

Orion eased the weight of his body from hers, moving to the side just a little. He brushed the tangled hair from her face and reveled in the glow he could still see coloring her cheeks and brightening her eyes. He had pleasured women before, but he had never taken as much pride in the fact as he did now. Then he watched her gaze clear a little as she looked at his shirt and then his breeches. That soft glow of pleasure faded fast.

"You do not like to be naked?" she asked as she tugged up the covers to hide her own nakedness as best she could while struggling through the lingering haze of sated passion to try and understand why he had remained partly clothed.

For a moment Orion considered telling her what he usually told women, and then he sighed. It was necessary for him to be honest, just as honest as Catryn always was with him. Just telling her that he had scars might be enough to make her cease wondering why he kept some of his clothes on, yet he knew he would be disappointed in her in some way if that proved true.

"I have a lot of scars on my back," he said.

"Oh." She slid her hands beneath his shirt and around to his back. Beneath her fingers she could feel the ridges left by old wounds. "Were you wounded? I know you and Giles speak of how you are a king's man. Did something happen during a time when you were working for the king?"

"No. I have had them since I was a child."

"A tutor?"

There was a faint hint of hope in her voice and he wondered at it. "No, my mother."

"Your own mother beat you enough to leave scars?"

Suddenly he was being held tightly in her slim arms. "She was a rigid woman who wished to beat the devil out of me," he confessed even as he wondered why.

"How could a mother do that? No, no need to answer. I have heard of other sins mothers have visited upon their children and been just as puzzled. It was but a question that did not exactly seek an answer, for I do not believe there ever can be a satisfactory one. The same when it is the father who commits the crime."

"Spare the rod, spoil the child."

"Oh, I did not suggest one never discipline a child, but there are ways to do so without beating them to the point that they are scarred for life." She started to tug off his shirt. "Well, now that that secret is out, take this off. I refuse to be the only one who is naked."

"They are upsetting to—"

"It might be wise if you do not speak on the times you have taken your shirt off for other women."

"Ah, a good point."

"So? Off with the clothes." She blushed. "Unless you mean to return to your own room now, of course. I may be presuming too much by thinking you mean to stay here."

"Not at all. I just felt I should warn you."

"If you can accept my scars then I shall accept yours."

"You do not have any scars."

"I do." She touched the marks low on her belly.

"The birthing marks are still a bit stark, and probably always will be."

Orion bent to kiss each of the scars running alongside her hip bones. "Marks of honor. You survived and gave the world a bright, gifted boy."

Tears stung her eyes as she watched him stand up, but she fought them. He was tense as he began to shed his clothing. Catryn did not want him to think her tears were because of what he was about to show her and misinterpret the cause. The man was clearly very sensitive about his scars.

When he was fully disrobed, it took her breath away, and not just because she had never seen a grown man fully naked before. She had the passing thought that it was a wonder he could fit what was dangling between his legs inside her, and then she clenched her hands into fists because she wanted to reach out and touch him. The lustful cause of that urge ended when he turned around. His back was a mass of scars obviously made by a cane or a whip. They crisscrossed his broad, strong back from his shoulders to the tops of his well-muscled thighs.

Shock was her first reaction but she was glad she hid it, for she could see him watching her closely in the mirror over the fireplace. Then fury surged up through her. His mother, the woman who had given him life and should have cherished him, had done this to him. She heartily wished the woman was near at hand because she wanted to give the wretched excuse for a mother a taste of her own vicious medicine.

"Why? What possible reason could she think she had to do that to her own child?" she demanded, fighting the harsh images that tried to form in her mind.

Orion turned and stared at her. She was furious. He did not think he had ever seen anyone that furious before. Perhaps rumors about a redhead's temper were not as exaggerated as he had always thought. For a moment he had believed he was about to suffer that look of shock and horror he so desperately did not wish to see in her eyes. Instead he was seeing the urge to murder someone there, and he suspected it was his mother. He moved back to the bed and settled down beside her before pulling her into his arms.

"My mother is already dead," he said.

"How?"

"She was going to church as she so often did and was run over by the minister's carriage." He could not fully repress a smile at the look of angry disbelief she gave him, clearly believing he was making a poor jest. "Truly. She was so busy reading her prayer book as she walked that she stepped out right in front of him. The man was from our old parish, but my father had removed him after he found out it was one of the man's sermons that inspired my mother to try and beat the devil out of me."

"So your father put a stop to it?"

"Only if he happened to be around, and he rarely was. Recall how I said he died."

Catryn frowned as she slid her arms around him. "Do you think that your mother may also have been using you in place of the one she truly wanted to beat?"

"When I was older and understood how my father had betrayed her practically from their wedding night, I began to think that. At the time, I just thought I had the devil in me."

"That is utter nonsense. It was your gift, one you gained from your father, whom she married. Do not tell me she did not know the full truth about who your father was when she married him."

"She did, but as with too many who come from outside the family, she did not truly understand. I do not believe she knew she would be bearing a child with a gift, either."

"Oh, she knew. Even the most innocent of women, one kept utterly in the dark about men and women and marriage and babies knows that making a baby requires a man, and that baby could look just like that man or be like him, or look like her and be like her, or even a bit of each. She had family, correct?" He nodded. "And siblings?" He nodded again. "Then she knew. She was either trying to make you pay for the fact that your father was a faithless swine . . ." She grimaced. "Pardon."

"No need. He was a faithless swine."

She decided to ignore the hint of laughter in his voice. "Or because she believed the rantings of some minister about devils and all."

"It was probably a little of both."

"Is what happened to you typical of what your family suffers?"

"Not really, but not so rare, either. We are different and, to some, a bit frightening. There is no hiding the rest of the family after the marriage takes place, so there are even more things to frighten new spouses. Yet it does appear that bearing a child with a gift that frightens them causes that final break. It is as if the mother, or father if he is the one from outside the clan, just refuses to believe they created such a child. One of my cousins said he often wonders if some of them believed they could breed it out of us with their untainted selves and grew angry when that glory was denied them."

Catryn blinked. "Now *that* was truly, deeply cynical. Unfortunately, I now realize your cousin may be right. She had no right, Orion. Mother or not, she had no right to do that to a child and, God help me, I cannot be sad she is dead. Siblings?"

"None. She found out very quickly that my father did not have a faithful bone in his body. From what I found out later, she held the foolish notion that she could make him see the error of his ways with scold-ings and denying him the marriage bed." He nodded when Catryn stared at him in openmouthed shock for a moment and then rolled her eyes. "Oddly enough, I do believe she was an intelligent woman, just not where it concerned my father and our gifts."

"What was your father's gift?"

"He could see the colors that surround all people."

"I do not understand. What colors?"

"According to my father, each and every person has an aura, similar to the circle of light one can see around the moon from time to time, and each color within it implies something. He did a lot of study about it when he was not hunting a new woman for his bed. Wrote it all down and searched out anything any of our forefathers may have written about it. I have quite a large collection of papers and such in a box at my house. He once told me, just before my mother left us, that my mother's aura was flashing with the colors of rage and fear, that he was sorry for that because he knew he was to blame for it. It appears he had married her because he thought the colors around her indicated that she was a peaceful, forgiving person, but those colors began to change when she found him with the downstairs maid two days after they were married and were preparing to leave for their wedding trip."

"Oh dear. I think my colors would have changed as well. But it all makes no difference. She should never have done that to you. Never. And for a moment there I wanted to hunt her down and see it done to her until she was bleeding at my feet. Then I would kick her."

Orion laughed and held her tighter. He had only allowed a few to know what his mother had done to him. And even fewer women had seen him completely undressed, ever since the first time he had seen that look of horror and disgust. He was astonished at how much it mattered to him that Catryn had not reacted so. He had seen that hint of shock, which she had quickly hidden, but shock he could accept. It was her anger that touched him the most.

"So are you staying here then?" she asked quietly.

"Yes, although I will slip out before the maid arrives, so do not see any insult when you wake to find me gone. I will do my best to try and salvage your reputation."

"It will probably need some salvaging," she said as she began to stroke his skin, loving how it warmed beneath her hands. "We may not have seen anyone who knows us, but that does not mean that word of this journey of mine will not leak back to London and the gossips. It matters not. I would change nothing."

"Nothing?"

She looked into his beautiful blue eyes and slowly shook her head. "Nothing."

He knew he ought to say something, murmur words to assure her that she was not just some woman to warm his bed for a while, yet he was tongue-tied for the first time in his life. Orion did not wish to say things he was not certain he felt or promise something he might not be able to give, which left little else to say aside from empty flatteries. He decided to just show her again how much he desired her.

Catryn was a little disappointed that there were no sweet words for her, or even for what they had shared, but shook it aside. It was better if he did not try to stroke her with well-practiced words. She wanted no empty promises, either. When he kissed her, she decided this was what she wanted. This heat and ferocity they shared was not false or empty. After he was gone from her life, she would be able to enjoy memories of a passion untainted by lies or flirtatious mutterings that had been too often said to others. She would make that be enough.

Chapter Thirteen

"Come along, Cat. Our meal will grow cold."

Catryn sighed and moved away from the window. As he had said would happen, she had awoken to find herself alone in her bed. She had fought a brief sense of unease over how such stealth chilled the warm memories of passion savored and shared. It had to be done that way. They could not flaunt themselves or she would be utterly ruined. Worse, there could even be enough gossip that Orion would feel compelled to try and save her from it by offering to marry her. Tempting though the thought of him as her husband was, she had already suffered through one loveless marriage and had no intention of suffering through another. She allowed Orion to take her by the hand and lead her to the table where they would share a meal. The maid setting out their morning meal was plump and pretty. She was friendly as well, but not flirtatious. Her smiles were not weighted with an invitation for Orion to join her anytime, anywhere. It made for a pleasant change, Catryn thought as she sat down at the table.

"We are full to bursting," said the maid. "That cursed rain is keeping most folk here and bringing others in to shelter. 'Tis the same at the White Hart."

"I would have thought the rain would have caused people to stay where they were, at least until it eased." Despite their need to chase down Morris, it had taken only one look out the window to decide they would be staying right where they were, a decision she had not even attempted to argue with.

"That you would, m'lady, but some were already on the road when it turned this bad. Some folk have no sense of how the weather can turn on you. Some think it will stop before the road becomes too dangerous but 'tis naught but mud and ruts already." She shook her head. "Now they are cheek by jowl here."

"Meg," Orion said and smiled when the woman turned her attention to him, "where have you put everyone?"

"In the common room," Meg replied. "We have only the two private parlors, this one and the one Sir Tupperton and his family are using. I know some places would put the other gentry in here, too, but the owner prides himself on making certain that private means private. You paid for privacy and so you will have it."

Catryn looked around the large room she and Orion shared. They sat at a table near the fireplace, leaving two other small tables, a settee, and two chairs empty. She was about to speak to Orion about offering to share the room when he stood up and gently took Meg by the arm.

"Show me who is in the common room, Meg," he said as he escorted her to the door. "I may be able to ease the crowding in there by inviting a few chosen people to share this parlor."

A moment later, Catryn found herself alone, Meg's effusive thank-you to Orion still ringing in her ears. She looked at the food and decided she was far too hungry to cling to propriety and wait for Orion to rejoin her before starting. A night filled with lovemaking obviously left one ravenous. As she filled her plate she idly wondered who Orion would choose. One last look at the rain streaming down the window had her hoping he chose well. Catryn strongly suspected they would be stuck with his choice for the rest of the day.

Orion stood in the doorway to the public room with Meg at his side and inwardly shook his head. People were shoulder to shoulder in the room, and seeing the speed with which the men were downing their ale, he knew some had decided the best way to spend a miserable day was to get soundly drunk. His gaze rested on a small family huddled on a narrow bench in a far corner of the room. A young woman held a small girl in her arms. Beside her was an older, sturdier woman who was keeping two young boys close by her side. Their clothing marked them as gentry but not wealthy or highly placed, quite possibly the family of a younger son. The looks on their faces told him that they knew how quickly things could turn ugly if the ale continued to be consumed with such greed.

There were only two other women in the room, but

they were seated at a table and well guarded by four men. Considering their ages he suspected it was another family, but he would not be surprised if they were titled. Their clothes certainly marked them as wealthy, or very foolish with their money. They were also more comfortably situated than the other family, despite the crowd.

He turned to Meg and just as he was about to speak, an annoyingly recognizable feeling swept over him. His second gift was odd and a bit erratic, but he knew something was inside Meg. While she studied the crowd, he studied her, and then grinned, relief flooding his heart. There was definitely something inside Meg, but it was not disease as he had feared. For a moment he wondered if he should say anything, and then he took another look at the number of men drinking heavily and knew he had to say something, for she could not stay and work in here. Orion just hoped it was news she would welcome.

"Meg, I have chosen the ones I would like to share the parlor with Lady de Warrenne and myself," he said and watched her glance toward the more fashionable group, her sigh badly smothered. "Not them." He nodded toward the family trying so hard to disappear from view in the shadows cloaking the far corner of the room. "Them."

"Oh, thank you, sir," she said. "I was sorely worried about them, I was. I will go and tell them."

He gently grasped her by the arm to stop her. "I will escort you over there. You need to be careful, Meg."

"Oh, I do know it, sir. Most of these men were headed to a boxing match. Now they are stuck here and swilling ale as if it will all disappear tomorrow.

That might fill the inn's coffers but it could also turn ugly." She shook her head. "And, even if it does not, there will still be a fair old mess to clean up come the morning."

"You have some women to help you in that, I hope." When she frowned at him, uncertainty clouding her eyes, he decided to just be blunt. "You should not be around these men or doing a lot of vigorous work or heavy lifting. It is dangerous for a woman to do so when so newly with child," he finished in a near whisper and watched her eyes widen.

"With child? You think I am with child?" she whispered back. "How could you know that when I do not?"

"I come from a very, very large family." He shrugged in a way that implied he had no rational explanation for her. "You could present me with a courtyard packed with women and I suspect I could find everyone within the mob who was with child. Trust me in this, you are carrying. Will you lose your job?"

Meg looked toward the young man filling tankards for the crowd and slowly shook her head. "No, Kenton and I are promised and he is the innkeeper's only son. His da is always pushing us to hurry up and marry, even got us a wee cottage only a short walk from here, but it is a bit rough and we wanted to make it finer, get a few nice things for it, repair a few things and all, so were waiting for a bit."

"Ah, then I am sorry but I think you must now reconsider the waiting." Her smile was so big and bright Orion lost the last scrap of the unease he had been suffering over giving her the news.

"You are right about that. Now, best we give that

poor, frightened little family over there the good news
that they can get away from these rowdy idiots. Oh
dear," Meg said when the older man from the other
family approached them.

"There must be another place my family can go to
in this inn. This is intolerable," the man said.

"I told you the private rooms and all the bedchambers are taken," Meg said. "Three times I done told
you that and it is still true. No one is leaving here in
this weather, now are they?"

"You could put us into one of those private parlors.
Just go tell whoever is in there that there is no choice."

Meg shook her head. "Those are private parlors and
the inn promises the guest who lets them that they will
not be bothered or forced to share. We stand firm on
that. Now, I can go and ask if Sir Tupperton—"

"Tupperton? I know that man. I am Lord Rishton.
Take me to him. We have done some business together and I am certain he will be willing to share the
parlor with me and my family."

"No, *I* will be doing the asking first. That is the
rule."

"And she is also busy assisting me at the moment,"
Orion said when the man looked prepared to loudly
berate Meg.

"Who are you?" demanded Lord Rishton.

"Sir Orion Wherlocke," he replied, bowing slightly,
and for once smiled with pleasure when the man took
a step back.

"I suppose it is you then who holds the other private parlor."

"That I do, and I am about to go and invite that
family over there to share it with me." He nodded

toward the group still huddled in the corner of the room.

"Them?"

The scorn in the man's voice irritated Orion. "Yes, them. They have no men to protect them."

The way Lord Rishton flushed and then sighed in resignation, silently recognizing that truth, softened Orion's dislike of him just a little, but then Rishton scowled at Meg. "If you can tell Sir Wherlocke to share his parlor then you can go and tell Tupperton that he has to share his."

"I did not tell Sir Wherlocke to share, m'lord; he offered and came here to see who might need it the most. When I am done helping him get that family settled, I will go and ask Sir Tupperton if he wishes to share with you and that you will also share the cost if he does."

Lord Rishton harrumphed. "You take a lot upon yourself, girl."

"I am the maid for those parlors. It is my job. Now, as I said, I will return when I am done with all I need to do now and then let you know what Sir Tupperton's answer is."

"Maid of the private parlors, are you?" Orion asked Meg as Lord Rishton strode back to his table and they started winding their way through the crowd toward the small family in the corner.

"I am now, and will be from now on," said Meg. "Gentler work that, and I will not have to be dealing with this lot." She glanced at Kenton. "Best to have a word with him, too, before much more time passes, as I have to tell him and his da that I will not be working in here now."

Orion looked at the family they approached and could see that they had spotted him and Meg. The two women were frantically whispering back and forth, pausing only to stare at him for a moment before starting their whispered conversation again. The closer he got the more sure he became that he saw hope in their glances toward him, but that made no sense. They did not know him and few people stared at him with hope, so few that he could not immediately recall a single one.

"Mistress Pryce, this is Sir Orion Wherlocke," Meg said when they reached the family. "He is in one of the private parlors with Lady de Warrenne and he has kindly offered to allow you and your family to shelter in there."

Both women had stood up when he arrived and were attempting to untangle themselves from the children, but the younger one still managed a credible curtsy, while the older woman managed to bob up and down a little while the boys still clung to her. "I am Mistress Mervyn Pryce, sir," said the younger woman, "and this is my mother, Mistress Anna Pugh." Mervyn smiled tentatively, watching him closely.

"Ah, fate is a funny thing, is it not?" He smiled at them, kissed Mrs. Pryce's hand, and then kissed Mrs. Pugh's. "A Pugh. I did make a wise choice." He glanced at the younger woman. "I do not recall the Pryces though."

"Fine people, sir," said Mrs. Pugh. "They are kin to the Pughs. Your cousin, the Duke of Elderwood, has a few of them working for him."

"Does he now? Excellent. Gather your belongings and come with me then. Did you come by stage?" he asked as he took a large bag from Mrs. Pugh and then began to herd them through the boisterous crowd.

"Oh, nay, sir," answered Mervyn. "His Grace insisted that we make use of his carriage. He said he would never allow women and children to ride about on the public stage. The driver and his son are staying in the stables, as he believed it would be very wise to keep an eye on the team and the carriage. I was near ready to take us all and go join them there."

"I believe you will find this much more to your liking." He opened the door to the private parlor and waved them inside before turning to Meg. "I think we will be in need of more food and drink."

"And some bedding for them," said Meg, "so they can be comfortable in the night."

"They can take my bedchamber. Just move my things over to Lady de Warrenne's so that they are not cluttering up the room." He just cocked one brow when she looked at him. "I can bed down in here or, if the crowd becomes too rowdy, go and guard my lady." He knew she was not fooled by his words but, despite the smile in her eyes, she just nodded and hurried away. Orion hoped Catryn accepted his plan with equal calm.

When he stepped into the room it was to find that Catryn had already introduced herself. The children were seated at the table while the women cut some bread and buttered it for them. Orion smiled at Catryn when she walked over to him.

"You chose very well," she said. "I could almost feel their relief when they entered this room."

"I chose even better than I could have anticipated. It seems they are from Elderwood, the family seat of the Vaughns and the Wherlockes. One is a Pugh, a family that has long served mine and the Vaughns, and the younger woman is a Pryce, relations of the Pughs, and one of another family that has people working at Elderwood. We can also relax and not worry about what is said. Watching one's every word can be wearying."

"Why are they so far from home?"

"Perhaps we can discover that while we all eat. Here comes Meg with the additional food I requested."

"It is needed." Catryn blushed as she watched Meg set out the food. "I was rather hungry." She ignored his grin as she moved toward the table.

Once the food was served and everyone had a plateful before them, Catryn asked, "Where are you traveling to, Mrs. Pryce?"

"To Portsmouth," she replied, "and please, call me Mervyn, m'lady."

"Thank you, and you must call me Catryn." She could tell by the looks on both women's faces that they might have trouble doing so comfortably. "Are you taking a journey?"

"Nay, we are collecting my husband." Mervyn sighed. "He was taken up by the military press gangs when he was on a journey to gain something for His Grace. It was months before we knew what had happened to him and more months before His Grace could get the authorities to get him free of service and returned. I fear he was wounded or injured in some way. His letter to us when he knew he was being sent home was not all that clear. They had sent him to India. My Llywd, who rarely went beyond the Elderwood lands." She shook her head. "I am not sure what will happen to us now."

"You will return to Elderwood, will you not?" said Orion.

"But to what kind of life? My Llywd may be seriously wounded or sickly. His Grace . . ."

"Will find something that he can do to earn his keep and find pride in the doing of it."

"Are you certain of that?"

"I am. He chose your Llywd to work for him. As what, may I ask?"

"Oh." Mervyn's smile was a little shaky. "My Llywd is an educated man and His Grace chose him to help with the books and, on occasion, in seeing to some of the books from the other properties; or even finding the best price for our wool or horses. The pressers must not have believed him when he told them he was the Duke of Elderwood's man of business."

Mrs. Pugh grunted in a soft sound of disgust. "They did not care. They saw a big, strapping man and wanted him to fill their ranks. He would not take the shilling so they just took him. It is near to a miracle that His Grace found him as quickly as he did."

"It did not feel so quick, but aye"—Mervyn nodded—"I understand how easily we could have lost Llywd forever."

"Modred will find work for him," Orion said again and looked right at Mrs. Pugh. "It is not easy for my cousin to find ones he can work with or be around for any length of time." When the older woman frowned and then nodded in understanding, he looked at Mervyn. "No matter how serious a wound your husband has suffered, Modred will not cast him aside. He is much too valuable to him, for his work and for the fact that my cousin can actually work with him. And Modred is also a very loyal man to those who have served him well."

The rest of the meal went quickly, conversation moving to more traditional topics such as the weather. Catryn watched the boys play and inwardly sighed, missing her own son. She was apart from him for a good reason, however. Until the threat Morris presented was ended, in whatever way necessary, Alwyn would always be at risk and she would not tolerate that.

"I think they suspect that we are more than traveling companions," said Catryn as she readied herself for bed and peeked around the privacy screen to look at Orion.

She was pleased that he had offered his bedchamber to the women and children but still felt a little awkward over how that must look to Meg and the family now using his bedchamber. Although she had decided she could risk her reputation, she was uneasy about doing so in such a blatant way. There was no doubt in her mind that neither Meg nor the other women believed he would spend the night in the parlor.

"I would say that *suspect* is the wrong word," he said. "'Tis more like a certainty."

She blushed and ducked back behind the screen. "Whenever that realization struck them, it did not appear to change how they treated us."

"Of course not. They are not of society and have a

much more practical nature. What you and I do, as adults, a man and a young widow, is not something they consider their concern. Then, too, one of them is a Pugh and I suspect she is well versed on my clan, both the Vaughn side and the Wherlocke one."

"By well versed you mean that she knows there are a lot of rogues within your family?" she asked as she hurried across the cold floor and slid into bed at his side.

Orion bit back a smile when she curled up by his side and he wrapped his arms around her. She wore her maidenly night shift, her hair properly braided. Despite that appearance of utter innocence, she did not hesitate to join him in the bed or curl up in his arms. Her small hand stroked his chest with obvious pleasure. He knew that when he started to make love to her, all that maidenly sweetness would disappear and she would become a fiery wanton in his arms. It was an odd mixture that he suspected could fascinate him for a long time.

"She has undoubtedly heard a few tales. We breed mostly boys, and that means there are always a goodly number of single young men doing what single young men are apt to do."

"Ah yes, the type of things that so many like to tsk-tsk over even while they gather up and retell every tale they can and do so avidly."

His eyes widened when she slid her hand down over his stomach and curled her soft fingers around his erection. There was a hint of tension in her body and he knew she was awaiting rejection, so he did his best to remain still and as calm as he could be with those long, delicate fingers shyly stroking him. The tentative way she explored him so intimately told him that she had never done such a thing before and that only made his desire burn hotter.

Catryn heard Orion make a soft murmuring sound of pleasure as she stroked him. It was enough to banish all her hesitancy. This part of a man had fascinated her since her wedding night. She had never seen a grown man naked until Orion, who plainly had only pretended modesty due to his scars, and she had never touched her husband in such a way during those silent, uncomfortable couplings in the dark. Until Orion she had never thought it something that could bring her any pleasure, either, and had decided its only use was to allow a man to relieve himself and to breed children.

The way Orion intimately touched her brought her a wondrous pleasure and she had suddenly wondered if she could give him the same. He had certainly hardened quickly when she had touched him. What surprised her was how her own desire grew stronger as she stroked him. She soon wanted to be in his arms, to feel the heat of their flesh blend. As she shifted to move up his body, she impulsively kissed him. He groaned and threaded his fingers in her hair, gently holding her in place. Catryn daringly ran her tongue along his length. Orion's reaction to that intimate caress was all the encouragement she needed to continue.

It was not until she took him into her mouth that her play was abruptly interrupted. Orion caught her up under her arms and dragged her up the length of his body. She opened her mouth to ask if she had erred only to have her question smothered by her night shift as he pulled it off over her head. And then she was on her back and he began to intimately caress her as he kissed with a hunger that had her heart pounding with anticipation. Since he was not acting as if she had shocked or offended him, she wrapped her body around his and let him lead the dance that always left her so well pleasured she could barely think.

Orion finally regained his senses enough to breathe more evenly and start thinking again. He quickly made certain that he had remembered to fall a little to the side when he had collapsed from the strength of his release so that he did not crush Catryn beneath him. Then he smiled. She was splayed out beneath him as if she had been knocked unconscious, the only sign of life being the way she was still panting. As he watched her breathing grow more even, it was a relief to realize that he had not shocked or frightened her with his sudden, fierce need to be inside her. When she slowly opened her eyes, he kissed her.

"Well"—she cleared a lingering huskiness from her voice—"that was very energetic of us."

He laughed. "True. I fear your ardent attentions to my eager body made my need for you grow rather fierce."

"Ah, so I did not do anything wrong." She blushed as she realized she may have just initiated a discussion of intimacies that she was not sure she was ready for.

Brushing a kiss over her blush-warmed cheek, he said, "No, you did nothing wrong." He nipped her earlobe. "A little more practice, a few careful instructions,

and you will succeed in leaving me too sated to move
for days."

She felt the warmth of his breath warm the side of
her neck as he laughed, and swatted him on the arm
in retribution. "Rogue. I do not think you should be
saying such improper things to me."

"Cat, we are naked together in a bed. I believe that
gives us leave to speak of almost anything."

"Ah. There is that."

He was still chuckling when he got out of bed,
washed up, and then came back with a damp cloth to
clean her off as well. It was a very gentlemanly thing
for him to do, but Catryn had to fight the urge to hide
beneath the covers. When he got back into the bed,
she was still a little tense with embarrassment, but relaxed when he pulled her into his arms. It felt too
good to be there with him, skin to skin, to let something like acute modesty ruin it.

"Such a modest lass," he murmured and kissed the
top of her head, then laughed when she gave the hair
on his chest a punitive tug. "I find it sweet."

"Sweet?" She frowned. "I am naked in a bed with a
lover. I am not sure I wish to be thought of as sweet."

"And what would you like to be thought of as?"

"Wild? Seductive? Intriguing?" She smiled when he
laughed again.

"You are all of that with a touch of sweetness."

For a few minutes she simply enjoyed being held in
his arms. If anyone had ever told her that she would
enjoy being naked with a man, she would have
laughed heartily. Curiosity would have made her willing to take a good look at a naked man, but she could

never have imagined how good it would feel to be skin to skin with one. Then again, she had never imagined she would find herself with a lover like Orion. He was a man who could tempt the most saintly of women into behaving badly.

That made her think of just how many women he had tempted and how few he had refused when they had invited him into their beds. It was not a pleasant thought. She could not help but fear what comparisons he might have made and how she might have suffered in those comparisons.

Shaking that thought aside, for it was far too depressing to dwell on, she then wondered how and when their affair would end. As a married woman and then as a widow, she had become privy to a lot of gossip about men, husbands, and lovers, and even some men to whom women claimed they would give a fortune to have as a lover. Some women suffered for taking a lover, while others appeared to be forgiven for having a whole string of them.

She had also learned that the end of an affair could be painful and very messy. She would not allow her time with Orion to end that way, she vowed. Catryn thought on how, right after she had given Henry a son, several women had advised her on the matter of conducting an affair properly, as if they had no doubt that she would soon enter into one. Discretion, she had been told, was a must. She grimaced, knowing she had already failed miserably in that. The other rules had been much simpler. Do not cling to the man. Do not expect love and devotion and never,

never demand it nor give it. Do not expect the affair to last.

It had all sounded so very sordid and even sad, yet here she was with a lover. Catryn decided she would do her best to follow all those rules but knew she would never be able to control her own heart. All she could do was try very hard not to make a complete fool of herself.

Chapter Fourteen

Catryn woke and looked at the man she was curled around. He looked so handsome even in sleep that she could easily have found that annoying. No one should look that good while sleeping. She grinned at such nonsense and idly wondered what would be the best way to wake him up.

The man had turned her into a wanton, she decided as she rested her cheek against his chest and began to trail her fingers down to his taut stomach. Before this, if anyone had suggested that she would enjoy being naked with a man, including her husband, she would have been shocked right down to her slippers and then had a hearty laugh.

Henry was the very last person she wished to think about while lying in bed with Orion, but memories of the nights spent with her husband were suddenly crowding into her mind. Darkness, very little touching, and only the parts necessary for breeding bared when it was time for the joining. It had been a chore, not a pleasure or even a true bonding between a man and his wife. Worse, too many of those times were now memories seen through a thick fog. It was as if she had dreamed those times Henry had come to her bed, but Alwyn was proof that he had.

Uneasy now, she struggled to bring those memories more clearly to mind, but that proved impossible. She could always recall that she had gone to bed, even how she often fretted over the possibility that Henry would join her, and then nothing until she woke in the morning with an ache between her thighs. The puzzle was about why she had not fully woken up when her husband had climbed on top of her. It could not be usual for a woman to sleep through such an activity. She had not slept through far less intrusive things, such as the maid coming into the room to light the morning fire.

"Ouch."

Catryn looked up to find Orion frowning at her. Then she looked down at where her hand rested on his stomach. She was no longer lightly stroking that smooth, warm skin. Her hand was partly clenched, her nails prodding his flesh. She blushed and tried desperately to relax her hand, but the thought of how Henry had crept into her bed at night would not be shaken from her mind and kept her tense. There was something wrong with what she was recalling, but she could not think what it could be, and that only added to her rapidly growing unease.

Orion reached down and took her hand in his. "I was enjoying your caress and about to request that you take it lower. Pleased I did not." He kissed her palm when she gave a shaky laugh. "What troubles you?"

She flopped onto her back and stared up at the ceiling. "I suddenly thought of Henry."

"Obviously not in a pleasant way." Orion nearly winced and then told himself not to be a fool as it was obvious that her memories of her late husband were neither fond nor welcome.

"No. I rarely think of Henry in a pleasant way. He was not a husband one recalls fondly. He inspired no fondness when he was alive, either. No, I just remembered how I never spent time abed with him like this, never saw him unclothed save once when he was shirtless only, and never touched him like this. Nor he me. Then I recalled that I can barely remember the beddings."

She blushed even as she scowled, uneasy about speaking of such personal matters yet feeling compelled to do so. "It is as if it all happened in a dream. I would go to bed a little concerned that Henry would come to visit, which was never a pleasant matter, and then wake up in the morning knowing that he had, but not truly knowing what had happened and when. It was as if I had dreamed the whole thing, yet I know I did not because of that pain." She looked at him. "Surely a woman cannot sleep right through such an event?"

"I would not have thought so and, thank God, I have never had any proof of it." Orion was pleased to see her smile but he did not like the implications of what she was saying, yet could think of no reason for a man to drug his wife just to bed her. "Were you a nervous bride, afraid of the bedding? One who would shake or cry?" It was hard to think of the passionate woman at his side as a terrified bride, but he had not

known her then, could not know how she may have
changed since her wedding day.

"Every bride is nervous on her wedding night, but
I was prepared. Even when it proved to all be such a
severe disappointment, I was accepting of that, too. I
wished to be a good wife and I wanted children. It
was never a pleasant duty, however, so I am puzzled
by how little I remember of it. One always recalls
unpleasant things clearly, as if the mind wishes for
you not to forget and thus fall into the same trap
again and again. And one always recalls what it is that
causes pain."

"Did you have anything to eat or drink before you
settled down to sleep?"

"Of course." She pointed to the small tankard of
cider on the small table by the bed. "I always have a
nice drink of some hot tea or spiced wine or cider as
I read a little before sleeping. It helps me to push
aside all those little irritations of the day that can keep
one awake for hours."

"It sounds to me as if your husband may have put
something into your nightly drink."

The moment Orion spoke that suspicion aloud,
Catryn knew it for the truth. There had been a time
or two in her life, such as when she had been sunk
deeply in grief over the loss of her mother, when she
had been given something to help her sleep. She had
strongly disliked it and never taken it again, hating
the way it pulled one into sleep against one's will and
left a person groggy, one's thoughts all in disorder, in
the morning.

Catryn was embarrassed that she had not recognized that she had been suffering the same sensations.

Now that she examined her fog-shrouded memories carefully, she knew it was exactly the feeling she had had in her marriage bed, right up until the moment she had gotten with child. The dark-of-night beddings had ceased then, too, and she had no trouble recalling everything that had happened during the nights following that moment. Never again had she awoken sore and her mind cloudy, with no more than a few scraps of memory to explain why she was experiencing that discomfort.

"That bastard," she hissed, clenching her hands into fists and wishing Henry was there so that she could beat him senseless as he so richly deserved. "But why do that? I did not refuse him or scream or weep."

"I have no answer for that and, since the fool is dead, I fear the reason is lost." He leaned over to brush his lips over hers. "Do you think we can kick the late, unlamented Henry out of our bed now?"

She laughed and pulled him into her arms. "With pleasure."

"That was my plan."

"And you always have such wonderful plans."

Catryn gave herself over to his kisses and caresses, letting the pleasure he brought to her banish the troubling memories of the past. When she was more than ready for Orion to join with her, nearly panting with the need to feel him inside her, he suddenly turned onto his back, still holding her in his arms. Sprawled on top of him, she was just about to ask him what he was doing when, after some fondling and adjusting of her body that nearly caused her to forget her questions, he grabbed her by the hips and plunged inside her.

Gasping with shock and pleasure, Catryn placed her hands on his chest. "I am on top."

"Aye, you most certainly are," he said, his voice low and rough with passion. "Now you ride me."

Realizing how exposed she must be, Catryn glanced down at herself. At some point during their love-making Orion had undone her braid and her hair provided enough covering that the brief chill of modesty quickly faded. She clenched her body around him and he growled. She decided she liked this position and not just because he filled her so thoroughly. It gave her a sense of power, even though she knew it for a pleasant delusion, for the power was a shared one, as their passion was.

"Are you just going to sit there all day?" he asked as he stroked her thighs.

"Now there is an interesting idea." She squirmed on top of him, delighting in the way he groaned softly and his eyes closed. "I do think Meg might be reluctant to serve us our meals here though."

She was startled when he suddenly sat up, licked the hard tip of each of her breasts, and then looked at her, his eyes darkened with a mixture of passion and amusement. "M'lady, would you be so kind as to begin moving?"

"Well, when you ask so politely, how can any lady refuse?"

She began to move and was soon lost to the desire that flared so quick and hot between them, one she was beginning to fear she would only ever be able to share with him.

* * *

Orion tugged on his boots and looked at the privacy screen Catryn had slipped behind in order to wash up and dress. He was in trouble, the sort of trouble he suspected many a man who had contemplated a long, happy life of bachelorhood faced at some time in his life. It embarrassed him a little bit to admit it, but he had been with a goodly number of women, yet none had given him the pleasure Catryn did. None had left him as sated. And not one had been a woman who could make him smile just by being there at his side when he woke up in the morning. She had more than filled his bed, she had conquered it.

He had gotten Catryn in his bed, but she had wriggled herself into his soul. He had certainly not been searching for any such bond. Orion knew that he had finally found the woman he could not walk away from. Even if he tried, she would forever be in his mind. His body would never stop craving the warmth and welcome of hers.

A heavy sigh escaped him. He still did not know if what he felt was love, for he had never really believed in the emotion, having seen so little of it as a child. He faintly recalled his father, who was away far more than he was at home, and thought that the man had loved him in his way. There were no bad memories there; he remembered feeling contentment when his father was there to stand between him and his mother and a touch of sorrow over losing him. What he knew was that he wanted to keep hold of the passion he and Catryn shared; he liked her, enjoyed her company, and she accepted all that he was. Those were not things to ignore or toss away just because he would not give up the idea of spending his life free of any woman's claim; but neither were they sufficient to convince a woman to stay with him.

"I hope Mervyn and Anna have not left yet," Catryn said as she stepped out from behind the screen. "I wanted to wish them a safe journey." She paused before the door and looked at him. "You are truly certain that your cousin will allow her husband to work for him again, no matter how badly wounded he is?"

"Very certain," he replied, "and if you had ever met Modred, you would be as well. He takes few people into his home because his gift does not allow it, not if he wishes peace in his own home. Elderwood is his haven from the world, a place where he is not constantly battered by the thoughts and emotions of others. This man was allowed in. He will always be allowed in."

She shook her head. "That is so very good of him, but I do feel badly for your cousin. That gift of his sounds much like a curse. And that is what you fear may be in store for Giles, is it not?"

"Yes, but I believe Giles already has shields, formed as he grew up surrounded by the poorest of the poor and criminals. If his ability to sense how a person feels grows stronger, I will send him to Elderwood to have Aunt Dob train him as she is training Modred. I just hope Giles does not fight me about it."

"It is a good plan, and if you need anyone to help you convince Giles, I am more than willing to try. I hope this Aunt Dob is as good as you believe her to be."

"Oh, she is. We have all decided that her gift is to teach all the rest of us how to correctly use our gifts and save us from their power," he said as he escorted her out of the bedchamber and headed toward the parlor.

"That is, I believe, a very powerful gift indeed."

Orion thought of where some of his family would be if not for Dob, and nodded. Ones like Modred would undoubtedly have ended up in a madhouse, the emotions and thoughts in such a place only ensuring that they never shook free of the madness. Others would have become little better than hermits, bruised in spirit and fated to remain alone. She saved them with her gift, her training, and her deep understanding of each and every gift their family had.

"Yes, it is, and I think we owe her more than we can ever repay." He noticed the Pryces and Anna Pugh coming out of the parlor. "You are just in time to say farewell."

Catryn hurried over to help Mervyn with the children while Anna went to speak to Orion. There was a very close bond between the Wherlockes and the family that served them. She stared at them in fascination and realized she envied them that. Eccles was more family than servant, although the line was clearly drawn. She could see both advantages and disadvantages to having servants who were so close to the ones they served that that line could become blurred, yet it obviously worked for the Wherlockes.

"Do not try to understand it," said Mervyn and laughed when Catryn blushed. "I am a Pugh and I can puzzle over it."

"I was just, well, rather envying it," Catryn admitted as she took the hand of the taller of the two boys and followed Mervyn out to where the carriage waited in the morning sun.

"We certainly see the advantages. I doubt there are many in the serving class in this country who can depend upon their employers as we can. There is a long history between the Pughs and the Wherlockes or the Vaughns. 'Tis the same with the Jones family."

"That is what Orion told me and from all he said, it was honed under fire, so to speak."

"It was that. We lost some of our own to the ones who came after the Wherlockes and Vaughns. It was a war, and it lasted for what feels like forever. Not sure it is truly over, either."

"It may never be fully over, for it is born of fear of what the family can do, perhaps even some resentment concerning the power their gifts give them."

"Ah, I ne'er gave that a thought. Jealousy."

"The laws have finally changed, however, and with that change a lot of the danger has passed as well. One just needs to learn how to be, well, reticent and not march about boldly showing the world what one can do."

"You are one of them, aye?" Mervyn frowned as she studied Catryn and then nodded. "It is in the eyes."

Catryn sighed. "A drop or two several generations back. Sir Orion told me that he has a few cousins with eyes similar to mine, ones that cannot decide whether to be blue or green. I only just discovered that truth, too, as it was very well hidden."

Mervyn nodded. "As it always was. Had to be. The Pryces have a drop or two, also. My Llwyd says numbers speak to him. 'Tis his wee jest, but he does understand numbers as few others can, and not just the adding of them. If a matter can be reduced to numbers, he can see where to go with them to win, or to lose. 'Tis not a skill I can understand no matter how often he tries to explain. I but pray that whatever hurt he was given in India has not stolen that skill. Llwyd loves his work, purely loves it."

Seeing the deep worry on the woman's face, Catryn gently patted her on the back. "He wrote you a letter, so we know his mind is still sharp."

"That is some comfort, but what if he has been maimed in some way?"

"Then you both learn how to live despite his wounds. Try not to worry yourself ill over it. Did it not occur to you that he may have kept secret exactly what sort of wound he suffered because he wishes to see an honest, unprepared expression when you first see him and how he may have changed? Men have some vanity about how they look, just as women do."

"I just want to see him again, to know that he is truly alive and home with us again."

"Then think only on that. Trust me when I tell you that men can be as sensitive about scars and faults as any woman. It will be fine as soon as he feels assured that you still love him."

"Of course I do. He is a very good man."

"He sounds so. You are a very fortunate woman." Catryn admired the way Orion moved as he escorted Mrs. Pugh out of the inn.

"Sir Orion is a good man, too." Mervyn laughed when Catryn blushed and then grimaced. "You should keep him."

"Um, it is not like that between us. He is a bit of a rogue . . ."

"And how could he not be when he looks like that? M'lady, do not look so distressed. You are a widow, not some young girl tossing her good name and future into the wind for the sake of a pretty face. And, as my mother said, you are not one of those loose widows . . ."

"Am I not?"

"Nay. You are not some roguish flirt. You follow your heart, I think. And Sir Orion *is* a very good man despite his great enjoyment of his bachelor life thus far. When he came into the common room I expected him to either join those fools drinking every drop of ale in the place, or ask the lordling and his family to join him in his private parlor. I was that surprised that he not only saw us but then chose to invite us to share that fine room with you. Then my mother said she was certain he was a Wherlocke or a Vaughn and she was arguing about how one of us should go and let him know that we worked for the head of the whole family. Still arguing over that when he walked over to us."

Mervyn crossed her arms over her chest and gave Catryn a fierce look. "He is gentry and so are you. Me and my mum are not. Another of your class would have chosen that lordling, thinking nothing of leaving me, my mum, and my babes in that common room, unprotected and surrounded by men who were drinking too hard. I watched Sir Orion make that decision, watched him look at his lordship's fine family and then look at me and mine. I know why he chose us before he even knew who we were."

"Because you were two women and three babes alone and unprotected, surrounded by rowdy men."

"Aye, and that is what tells me he is a good man. And that good man is not giving you the rogue's eye."

"The rogue's eye?"

"That look that is hot but the fire doesn't burn long

or too deep. Nay, he looks at you like a man who is thinking that there is a woman who would make any man a fine partner. I know you do not see it, but at least consider the matter, since we both know you will go right back to being a proper lady once you are home again."

"I will attempt to consider it. And you remember to think only on the fact that Llwyd is alive and home with you."

"I plan to." Mervyn frowned toward where her mother stood and talked to Sir Orion. "I wonder what she is so busy whispering about?"

Catryn studied Orion and Mrs. Pugh. The woman was intent, obviously considered what she had to say to be of the utmost importance, and not at all intimidated by the fact that Orion was a knight. Despite that wide difference in their stations, Orion gave Mrs. Pugh the courtesy of listening and responding to whatever the woman was saying.

Mervyn was right. Orion was a good man. A man a woman should fight to keep. It was a lovely thought, but Catryn was certain that, if she tried too hard to hold on to Orion, he would slip through her fingers like smoke.

"His fingers?"

Orion was not surprised to discover that Mrs. Anna Pugh knew more about the health and fate of her daughter's husband than her daughter did, including the nature of the man's wounds. All Mervyn's thoughts had been on her husband, his health, and the fact that he was free again. Anna Pugh had needed to know more and had done an excellent job of investigating.

"Two. Cut them off down to the knuckle and he badly hurt his knee in the same incident, so that could leave him with the hint of a limp. And I think he is a wee bit bruised in mind and heart. Bringing home some dark with him."

"That is not surprising, Mrs. Pugh," Orion said. "You told us he grew up at Elderwood, only left it to go to the Cambridge and he loves to work with numbers. Not a man to be hardened to the ugliness of the world, yet he was suddenly dragged unwillingly into the military and sent to a foreign land. But, Mrs. Pugh, he is coming home now, a bit bruised and weary, but still having most of his parts, plus a wife and three children who are anxious to see him again. I suspect he has a goodly number of other Pryces waiting as well."

"But his fingers and his knee . . ."

He still has eight fingers and two legs." He was startled when she abruptly hugged him. "Just the truth, Mrs. Pugh."

"I know, but I needed it said, for I was not seeing what he still had, only what he had lost." She looked to where Mervyn and Catryn kept the children entertained. "She is a very good woman, Sir Orion."

He knew she was not referring to her daughter. "I know that, Mrs. Pugh. I know that very well indeed."

"Good. You do have some good sense despite being a man. Try to use a bit of it to see what is best for you."

Orion was torn between laughter and a sense of insult as he watched Mrs. Pugh say farewell to Catryn. The woman then bustled her family into the carriage as if it was their fault that she was still standing in the innyard. Catryn waved farewell as the carriage pulled away and Orion caught her hand in his when she returned to his side.

He glanced down at Catryn as he walked her back inside the inn, where he hoped a meal would be waiting for them. The outrageous Mrs. Pugh was right. Catryn was a very good woman and she would be an excellent choice for a wife for any man. Orion was just not sure he was that man, for he knew nothing about marriage save what a disaster it could be.

It was a relief to find the parlor empty again and the food set out for them. As they had walked he had tried to think through all the marriages in his family, close and not so close, and it was a dismal tally. It was not just his parents who had shown him what miserable chances there were for marital harmony for Wherlockes and Vaughns. His entire clan was riddled with miserable marriages, the good ones so rare as to appear nearly miraculous. Orion did not dare see the recent spurt of happy unions among his family as a sign of great change, of a better future. Therefore it was wrong to think of dragging any woman into such an ill-fated union.

Once they were seated and helping themselves to the food, he turned his thought to the matter of Morris and relaxed. "Today we will try to make up for the day we lost to the rain," Orion said.

Catryn watched him as he slathered butter on a piece of toasted bread, and then sighed. The very last thing she wished was for this adventure with him to end, for she strongly suspected that their affair would end as well. Yet it did not seem right to keep him

working so hard to help her. Morris no longer held
her son and Orion had to have a lot of personal and
government business he was neglecting.

"Perhaps we should just stop," she said. "Alwyn
is safe and I could just take him home, stay with my
father, even hire some very large guards."

"You would remain uncertain of if or when Morris
might try again. Is that truly how you wish to live your
life?" He saw uncertainty cloud her eyes. "Is that how
you wish Alwyn to live?"

The mere thought of having to weigh her every
move, to keep Alwyn constantly under guard, chilled
Catryn to the bone and she shook her head. "No, I do
not, yet I cannot feel it right to hold you to this hunt,
which begins to look as if it is unending."

"My time is my own."

"But . . ."

"Cat, I cannot, in good conscience, walk away when
I know that stopping now would leave a woman and a
child in danger. The fact that the woman is you and
the child is Alwyn makes it far more than a matter of
conscience anyway. This is now personal. We will
continue until I am satisfied that Morris is no longer
a threat."

She desperately wanted to ask why the fact that it
was her made it personal, more important to him.
Then she recalled the advice she had gotten from
other women on how one should conduct oneself
while having an affair. Unasked-for though that advice
had been, that did not dim the truth or usefulness of
it. Do not push for love or promises, she had been
told very firmly. Pressing Orion to explain why he

considered her problem personal could be seen as pushing.

"I am still not sure how we end the threat without killing the fool," she said, "and I do not want you to get blood on your hands because of me."

Orion smiled and she could see the sadness behind it. "There is blood there already, Cat. Do not forget who I have worked for. I will add more blood gladly, without hesitation, if it will gain you and Alwyn a safe, peaceful future. But I have hope that I will be able to scare the idiot into leaving you alone."

"How can you do that? You have implied that before, yet I simply cannot think of how it can be done." She sipped her tea and added, "And Morris might not have the good sense or intelligence to stay scared."

"I have scared the heart for the fight out of a few people in my time. Working for king and country as I do, it is not that hard to make someone believe he will always be watched and never know when the blade will fall or who will wield it. Morris is not the bravest of men."

"Oh no, most certainly not. Alwyn talking to his Papa terrifies him."

"Which brings me to my next idea. We will do our own hunting for another day, maybe more, and then I will send for some of my family."

"Will they not also run into this wall or shield you believe Morris possesses?"

"Some, but I have been considering the ones who might not be affected. It occurred to me that what I do, while not reading a person's mind or reading their heart or the like, is intrusive in a way. So I thought of which of my family could be helpful yet have a gift that is not intrusive."

Catryn thought on what Orion's gift was in an attempt to understand what he was saying, and then nodded. "Your gift reaches out too much, intrudes a little too deeply, for you need to understand the way your prey thinks."

"Exactly." Orion had to fight hard to hide his utter delight over how she accepted such gifts so thoroughly, she could now discuss the way they worked with calm and intelligence. "There are ones in the family who could track Morris almost as a hound does a fox. They can read a trail almost as one reads a book, by what is on the ground and even in the air around the trail. A few others simply have normal skills, outside their gifts, that could help. Any one of them could assist me in terrifying Morris into leaving you alone."

It did not take Catryn more than the space of a heartbeat to understand Orion's plan and see just how easily it would work on the highly superstitious Morris. "Oh mercy, he will want to move to a cave in the far hinterlands of Russia."

Orion laughed. "So I thought. Eat up, love. We need to be on our way soon if we are to get in a goodly number of hours on the hunt."

Catryn turned her full attention to her meal to hide the rush of emotion stirred by the way he had called her *love*. She knew how easily men could use such endearments. They were lovers now, and he could not continue addressing her formally even when they were private together. She would have to learn how to accept such pet names, to not take them to heart and fool herself into thinking that what she and Orion shared was any more than lust and friendship. It was the only way she would survive this adventure with him without suffering the sort of self-inflicted wounds that never healed.

Chapter Fifteen

Orion frowned as he entered Catryn's bedchamber to escort her down to the parlor. She was sprawled on the bed with one hand on her stomach and the other holding a wet cloth to her forehead. He cautiously approached the bed, noted how pale she was, and began to worry. He could sense no disease within her, although that talent was inordinately quixotic. It would be no surprise if it failed to show itself just when he needed it most. An illness would explain why she was abed on such a fine day and had so obviously welcomed his decision to stop early in their travels.

"Catryn, are you ill?" he asked quietly as he sat on the edge of the bed and took one of her limp, cold hands between his and began to try and rub some warmth back into it.

"'Tis nothing terrible, Orion," she said, peering at him from beneath the cloth. "'Tis but a woman's troubles," she whispered.

"Ah." He almost smiled at her blush, but that touch of color on her cheeks looked too similar to a fever's dangerous kiss to be amusing. "Is there anything I might get for you? Some tea, perhaps?"

"No, but thank you kindly for thinking of it. Tea does not appear to cure all my ills, at least not the tea you offer. Once I am a little less miserable, I will have you take me to a place I saw in passing a mile or two back down the road. It could be farther than that, as I did not take careful note of how far we traveled before stopping here. But it had all the things growing there that I need to make myself a nice, soothing tea."

"I can fetch them for you," he offered. "All you need to do is write down just what you need."

"You would recognize what I ask for?"

He moved to get her some writing supplies. "I will ask if I do not recognize something on your list, but over the years I have gathered quite a lot of knowledge concerning plants and herbs for healing potions and salves."

"An odd thing for a king's man to know." She sat up and wrote out a short list, nodding in agreement when he briefly described each one, and then silently handed him the list before settling back against the pillows.

"There were times when knowing how to doctor oneself was very convenient." He kissed her on the forehead and then placed the lavender-scented cloth back there. "A mile or two back down the road?"

"Yes, although it could be a bit more than that. The spot will be on your left, for it was to my right as we rode past it. A rather sad, crooked willow sits in the midst of a clearing. Someone must graze some sheep there from time to time, I am thinking, but not for a while, as around there grows everything I need. I hate to ask this of you as you have only just returned from hunting Morris . . ."

"It is no bother. I will return as quickly as I can. Rest for now."

She waited until the door closed behind him before taking the cloth off her forehead. It had not been completely necessary. Her head had ached, but the pain was already no more than a dull irritation, the first sharp pain of it fading away. Catryn suspected she had looked appropriately ill as well. The foreboding that had struck her had been a very strong one.

It was odd, but this time she had actually seen something. Catryn could not say it had been a true vision, but it had been very close to one. She had seen Orion on the ground, the front of his shirt soaked in blood and his sightless eyes staring up at the sky. Rubbing her upper arms, she could still feel the rough hands dragging her away, although there had been no movement in what she had seen. It had been like some gruesome painting seen through an open door just before that door had been slammed in her face.

Orion was going to be furious when he realized she had tricked him into leaving, but she had had no choice. The moment the foreboding had eased its grip on her she had known what she had to do. Somehow she needed to get Orion far enough away from her that he could not reach out to attempt to help her when Morris's men arrived. It appeared she had succeeded.

Moving to the window, she stood to the side and peered around the edge of the heavy drape. She could just see the stable doors and waited to see if Orion rode away. When he appeared a few minutes later, she cursed. He was riding a horse hired from the inn, one that looked capable of galloping at a goodly speed, at least for a while. Catryn had hoped that he would take the carriage, for it would make a rush back to the inn a lot slower, if only because it had to follow the road. If he guessed what she had done before the danger she had seen was past, he could make it back in time to meet the fate she had foreseen.

He set a fine figure on a horse, she thought, and sighed. There was no doubt in her mind that he would hunt for her when he found her gone. She hoped she would be gone because she had escaped the threat coming her way, but what hope she managed to stir up was very weak. Those hands on her arms had felt like shackles.

After watching Orion ride away, Catryn gathered her things. She might hold little hope of escaping what was coming, but she had no intention of just sitting there and waiting for it. Her attempt to escape fate might well resemble a fly struggling in a spider's web, but her pride demanded she make that struggle.

Catryn was only halfway down the stairs when she heard a rough voice demanding to be told where she was. Cursing softly, she raced back up the stairs and down the hall, praying every step of the way that Morris's men did not have the wit to guard the back way out. Her prayers went unanswered. Catryn was barely three steps down the narrow stairway the servants used when she heard a man ordering the women in the kitchens to get out of his way. Behind her she could hear men in the hall cutting off that route of escape as well. Catryn hurried the rest of the

way down the stairs and waited until she saw the door
latch move. With all the strength she could muster,
she slammed the door open. A loud thud, cursing,
and a crash told her she had struck a telling blow. She
ran through the door into the kitchen. Without a
word, the cook opened the door to the kitchen garden
and Catryn kept right on running.

It did not surprise her when a loud cry went up
before she had even cleared the length of the inn.
Catryn did not stop, however, well aware that even
looking behind her could slow her down. She could
hear the thud of booted feet behind her, gaining on
her, as she raced toward the woods. The fact that the
inn sat on the very edge of the village, bordering a
pretty wooded area, no longer seemed an advantage,
something providing a lovely view. She was sure the
village would have provided her with a better chance
of escape, perhaps even someone to come to her aid.

She had barely entered the woods when a heavy
weight slammed into her back. Catryn hit the ground
so hard she lost the ability to breathe. Even when the
heavy weight on her back eased and she was yanked to
her feet, she struggled to catch her breath. She finally
did so with a shuddering gasp.

"Get her things," the man holding her arm ordered
the two panting men behind him.

"Here now," cried out the innkeeper as he and two
of his stable hands ran up. "You let that woman go!"

If Catryn had not still been struggling to breathe
properly she would have sighed. The three men who
had caught her pulled out their pistols and aimed
them at her unarmed defenders. She did not really
blame the innkeeper and his men, paling as they took

a hurried step back. The innkeeper carried far too many pounds on his short body and his companions were little more than boys. The men had tried to help her and she was grateful for that.

"No need for that," she managed to say to the man holding her. "I will go with you."

"Where is that man you have been leading about?" her captor demanded.

Catryn shook her head over that description of Orion. "Gone. Rode off a while ago and I have no idea when he will return."

"Shame, that. Morris wanted him dead. He will be sore grieved."

"Well, at least one good thing will come of this."

Her captor glared at her even as his companions snickered. "You been causing him a lot of trouble."

Catryn did not even bother to answer that remark as she was dragged toward a sad-looking carriage. Even though her attempt to escape had been an utter failure, one good thing really had occurred. There were witnesses. When Orion returned, there would be a lot of information for him to gather.

He would also be furious, she thought, and cursed when she was roughly shoved into the carriage. There was a chance he would blame himself for what had happened. Orion may have accepted her as his compatriot in this adventure they were on, but she knew he had also accepted all responsibility for whatever happened to her. He would be furious that she had tricked him into leaving, but even more angry at himself for believing her ruse. It was better than him being dead, she told herself.

The carriage jolted into motion. Catryn fought

to steady herself as she moved to the door of the carriage. It did not surprise her to discover they had somehow secured it shut from the outside. There would be no escape through the doors, even if she had dared to hurl herself out of this swiftly moving carriage. She braced herself for a rough ride and tried to prepare herself for the upcoming meeting with Morris.

Giles opened his eyes and frowned up at the ceiling, wondering why he was in bed when it was not yet nighttime. Then he recalled that he had been reading a book to Paul and Alwyn while they rested, as Lady Penelope had ordered them to. It made him smile to think of it, for they did not care how he stumbled over the words, even helped him from time to time, and it felt good to be just the three of them for a little while. They were becoming a family, he decided, and hoped Hector would overcome his lack of trust and join them.

He looked around but saw no sign of either boy and slowly sat up. They should have wakened him, if only with their movement as they had gotten out of the bed or the sound of them leaving the room. Giles began to get a very bad feeling.

Cursing softly, he left the room to search for the two boys. The last thing Giles could recall was hearing Paul and Alwyn whispering, and feeling Alwyn's growing fear. He had thought on how he needed to ask them what they were talking about, and that was the last he remembered, so it must have been when he

had fallen asleep. Giles was still certain the two boys
had been plotting something.

After finding no sign of the boys inside the manor,
and being very careful not to allow any of the adults
to sense his urgency, Giles headed outside to continue
his search. It helped that the Radmoors had taken a
lot of the boys into the village, including his mates.
He would never have been able to fool them.

The fact that Hector was not around began to
bother Giles as well. Although Hector was having
some trouble accepting him as yet another brother,
Giles was sure the older boy would have stopped Paul
and Alwyn from getting into too much trouble.
Hector would also listen to Cousin Ezra and Paul,
however. If those two claimed some vision or warning was pushing them to do something, Hector would
follow their lead without question.

"I do not want to go!"

The fear behind those words was so strong Giles
could almost taste it. Alwyn was being forced to do
something he did not want to do. Since the only thing
that frightened Alwyn at the moment was the chance
of being grabbed by Morris, Giles started to run to
catch up to the others.

"You *have* to," said Ezra.

"No! Alwyn does not have to do a bloody thing if he
does not want to," yelled Giles as he stumbled to a halt
next to Alwyn and glared at Hector. "What were you
thinking?"

"That Paul and Ezra had the same vision and that
means it has to happen," replied his half brother,
eyeing Giles's clenched fists warily.

"What has to happen?" Giles demanded of Ezra,

trying not to be too pleased at the fear in his cousin's big brown eyes.

"Alwyn has to be here so that Morris's men can grab him again," replied Paul and Ezra vigorously nodded.

"Don't be a clodpole."

"I am not a clodpole! It *has* to happen this way."

"You are a clodpole if you be planning to hand the lad o'er to that bastard!"

When Giles reached out to grab Alwyn, Hector grabbed hold of him. He was not sure exactly who started it, but the next thing Giles knew, he and Hector were rolling around in the grass punching, kicking, and scratching each other. Hector proved to be the better fighter in the end and Giles soon found himself pinned beneath his half brother. The angry humiliation he suffered was eased when he saw that Hector had a bloody nose.

"Just listen to Ezra and Paul," said Hector as he cautiously released Giles and stood up.

As Giles stood up to brush himself off, Ezra started talking. "Paul and I both saw something. It was a man, and we think it was Morris, and we knew he was the threat. We both agreed on that. But Paul saw your father bloody and on the ground, and Morris had Lady Catryn. I saw your father standing over Morris with Lady Catryn by his side *and* with Alwyn there with them."

The thought of his newfound father bloodied on the ground made Giles's heart clench so badly he wanted to howl, so he thought hard on what Ezra had said. "But what does that mean and why would you each see something so different?"

"We decided it means that Alwyn has to be there, too." Ezra shrugged. "Do not know why, but Alwyn being there changes something. It was impossible to see just how, as he is only a little boy, but *my* vision put him there and *my* vision had your father being the victor. I also saw what I did *after* Paul saw what he did, and the only difference was that Alwyn was there; so he has to be why your father is left standing."

"But I do not know how to fight," said Alwyn.

Giles looked at the boy. Alwyn was pale, his eyes wide, and fear filled his little body. He could not believe this small, terrified child was who would keep his father alive, either. Yet he did not dare to question Ezra and Paul. If he denied what they saw and refused to allow them to do what they thought they had to, his father might die.

"I do wish you had seen *how* Alwyn makes a difference," Giles muttered and scowled at Ezra.

"So do I." Ezra dragged his hands through his hair, leaving several strands standing straight up.

"We best decide," said Paul. "They are coming."

"I will go," said Alwyn, standing up as straight as he could. "My mother would be sad if Sir Orion got bloody and he helped me get away from Morris and helped my mother find me. And I think Giles would be sad if his father got hurt, too, and Giles saved me. My mother will be with me so it will all be fine."

It would not be fine at all, thought Giles, but he said nothing. Ezra and Paul had the sight. It was not wise to ignore their words. This plan was going to make every adult around them furious, however. Giles also had to think of some way to stay with Alwyn and yet not be caught by Morris or his men. He had no doubt about his own fate if he was caught. No one needed him alive to claim Alwyn's fortune. Then he heard the faint sound of a carriage approaching at a quick pace and knew he had to make his plans fast.

"We have to get him nearer to the road," said Hector.

Giles grabbed Hector by the arm to stop him. "You cannot put the boy out by the road as if he is some Michaelmas gift just waiting to be gathered up." He looked at the boy trying so hard to be brave and decided he would be a good brother to have, if his father was smart enough to marry Alwyn's mother. "Only Alwyn goes. Alwyn, walk toward the road and pretend you are looking for some of those stones you like to collect. The rest of you"—he glared around at the other boys—"keep back some, so that if the men catch sight of you, they do not see you as something they need to be rid of."

"Will they not be suspicious if they find him wandering about alone?" asked Hector.

"He will not be alone, just separate from the pack. Once they grab him, the rest of you can make an outcry and act like you are going to chase him down and get him back. Just do not get too close. I want you all to make as much noise as you can and appear to be trying to get to them before they can get Alwyn in the carriage."

"How do you know they have a carriage?"

"I can hear the bloody thing. Now, my plan? You understand it?"

"Why is it your plan?" Hector studied him and his eyes slowly narrowed. "What are you going to do while Alwyn gets grabbed and we run around like headless chickens, yelling like we are actually a threat?"

"I am going to get on that carriage," Giles said.

"How can you do that without being seen?"

"Thought you lived in the city," drawled Giles, but then hastily explained when Hector glared at him. "I am jumping on the back so I can go where they go. Do it all the time in London. Usually a little perch there for a footman."

"That will not be a city carriage."

"Have not noticed a big difference in carriages. I can just hang on the back if I have to. Now be ready to do what I said."

Giles moved closer to the road, doing his best to stay out of sight. He was not fond of riding on the back of a carriage, but he could not allow Alwyn to go into danger without him. If his brother and cousin were right, Lady Catryn was in trouble, too, and his father would not want her to be alone, either. Hector had not spent days traveling with the two of them and did not know that Lady Catryn could become their mother. Giles was still hoping his father had enough sense to see that it would be a good choice for all of them and that he would regret it if he let her walk away.

The carriage had slowed somewhat as it neared the manor, then stopped suddenly when the man riding with the driver bellowed in surprise. If Alwyn had stayed in the manor or even in sight of the residents at Radmoor, they would never have had a chance. It also appeared that Morris's men were not bright enough to question why the boy was outside, near the road, all alone. Anyone with a drop of sense would see the trap waiting there, Giles thought as he got ready to run to the back of the carriage.

The man who had yelled jumped down and grabbed Alwyn. Giles almost smiled at the way the boy carried on, and the others quickly did as told. The noise was a perfect distraction and he ran, hopping onto the back of the carriage and tucking his body in as close to the wood as possible so that he would not be spotted.

He listened as the man shoved Alwyn into the carriage and slammed the door. And odd noise told him that the door was being secured in some way. Then he pulled out his handkerchief and hastily tied it over his mouth and nose. Just as he finished, the driver snapped the reins and the carriage jerked into motion, within moments reaching a speed that frightened him a little.

As soon as he began to feel more secure, Giles inched up until he was standing. He peered into the little window and saw Lady Catryn hugging Alwyn. The smile the little boy gave her showed he was proud that he had done his part in the plan perfectly. Lady Catryn looked horrified and Giles hoped it was because she did not know the whole story.

When she struggled to her feet, he tensed, knowing she would see him in a moment. He tried to think of a way to tell her everything was fine. It was not, and she was too quick-witted to believe that, but he would try to reassure her. Then her eyes met his and widened. He grinned.

Catryn jerked awake, stunned that she had actually gone to sleep for a while and blamed the surprisingly steady sway of the carriage. A quick look out the window revealed that it was late in the afternoon. She had thought Morris would have been lurking a lot closer to the inn where she and Orion had stayed. Although Orion had difficulty using his gift to find Morris, he had still been certain that the man was close when they had stopped there. It was why they had stopped much earlier in the day than they had planned, for Orion had wanted to take some time to seek out any clues to Morris's presence in the area. They were miles away from there now.

She wished she knew how long she had slept but could only guess. Then she realized the carriage was beginning to slow down and she returned to looking out of the window. Her heart sank, for she was certain she recognized where they were. Despite how firmly she told herself that one could not tell one larch from another, she could not shake her certainty that she knew the place, and the small clearing they were now passing by.

The truth struck her hard and she gasped. They were near Radmoor. Catryn was torn between hope and fear. Were they just passing through on their way to London? Were they here to try and get Alwyn? Did she have even the smallest chance of getting one of the doors open, leaping out of the carriage without breaking any bones, and running for the manor and safety? Just as she decided to try the doors again, the carriage came to such an abrupt stop she was tossed off the seat and landed hard on the dirty floor.

Catryn cursed as she struggled to get untangled from her skirts. She could hear the men talking and there was an urgency in their voices that told her something important was about to happen. There was a chance that they would open one of the doors and she needed to be ready to try and get out, no matter how slim the chance of success. Scrambling to her knees, she was just about to get to her feet when the door was yanked open. Her lunge for the door was halted by the impact of a small body, which sent her slamming back to the floor. She knew who she held even before she looked up into blue eyes as familiar to her as her own.

"Do not look so sad, Mama," Alwyn said as the door was slammed shut and the carriage began to move again. "This is where I must be. Even Papa says so."

Catryn fought back the urge to weep. Her one comfort had been that Alwyn was safe. Just why that was no longer true was a question she needed answered but was not sure Alwyn could do so. At times he could seem much older than he was, but she now wondered how much of that was actually his spirit companion and how much was Alwyn.

"Why must you be here?" she asked her son as she started to struggle to get to her feet without letting go of him or tearing her gown.

"Because Paul and Ezra saw it in a dream. If I am here with you then Sir Orion will not end up on the ground and bloodied."

She nearly fell back onto the floor. "They saw him dead?"

"They did not say dead. They said on the ground and bloody. But if I am with you it will be Morris who is on the ground." He frowned. "They did not say Morris would be bloody and I think he should be. He is behaving very badly."

"It was still foolish of you to allow yourself to be

caught. We left you at the Radmoors so that Morris could not grab you again, and yet here you are."

Alwyn patted her cheek. "I will be fine. They saw me standing with you while"—he paused and looked thoughtful as he always did when his spirit spoke to him—"that cowardly pile of pig muck will be squirming on the floor in terror as he damned well should be." He then smiled and nodded. "Papa is right again."

"Papa needs to grow a little humble."

Finally on her knees, Catryn started to push herself to her feet. She looked to the long narrow window at the back of the carriage and froze. Giles was looking back at her. She blinked and shook her head, but that boyish face with its mischievous grin was still there.

"Giles, what are you doing?"

It did not surprise her when his answer was a few awkward jerks of the fingers of one hand, and then he slowly disappeared from view. She sat down on the seat and kept Alwyn pinned to her side. How could everything have gone so wrong so quickly? What bothered her even more, aside from the gnawing fear that Giles would die on the back of that carriage, was that Orion would soon learn the ones he had been working so hard to protect were now in the hands of their enemy. The fact that she had tricked him into leaving her alone so that Morris grabbed her first was going to make him even angrier.

"Alwyn, we need to pray that Giles stays safe on the back of this carriage," she said.

"I will. Papa says the lad will do fine as he is a boy who has learned a fine skill or two while fighting for his life in that hard-hearted bitch of a city."

"Aeddon Vaughn, you will cease teaching my child those words," she snapped and then sighed. "And now I am talking to a spirit I cannot even see. This disaster has clearly disordered my mind."

Perhaps, she thought wearily, that would be her plea when a furious Orion finally found them.

Chapter Sixteen

After making certain he had all Catryn had asked for tucked securely in the small sack, Orion tied it to his saddle. He stared at it for a long moment, wondering what bothered him about it. Everything about Catryn's request troubled him, causing a nagging uneasiness that grew stronger the longer he was away from the inn. It was as if he were acting out a part in some play. Yet he could not see what was wrong, what misstep had been taken.

His heart clenched as he battled the fear that he had lost his gift. Not only was he surprised how much that bothered him, as if someone had cut away a piece of him, but he had never heard of a single person in his clan having that happen to them. Considering how their ancestors had suffered for what they could do, Orion was certain he would have heard or read of someone who had found a way to kill the part of them that made them so different from everyone else. He was allowing his difficulties with Morris to prey on his mind. It was also a bad time for his gift to become

so tempermental as he needed it in his battle to keep
Catryn and Alwyn safe.

Catryn had been ill and he had come to collect
what she needed to help her feel better. It was as
simple as that, he told himself, yet a part of him still
refused to accept that. He could almost believe he
had begun to gain a third gift, something none of his
clan ever had, and was having a premonition or fore-
warning. That pinch of panic was growing stronger
and a part of him was increasingly urging him to go
back to the inn as fast as he could.

Deciding he would heed that intensifying urgency,
Orion mounted his horse and rode across the field
toward the road. He had just reached the edge of the
road when he spotted three horsemen riding his way
from the direction of London. He kept his hand on
his pistol until they drew close enough for him to
recognize.

At first he was delighted to see some of his family,
especially three men he rarely saw but liked well.
Then he thought on how unusual it was for three of
his clan, large though it was, to be on this road at this
particular time, and just when he was really in need of
some help. All pleasure in seeing Bened, Iago, and
Gethin rapidly faded. His smile of greeting was no
more than a memory by the time the three men
reined in before him.

They did make an impressive group of men, Orion
thought as he waited for one of them to speak. Bened
Vaughn was the biggest, taller than the other two by
several inches and broader of shoulder. Dark haired
and dusky skinned, Orion had no doubt the tale of his
gypsy blood was true despite his silvery eyes. The man

could sense danger or an enemy and could read a lot in the weakest of trails. Iago Vaughn looked the elegant man of society many thought him to be, with his thick black hair; tall, lean, and well-dressed frame; and hazel green eyes. But Orion knew the man had strength and courage. He had to possess such qualities to deal with a gift that showed him the dead, revealed ones standing in the shadows of approaching death, and could even show him people connected to death in some way, usually from the dealing out of it. Gethin Vaughn looked a lot like his sister Alethea, now the wife of the Marquis of Redgrave, with his black hair, ivory skin, and silvery blue eyes. The last Orion had heard of the man, Gethin had been roaming through the wilds of America learning everything he could about medicines, potions, and anything that hinted at the mystical. Every one of the men was closely connected to Alethea, who had the powerful gift of foresight, and who was in London at the moment.

"Thea sent you," he finally said, fighting to hide the fear for Catryn that gripped him.

"She did," said Bened. "She said you had need of us. Told us you were being blinded by a man you need to stop. Did fear she meant that literally, but then she explained herself. Man has a shield and your skills cannot get past it. She thought ours might."

Orion grimaced and scratched his chin. "That is the sad truth. Yet if he is shielded from me then he will be shielded from you, will he not?"

"I thought so," said Gethin, "but my sister just said we had to come here, to the field with the crooked willow. She was insistent on that. I am thinking Bened's gift for reading a trail might be something no one can truly protect himself from. I have also gained some knowledge of the same in my travels. I decided Iago was sent along as the pretty trimming for this mighty army."

"How kind of you to acknowledge who is the fairest of this group," drawled Iago, but the look he gave Orion was intensely serious. "My gift would be useless as far as I can tell, but when Thea says to go, one goes. I will say that I have never encountered anyone who can repel my gift." He smiled faintly. "Death conquers all, they say. I do, however, have some other uses."

Knowing Iago referred to his work for the government, Orion nodded even as his stomach became knotted with worry about Catryn. "What did Thea see?"

"All she told us was that we are needed here."

"No, we need to be at the inn."

Orion could wait no longer and spurred his mount into a gallop. He now knew what had been nagging at him. Catryn had looked the same as she had when she had felt a strong foreboding. She had seen that danger was headed their way and found a way to send him off, to get him away from the looming threat. While he had been prancing through a field collecting plants she did not need, she had been alone at the inn, facing whatever Morris had decided to send against them this time.

The sound of his relatives following him gave him some comfort. If more of Morris's men were coming for him, he could meet them squarely now. All that really mattered was that he reach Catryn before the threat did.

When he reined in before the inn, he knew he was too late. The innkeeper and several of his workers were waiting for him. Orion dismounted, pushed by them, and went straight up the stairs to Catryn's bedchamber. He knew he would not find her there but hoped he might find something, anything, which could tell him who had her and where they were taking her.

Her bedchamber held nothing of hers except for her lingering scent. It was obvious that she had gathered her belongings in a hurry, though. It did him no good at all, but he could see her plan clearly. First she put him out of harm's way, and they would be sure to have a discussion about that when he got her back, and then she would hide wherever she could. Knowing he could be used against her because she cared for him, she would try to lead her enemy as far from the inn as possible. He also knew, his gift acting just as it should for the first time in far too long, that she would try to get to Radmoor, where she would be safe with her son.

"I am sorry, sir," said the innkeeper.

Orion looked behind him and realized that his kin and the innkeeper had all followed him to Catryn's room. He fixed his gaze on the innkeeper. "Did she get away?"

"Nay, sir," the innkeeper replied. "She gave it a good run, she did, but one of them knocked her to the ground. Then we, me and the lads, tried to stop them from taking her, but they pulled pistols on us, threatened to shoot us. Your lady said she would go with them then. They tossed her into a carriage and headed for London. Well, headed off in that direction and all. Right sorry we failed in stopping them."

"They would not have hesitated to shoot you. You did the right thing and so did she."

Resisting the urge to shove everyone out of his way, Orion politely nudged his way through the blockade formed by the innkeeper and three Vaughns. He went into the room next to Catryn's, the one he had taken for the sake of propriety only, since he had had every intention of spending a long, luxurious night in his woman's arms.

His woman, he thought as he hurriedly packed his belongings. Orion shook his head. She was his and it was past time he just accepted it, stopped wondering over such things as love. He knew he would be a good husband and that was all that mattered. Catryn was his and Morris would pay dearly for frightening and hurting her.

"Where do you think they took her?" asked Iago as they started out of the room.

Orion stopped and looked behind him, realizing that he had been so involved in his own thoughts he had not even paid heed to the fact that his relatives had been following him around. All three watched him with concern, and a touch of amusement. He suspected the concern was mostly for Catryn and the amusement came from the knowledge that he had been firmly caught, his bachelor days soon to come to an end.

"He is taking her to London," he replied, turning and starting out of the room. "The man does not plan anything. There is no order to what he does, which is one reason he has been so difficult for me to stop.

That and what I suspect is a natural shield against such gifts as mine. One thing remains constant. He wants my Catryn."

"So he will not hurt her."

"Not yet. If he can force her to marry him, get what he wants, I cannot be certain what he will do after that. Catryn and Giles say he is similar to the very worst of spoiled children, intellectually and emotionally. What does such a child do if he gets what he wants and then decides it is actually not what he wants or becomes bored with it?"

"Tosses it out or breaks it."

"So I thought. Catryn is safe enough for now, at least until the vows have been said. So is Alwyn." He stopped short and stared blindly at the horses waiting for them, absently noting that the animals had been tended well by the inn's stable hands. "Alwyn," he muttered. "I think we will need to make a stop at Radmoor. The boy is there and he is the other thing Morris badly wants."

"So Thea said," Bened said as he moved to his horse and swung up into the saddle.

"I thought all she told you was that you needed to be here to help me because I was too blind to do it myself." Orion secured his pack to his horse and mounted.

"That and the fact that it is not just because of the woman. The boy needs help and he is one of us. That she did not explain."

"And I have no answer. There is a very distant connection between the Gryffins, Catryn's family, and ours, but the boy has a very strong gift." Orion started to ride in the direction the innkeeper said the kidnappers had gone, keeping his horse at an easy pace. "He has a spirit attached to him whom he calls Papa." He explained all about Aeddon. "For that I have no answers either."

"You do not believe Catryn cuckolded her husband though."

"No, Bened, I do not. Yet, it is evident that her husband drugged her every night he planned to visit her bed, and there was no reason to do so. I begin to fear that there is a very ugly truth behind what he did, one that is going to cause Catryn a lot of pain."

Bened nodded. "No racing to the city?"

"No. Morris will go there and I believe he will go to his own home as well. Might already be there and it is just his men we chase now. Morris thinks I am the only threat to his plans, and I have yet to prove to be a truly serious one, sad to say. There is no need to exhaust ourselves or our mounts."

When not one of his relatives objected to that plan, Orion relaxed again at that silent agreement. He wanted to race to London and snatch Catryn away from Morris as quickly as possible, but he knew it was an unthinking urge. At the pace they had set they would not arrive in London all that much later than Morris's men, who would have to change the team pulling the carriage at least once, perhaps more if they pushed the horses hard, and they also had to follow the roads. He and his family had some time to plan what to do when they did find Morris.

And once he got Catryn free of Morris and all the trouble he was causing, Orion knew he had to make a decision. Stay free or stay with Catryn. There was no way he could do both. His heart told him to stay with her, marry her, become a faithful husband. Despite the fact that he wanted no other woman, his mind had stubbornly clung to the idea of maintaining his freedom. The gut-wrenching fear he felt over her being in Morris's hands told him he was just struggling a little against the inevitable.

"Appears to be some trouble at Radmoor."

Iago's voice pulled Orion from his thoughts and he realized they had ridden miles already while he had brooded. He was briefly grateful for the respite until he realized the import of his cousin's words. Looking ahead, he could see Ashton arguing with some of the boys while Pen sat on the grass with a wide-eyed Juno at her side. A cold, hard knot settled in his belly as he nudged to the front of the pack and rode over to the group. The looks on their faces when they saw him only made that knot colder and harder.

"What has happened?" he asked and then noticed that Alwyn and Giles were not there. Knowing his son, Orion was certain the boy would be in the midst of this trouble, if only to watch it. "Where are Alwyn and Giles?"

"Morris has Alwyn," answered Ashton as he stepped closer to the road.

"He had to go," said Paul, moving to stand next to Ashton.

"Are you telling me that you knew what would happen and did nothing to stop it?" The way Paul turned pale told Orion that his anger was too clear to see, and although he felt guilty for scaring the boy, he was not sure he could bury the fury burning inside of him.

"We could not stop it," said Hector as he stepped up beside Paul and put his arm around the younger boy's shoulders. "Paul saw you dead at Morris's hand and Morris holding Lady Catryn. Ezra saw Morris as the one who would fall, and you holding Lady Catryn. With you stood Alwyn."

"Oh hell," muttered Ashton, and Orion could hear his companions echoing the sentiment weighting Ashton's curse.

The boys had read the signs the only way one could read them. Paul and Ezra were already gaining a reputation within the family for the clarity of their visions and forebodings and the way they worked together so well to understand them. If Orion was to survive the final encounter with Morris, then Alwyn had to be there. It did not make any sense to him, for he could not see how a small boy could be of any help, but he doubted either Ezra or Paul had seen the sort of detail that would make it all clearer. Nor did any of it make the knowledge that Morris held Catryn and Alwyn any more palatable.

A tug on his boot drew his attention. He looked down to find Juno staring up at him. She was a beautiful child and, strangely, just looking at her calmed him, if only a little. He glanced quickly at the boys watching them so closely, their bodies slightly tensed and their eyes narrowed. Orion knew they did not suspect him capable of cruelty to the child, that they knew him better than that, but they also did not want him to spit out his anger at her. He suddenly pitied any man who tried to woo her when she grew up, even if he was completely honest in his affections. The dishonest ones would deserve whatever hell her army of protectors visited upon them.

"I can help," said Juno. "If you take me with you and we catch up with the carriage, and then you make me sad or scared, a big storm will come up and stop the bad men and then we can save Lady Catryn and Alwyn."

It took Orion a moment to sort out that long sentence, but when he did, he said, "That is most kind of you, Juno, but I could never bring myself to make you sad or frightened on purpose."

"Oh. I was hoping it might help." She frowned. "But it might be bad because Giles would be caught outside in it, too, and I would not like that because he could get hurt."

Orion tensed and looked at the boys again. Even Giles's friends who had grown up on the hard, unkind streets of the city looked uneasy and took a step back. He knew he was not going to like the answer to his next question.

"Where is Giles?" he demanded.

"He had to go with Alwyn," answered Hector.

"He allowed himself to be taken as well? Those men did not want him, so that makes no sense."

"Well, no, he was not taken by anyone. He got on the back of the carriage."

Two things surprised Orion when he heard that. The first was that he was still mounted and had not fallen to the ground when his heart had stopped or his breath had caught fast in his throat. The second was the undeniable fact that he cared a great deal

more for his sons than he had allowed himself to
acknowledge.

"Giles is riding on the back of the carriage?" he
asked when he was able to breathe again.

"He is good at it," said Abel, the oldest of Giles's
mates at twelve, and his three mates nodded in agreement. "Got round the city that way all the time."

"Did he. Well, he is not on a carriage in the city
now, is he. One that winds its way through crowded
streets at, most often, a sedate pace. He is on the back
of a carriage racing over open roads as fast as Morris's
men dare to drive it without killing the team pulling
it. He is hanging on to the back of a carriage going
over roads with ruts deep enough to break a wheel
or axle, and roads that, if he loses his grip, could easily
break every bone in his body."

He was almost yelling by the time he finished.
Taking a deep breath, he let it out slowly in an attempt to calm himself. He knew it was his fear for
Giles that was feeding his anger. They were just boys,
after all, and he also knew that, even if they had
wanted to stop Giles they would not have succeeded.
Giles could be stubborn, and he had made himself
Alwyn's champion. Once Alwyn was placed in danger
there was no stopping Giles from doing anything he
felt was needed to help keep the boy safe.

"He had to be there," said Juno.

He looked down at the little girl again and then
reached down to pull her up onto the saddle. Orion
kissed her on the forehead and used her presence to
further calm himself. She was a sweet child and already loyal to the others.

"I thank you for your kind offer of assistance, Juno,

but I must do this myself." He glanced at his cousins who rode with him. "And with these fine fellows who know well how to deal with bad men." Carefully, he set her back on the ground and watched her run back to Penelope's side before he turned his attention back on the boys.

"You are absolutely certain of what you saw and how this must be?" he asked Hector, and also glanced at Ezra and Paul, who both quickly nodded.

"They are certain," replied Hector. "They came to me with it first and I battered them with questions, but they held firm in what they believe. Alwyn has to be with Lady Catryn or this could all go very badly for you."

"Yet they did not see these men, did they?"

When both boys shook their heads, Hector just shrugged. "That just means that nothing happens to them, that none of them are the ones who would be in danger."

Hector had obviously taken the time to learn about Paul and Ezra's gifts, each one's weaknesses and strengths. "That could be true. It does not matter. I suspect no one saw what Giles was going to do, either." Again Ezra and Paul shook their heads and Orion had to bite back a curse.

"He told us as soon as he knew what Alwyn had to do," said Hector, and idly, gently, rubbed his badly bruised nose. "I was the one who tried to keep it all secret from Giles, because I knew he was guarding Alwyn. He must have woken up sooner than we thought he would and came looking for the boy. Giles did not want Alwyn to go, but after he calmed down and listened to Ezra and Paul, he knew there was no choice. That was when he decided the boy and your lady would not be going alone."

"I do not feel anything bad," said Paul. "I have been thinking of Giles and his being on the back of that carriage, and there is no fear or worry about it. Even when he said what he was going to do, I did not feel anything bad."

"I will accept that as a hopeful sign." He looked at Ashton. "This is a royal mess, is it not?"

"It is, and I am sorry—" Ashton began.

"No, this is not on you. You cannot keep a constant guard on this lot. Too many of them if naught else. And every one of them is clever enough to get around you if he is determined to do so. As for Giles? The boy has a strong compulsion to help children he believes are in danger. There would have been no stopping him once Alwyn was taken up by Morris's men." He looked at his cousins. "It appears we must rescue my lady *and* her son now, along with my own wild child."

Iago smiled faintly. "Not to worry. We will manage."

They lingered long enough to get a few supplies and water the horses. Within an hour they were back on the road to London. Orion fought to calm his fears. His woman, her son, and his own son were all within Morris's reach. Paul's assurance that he had not sensed any danger to Giles did not completely ease his worries. Good as the boy was, there was always the chance of an error, or for his ability to see danger for those he cared about to fail him. All Orion could do was pray that Giles made it safely to London and that Catryn and Alwyn did not suffer too much before he could reach them.

Chapter Seventeen

Alwyn cried out when he was snatched from her arms and Catryn lunged for the man who had grabbed her son. Another man caught hold of her so tightly she gasped and immediately stopped struggling, terrified he would break something if she was not still. She would do Alwyn no good if she was injured.

It had been a long, rough ride to London. She was not surprised to hear the men who ran up to tend to the horses muttering about the sad state the animals were in. There had been only one stop for a change of horses and a chance for her and Alwyn to relieve themselves. Catryn had tried to get help, but one of the men had entered the carriage as she had stepped out and held a pistol on Alwyn. She had not even had a chance to try and see if Giles was still with them and unhurt.

Since she could not be certain that Morris wished to keep Alwyn alive, Catryn had obediently allowed herself to be led to the privy and silently suffer the humiliation of having a burly, silent man stand guard just outside the rickety door while she was inside. Alwyn had been held tightly and led just around the corner of the building, then shoved back into the carriage, the silent guard never moving the pistol he kept aimed at her son. Once the exhausted team was exchanged for a fresh one, the guard had left their side, shut and secured the door, and then the carriage had begun to move again. A quick peek out the back window had revealed Giles looking dirty and tired but still unharmed and, if his grin was any indication, undaunted. She could only pray he had remained so.

She was not a superstitious person, but Catryn began to think that Fate herself was pushing her to this place and time. As her captor dragged her toward the door to Morris's London house, she could only pray that Dame Fate did not have a dark future planned for her or her son. Telling herself it was a foolish way to think did not help, for she could not shake the feeling that this was all necessary, as if some important truth was awaiting her at the end of this trouble. It was a very strange way to think, especially at the moment, and she struggled to push it aside. All she needed to think about now was keeping her son and herself alive until Orion could reach them.

And he would come, she thought as she was shoved so hard into an ornate parlor she barely stopped herself from falling to her knees. Catryn had to move quickly to save Alwyn from a similar fate. She stood with her arms wrapped around her child and glared at Morris. Orion would come for her and she could not wait to see him deal with this fool.

Catryn realized she trusted Orion. After her marriage she had trusted few people, especially handsome men. The stories told by other wives and widows revealed few men could be trusted to hold to their vows and were often all too concerned with only their own pleasures. In some ways she had even felt that her father had failed her, although she now knew in her heart it was wrong to blame him for how he had kept himself apart from her in so many ways after her mother died. There was no doubt, however, that her grandfather had failed them all.

So, as the years passed, it had appeared to her more and more that a man was just not someone a woman could fully trust to watch her back. She began to believe that she could never really have a man in her life whom she could fully trust to be her comrade-in-arms. Yet, in the few days she had been with Orion, she knew he would do his best to find her and help her; and that trust was not because the man gave her so much pleasure, but one born from a deep faith in his word, his honor, and his strength. It surprised her to feel that way about someone she had known for so short a time, but she decided she liked how it felt. Orion had her back. That surety gave her the strength to do her part, to make sure she and Alwyn did not give Morris what he wanted and were ready for Orion when he came.

Morris sat in a heavily carved chair that was evidently intended to look like a throne. Catryn inwardly shook her head. There was nothing about the man that was impressive, not in his looks nor in anything he had ever done in his life. He obviously thought himself important, however, and she wondered if that could prove to be a weakness.

"Got them both, sir," said the man who had dragged her into the room.

"I can see that," snapped Morris and then he sighed. "Good work, Tom. Guard the doors, including this one. She has proven to be far more elusive than I had anticipated."

"Aye, sir."

Catryn watched Tom closely. He was unquestionably a criminal, but unlike the others Morris had used, this man appeared to possess some intelligence. That could prove a problem, but she decided she would worry about it if and when a chance to escape appeared. She would keep her attention fixed upon Morris for now.

"So, Catryn, here we are," Morris said. "Would you like something to drink?"

She was thirsty but the knowledge of how her husband, Morris's brother, had drugged her was still too fresh in her mind to trust in anything a de Warrenne served her. "No. This is not some social occasion, Morris."

"If you would cease to be so stubborn, it could be."

"You steal my child and now you kidnap both of us and you think *I* am being difficult?" She shook her head. "I begin to think your sanity has left you."

"I offered you a proper marriage, woman! You tell me no and then run about the countryside with a lover. You are in no position to question me!"

"I never would have met Sir Orion or had to run about the countryside if you had not beaten my father and stolen my child. And a marriage between us would never stand."

"It will if I do not try to go to a church in this

country. I looked into the matter after what you said and discovered that it can be done elsewhere with ease. Such a marriage would also be recognized here."

"Not if my father protested it and he most certainly would. Loudly."

"He would keep his mouth shut. I will hold you and the boy and that will give me the power to silence him. The man will not want to do anything if it could result in harm to you or that child."

There was too much truth in what he said for her to even bother trying to argue with it. "No matter where you try to marry me, it cannot be done as long as I refuse and claim it is against my will."

Morris moved so fast Catryn had no time to react. He was out of his ridiculous chair and yanking Alwyn away from her before she could stop him. She lunged for him, only to be painfully halted when Tom grabbed her braid and pulled her back. The situation was growing tense, even dangerous, and somehow she had to calm everyone down without giving Morris what he wanted. Catryn was not sure that was possible.

She could not marry the man, and not just because he was not Orion. Once married she and Alwyn would lose what little protection from Morris they had now. At the moment, he wanted something from her. Once he got it, he not only had no need of Alwyn, he would undoubtedly soon tire of her. At best she might be kept around until she gave him a child. The thought of him using her to breed him a son made her stomach churn, but she struggled to keep that vehement distaste from showing in her face.

"You cannot keep threatening people to get what you want," she said.

"Ah, well, yes. Yes, I can." He smiled at her. "Your father loves you, loves this brat. He will do all I ask of him if I make him understand that you and Alwyn will pay very dearly for any insult he offers me or any difficulties he causes for me."

"Papa says only a coward threatens women and children," said Alwyn.

"Henry is *not* talking to you!" yelled Morris as he shoved Alwyn back toward Catryn.

"Not Henry. A-E-D-D-O-N. Aeddon. He talks to me." Morris paled and stared at Alwyn. "Who?"

"I just told you. A-E-D-D-O-N. Aeddon. And he says he wants to pull your lungs out through your nose."

"Take them to the cellars," Morris ordered Tom and then glared at Catryn. "Maybe some time locked up down there with no food, no water, and no light will make you begin to think more clearly."

"Papa says—" began Alwyn as Tom and another man grabbed him and Catryn.

"Shut up! Shut up! Just bloody shut up! Get them out of here, Tom. Now!"

Catryn did not bother fighting the man who dragged her out of the room, past two more guards in the hall. Even if she could break his hold, she would then have to try and free Alwyn. The odds of doing both things and then getting out of the house were not ones anyone would bet on. She decided to save her strength.

She and Alwyn were taken down into the cellar. Catryn was held firmly by Tom as the other man used the candle he held to light several others in the dank room. Tom unlocked a metal cage and the men pushed her and Alwyn inside. She stumbled, and by the time she caught her balance and turned toward the door, it was locked and Tom was staring at her through the bars. He then looked at Alwyn, a look that held a touch of fear. Catryn moved quickly to put her arm around her son and hold him close to her side.

"You teach him that?" Tom asked her.

"Teach who what?" she asked, even though she had a very good idea of what he was asking about.

"Teach the boy to try to make folk believe he can talk to the dead."

"Do not be ridiculous. No one can talk to the dead. What an odd thing to believe."

"Well, Aeddon was odd."

Before she could ask what he meant by that, he left. She breathed a sigh of relief when he did not snuff the candles his compatriot had lit. For a while she and Alwyn would not be left in the dark. It was a small comfort.

Catryn looked around their prison. They were in a large metal cage which held several racks of wine and large barrels. A quick, closer look at the goods revealed it was all of the best quality, some of it obviously bought from smugglers. To the back of the cage there were several wooden crates with more bottles packed inside. In a far corner was one barrel standing alone. A peek inside revealed apples and she grinned, reaching down to choose two. It seemed someone wanted to be sure there were apples at hand and that they were not all eaten by the men Morris hired, or the servants.

"Come and sit, Alwyn," she said as she sat down on one of the covered boxes that held brandy. "I found us some apples. I think the cook hides them here so they are not all eaten before they can be used in cooking. It is also a good storage area for such things. These may be more tart than you like, but will ease any hunger or thirst you may have."

Alwyn sat next to her and began to polish his apple on his coat sleeve. "We could drink some of what is in all these bottles."

"We could, although I am not certain I can open them since I do not have the proper tools. But 'tis wine and brandy, love, and I would just as soon you do not have any of it. If our thirst grows too keen, however, I will not hesitate to try and find a way. I but hope we are not pushed to that need as you are too young to be drinking wine or brandy."

The look in Alwyn's face, one that told her he was deciding if he should remind her that he was not a baby, made her want to smile. Catryn turned her attention to her apple. To her relief it was not too tart and she slowly ate hers while studying their prison for any possible route of escape. It did not take long for her to know there was none. The key to the door was too far away, hung on a hook near the bottom of the stairs, and the cage itself was built strongly, the bars sunk into the stone floor. Morris obviously felt a great need to protect his drink as if it were liquid gold.

Catryn's thoughts then turned to Morris's reaction to Alwyn's talk of Aeddon. Morris had known the man. Considering what Tom had said before leaving the cellar, so had he. Although Henry had never mentioned the man, it was very possible that he had also known Aeddon. She was not sure why, since she knew there had undoubtedly been many people her husband had known whom she had never met or would have wanted to, but the fact that Morris, Tom, and quite possibly Henry had known Aeddon made her very uneasy.

She looked at her son, who was taking very small bites from his apple in such a way that it was leaving funny little patterns. The only way she could learn about Aeddon was to ask Alwyn, yet she hesitated. He was just a child and she could not be certain the questions she had would bring answers a child should hear. Aeddon had proven to be a rough-spoken spirit. Catryn realized she had no choice, however. This man Aeddon, whose spirit clung tenaciously to her child, was an important piece of the puzzle that had become her life. She was certain of it.

"Do you think Giles is all right?" Alwyn asked.

"He was when we stopped to change the horses," she replied. "The last part of the journey was not nearly as rough as the first part, and he managed to hang on all during that bumpy ride."

Alwyn nodded. "Giles is strong. Maybe he can rescue us or get us some help. It will all be fine."

She was not so sure of that but was not about to say so, and turned her thoughts back to the matter of his ghostly companion. "Alwyn, is Aeddon with you now?" she asked.

"He is always with me," Alwyn replied. "That is what papas do."

"I see." Since Henry had spent so little time with their son, she wondered if that was why Alwyn was so ready to believe his spirit friend was actually his father. "And you are very certain that he says he is your father? You believe that?"

"Yes. He is."

"But, love, I do not know this man. Mothers usually know what man helped them make a child, and I have never met anyone named Aeddon."

"He says you were sleeping and Henry paid him to make me."

Catryn had a sudden urge to be violently ill and then stiffened her spine. "Does he say why he would do such a thing?"

Alwyn frowned for a moment. "I cannot say bad words."

"This time it is allowed as I truly want to know what he has answered. It is very important."

"He says he was a reckless bastard and owed Henry money. He is sorry, but that was what was asked of him to clear his debt. Then Henry betrayed him as soon as he knew I was in your belly and cut Papa's throat and threw him in the river."

Catryn had so many questions, but she hesitated to ask her son any of them. The answers could well be things a five-year-old child should not hear, let alone repeat. It made no sense. If Morris knew about Alwyn's true father, however, it would explain why he was so adamant that everything should belong to him.

A tapping at the small window drew her out of her thoughts and she looked over to see Giles's dirty face peering in at her. He grinned and waved. Alwyn looked and waved back. Then Giles moved out of sight, yet she was sure he had not gone far.

"You were right, Mama. Giles is fine." Alwyn calmly returned to eating his apple.

Leaning back against the bars, Catryn wished she could share her son's calm. Her mind was crowded with questions and her heart ached. If what Alwyn said was true then she was not quite as pure as she had thought. She did not wish to even consider what Orion might think of her if he knew she had cuckolded her husband. It might not matter that the cuckolding was arranged by Henry and she was too drugged to know what was happening.

She had an urge to weep but did not really know why. Catryn supposed it was the knowledge that, from the very beginning, all Henry had wanted of her was a son. If what Aeddon the ghost said was true, Henry had been willing to use his own wife like a brood mare, even hiring a stallion to get her with child. It was both horrifying and humiliating.

It was not easy, but she forced all thought of that crime from her mind. She had a more immediate problem. Somehow she had to get herself and Alwyn away from Morris. Although she had no doubt at all that Orion was coming after them, it could only help if she and her son had already slipped away from their captor. That was what she had to fix all her thoughts on. Even if there was a chance to get some badly needed answers, she had to be ready to grab any chance for escape. Catryn chose two more apples, handed one to Alwyn, and proceeded to imagine every possible way a chance for escape could arise and what she would have to do to take full advantage of it.

The candles were sputtering, threatening to plunge her and Alwyn into the dark when Tom walked in. He glared at the candles, muttered something about what an idiot Harry was, and then unlocked the door to the cage. Catryn lunged at him, but he was ready for her.

He grabbed her by the arm and swung her around so hard she slammed back into the bars of the cage. Then he grabbed Alwyn before she could recover her sense.

Cursing softly to herself as she checked for any sign of blood on her face, she followed him out of the cellar. There was no choice since he held Alwyn and had a pistol in his hand. Wincing when she touched a spot that was already bruising on her cheek, she now knew why he had come after them on his own. He had a true skill in handling prisoners.

Once inside the room where Morris waited for her, Tom shoved Alwyn toward her. She held Alwyn close and watched Tom and another man shut the doors and take up a place on either side, pistols at the ready. Catryn then looked at Morris sitting in his pretentious chair. He studied her face and then glared at Tom.

"You have marred her," he snapped.

"She tried to escape," replied Tom. "I persuaded her to stay."

Morris narrowed his eyes but said nothing. Catryn realized that he was uncertain about Tom, perhaps even a little afraid. Unfortunately, she could not think of any way to use that.

"So, have you had time to reconsider your stubborn refusal to do as you are asked?" Morris sipped at a glass of deep red wine and watched her closely as he waited for her to say something.

"You have no right to keep us here," she said. "You have no right to order me to marry you. You had better let us go or you shall be very sorry, very soon."

"Sorry? I was sorry the day Henry married you. He

never should have married anyone. He and I had a bargain and he broke it."

"What bargain could you have had that would stop him from trying to find a wife and breed an heir? No man would willingly give that up."

Morris sneered as he leaned forward in his chair. "I knew his secret."

Catryn made soft sound, rife with scorn. "I suspect you have a few secrets of your own. Just how bad could that secret be that Henry would give up his chance to have an heir?"

"The fact that he could never breed an heir."

"And how could you be so very certain of that? Did he rut with anything in skirts yet produce no bastards?" The tension grew in her as she tried to push him to spit out the truth, but she resisted the urge to ask him any direct questions yet, for fear he would simply toss her back into the cellars until he could think of an answer. She knew Morris well enough to know that to uncover the truth one had to push him into a temper.

"He did indeed rut with anything in skirts, right up until he picked the wrong man's wife." Morris smiled in a way that gave Catryn chills. "No more rutting for dear Henry after that," he said in a singsong voice very like a child's.

She frowned as that implied an injury that had left Henry unmanned, yet she was certain she had glimpsed the appropriate shaping of his breeches from time to time, a shaping that strongly hinted that everything that should be there was. "Henry was not castrated."

"Ever see him naked?"

She blushed. "That is none of your business."

"Ha! Did not think so."

"Our wedding night—"

"Was performed in the dark with a mostly clothed man. That was me. In the dark, after a little laudanum in your drink, and you did not know the difference. Think old Henry was a bit offended by that. Sad to say, that time was a failure as you did not conceive that night. Henry would not let me try again. He decided he did not want me to sire his child, or perhaps he just did not like to share you with me. He never liked sharing his things with me."

Catryn slowly shook her head as she fought the nausea that threatened to swamp her. "I saw, well, the front of his breeches . . ." She struggled to think of the right words and was almost relieved when Morris interrupted her.

"Padded. But, yes, most of him was still there. Let us just say that Henry lacked what was needed to seed a child of his own. Of course, that was also why Henry stopped even trying to pretend he was a real man with some use for a woman."

She rubbed at her forehead where the dull throb of a headache was forming, one she doubted was caused solely by Tom slamming her into the cage bars. The way Morris kept answering her questions without really telling her anything was maddening enough to make her want to scream. If she was hearing him correctly, and correctly guessing what was not being said, then Henry had been gelded by an angry husband.

"What do you mean when you say he was pretending to be a real man?"

"He did not truly like or desire women. He tried and all it got him was mutilated."

"If he did not like or desire women, then why was he rutting with them so freely that a man felt the need to maim him? And where did he go nearly every night after we married if not to rut with some other woman?"

"I just told you that he fought his urges at first. After he married you he gave that up completely and often visited his favorite catamite."

"Henry preferred men?"

She could see that Morris was highly annoyed that she was not horrified, but then no one knew about her father's uncle and his *dear friend*. Her father had been the only one in the family who had not shunned the man when the truth of his preferences had slipped out. Her great-uncle had also been the only one in the family to visit her and her father regularly and to offer to help them when they were so close to losing everything. It was a shame that Henry had lacked the good heart her late great-uncle had had.

"Not men exactly, not children either, but boys barely into manhood. That is why he was stabbed."

"The men who stabbed him went to their deaths still claiming it was just their idea to rob Henry."

"Which they had to do if they wished to save their families. You see, Henry seduced the only son of a very powerful man. Even I have not been able to get the name, just that tiny bit of information."

"Well, none of this truly matters, does it?"

"It tells you, quite clearly, that your son is not the rightful heir."

"My son was recognized by Henry as his true and lawful heir. He was born while Henry and I were married, so the law recognizes him as the heir. Even the timing of the birth was all correct and acceptable, being that it was a year after Henry and I married. Alwyn is legally a de Warrenne, God help him, and it is past time you accepted that."

"That brat is no de Warrenne!" bellowed Morris as he leapt up from his chair.

Catryn pushed Alwyn behind her and braced for a possible attack, all the while praying that Orion would hurry up and find her.

Chapter Eighteen

With a swiftness Orion had to admire, Iago and Bened removed the two guards at the door. It was not a skill he would have thought the elegant Iago would have. The ones in the family who had gifts like Iago's usually avoided anything that brought them into too much contact with death. Such stealth and skill were of the kind taught to men who would go into battle.

"I believe our cousin Iago has a few secrets," murmured Gethin.

Orion looked at the man hiding with him in the alley across from Morris's town house. "I was just thinking much the same. Surprised me. The veil between the living and the dead is very thin for Iago. Would not have thought a man with such a gift would indulge in anything requiring the skill to put a man down with such stealth. That is a warrior's talent and few with Iago's gifts would ever wish to be near a battle of any kind, small or large."

"True, such skills do often go hand in hand with dealing out death."

"Exactly. Even if Iago does no killing himself, he must work with ones who do. But I will not quibble, for those skills have proven very useful at the moment."

When Bened appeared at the corner of the house and gave them the signal, Orion and Gethin hurried across the street. It worried him that he had not yet seen Giles, not at any point along the route from Radmoor to Morris's. Although he had not been overly concerned about the boy once they reached London and had found no sign of a dead or injured Giles on the road, constantly reminding himself that Giles's hard life had given him skills and a resilience other children did not have, that newly won calm began to fade. He should have seen some sign of the boy by now.

Pressing himself against the outer wall of the house, Orion watched the door. No one had rushed out when the two guards had abruptly disappeared, but he would give it a few more minutes just to be certain no alarm was sounded by those within the house. Entering a house none of them had been able to reconnoiter was dangerous enough. They could not even be all that certain that Morris was in there, except that the presence of two burly guards implied the man had come home. All that lack of certainty left them with only one real advantage, and that was the element of surprise. He wanted to be as certain as possible that they held on to that.

"Father, over here."

The whispered words immediately soothed Orion in a way he had not known he needed to be soothed, and he realized he had actually not put aside his concern, simply buried it beneath a thin layer of reassurances. He turned, looking into the shadows at the far edge of the house. It took him a moment to see the boy and he shook his head, torn between hugging the boy for being safe and shaking him until his teeth rattled for doing something so dangerous. He also knew now that Giles had undoubtedly been a very skilled little thief. He signaled the others and then moved toward Giles, confident that the others would quickly join them.

"You are very fortunate that we did not find your shattered body in the road," he said when he reached Giles. "Sneaking a ride on a carriage racing down country roads is not the same as doing so on one winding through crowded city streets."

"I know it," said Giles. "I took care, but I will never do that again. Too fast, too unsteady, and too long a journey for such a game as well. They are in there." He pointed to a large window on the side of the house and then tensed when Iago, Bened, and Gethin joined them.

"My cousins," Orion told Giles and introduced the men to his son even as he moved closer to the window Giles had pointed out to him.

"Window is open so we need to be very quiet," said Giles, staying close to Orion so that he could speak softly yet still be heard. "When Catryn and Alwyn first came here they were in there for a while, and then they were taken to the cellar, but I could not find a way inside. All I could do was let them know I was here. Morris had just sent for them again when I saw these fellows"—he nodded at Bened and Iago—"and waited to see if they were a new threat." He looked at Bened. "You are a big 'un."

"That I am," said Bened and smiled.

"And calm. So much calm in you," muttered Giles. "Is that a gift?"

"I have long thought so, or possibly just a necessity provided by my gifts to ensure that they can work as they should." Bened studied Giles for a moment. "I believe I know what your gift is, and it is quite strong already." He looked at Orion. "Planning for him to spend some time at Elderwood with Modred and Aunt Dob?"

"The time may come when it is needed," Orion replied. "Giles knows that." He tensed. "I believe Alwyn and Catryn are back in the room."

"If one of you can raise me up, I might be able to peer in and see something worth seeing," said Giles as he eyed Bened.

"Can you make certain you are not seen?" asked Bened.

Giles looked offended. "Of course I can."

"Then come along," Bened said as he moved to press himself up against the wall.

Orion watched as Giles climbed Bened like a tree. By the time the boy was standing on Bened's shoulders he was just out of reach of the window. Before Orion could express his disappointment, Bened, after a quick whispered exchange with Giles, grabbed the boy by the ankles and slowly raised him up until he could grab hold of the window ledge. Although he knew Giles was just a skinny boy of eight, Orion had to marvel at the ease with which Bened steadily held the boy over his head. It was a long, tense few moments, however, before Bened lowered Giles back down to the ground.

"You were right," Giles said to Orion. "They just brought Alwyn and Catryn back into the room. There are two men with them and they are standing guard at the door. Inside the room. Morris is sitting in an ugly chair to the right of this window. I know there are two more men at the back of the house, but I am not sure if there are any more inside."

"We will take care of the two at the back," said Bened and disappeared into the shadows with Iago.

"Once they are done with that, perhaps we could go in through the back of the house," said Orion.

"A good idea," agreed Gethin. "Once those two rid us of the guards back there we would only have to deal with whatever servants might be in the kitchen. From what you have told us of this man, I do not believe we will have to fear that the servants will be compelled by loyalty to risk anything to warn him."

Orion nodded and cautiously started toward the back of the house, Gethin and Giles following him. It did not surprise him to find Iago and Bened already finishing the binding up of the two unconscious guards.

"We are going in through the kitchens," Orion told them.

Bened nodded. "That will work. Let me go in first."

Before Orion could express the opinion that sending the biggest man in first might not be the best plan, Giles nodded. "He will make them all calm," he said, looking at Orion. "He has so much calm in him it just comes right out and touches people."

"Oh, aye, there is definitely a visit to Elderwood and Aunt Dob in your future," murmured Bened before he went down a short stairway to the door leading into the kitchens.

It astonished Orion when Bened simply knocked once and then walked right in. No one cried out in alarm, despite the sudden appearance of a large, dark-haired man in their midst. There was some murmuring, and then Bened briefly appeared in the doorway to signal them all to join him. Inside, Orion found what had to be all of Morris's servants seated at a table, obviously having been in the midst of eating a meal when Bened had walked in. They eyed him and his three companions a little warily but there was no outcry, no sign of any fear, just curiosity.

Giles was right. There was something about Bened that worked to calm people, even in situations where calm was the last thing they should be feeling. Then, too, Gethin was probably also right. The servants had no loyalty to Morris, for the man had done nothing to earn it.

"If what you are doing is going to make de Warrenne leave," said a thin young man in a footman's livery of the same colors as Morris's carriage, "can you make certain he pays us what he owes us first?"

"We will do our best," said Orion, "but I fear that might take time, even if he agrees to do so."

The man shrugged. "We can wait. Got nowhere else to go."

And that, Orion thought, was probably why Morris still had servants. They would have left him long ago if they could have found other positions. By the looks of the very fine meal laid out on the table, they had found at least one way to gain some compensation for their work.

Leading the others, Orion started to make his way toward the room where Catryn and Alwyn were being held. As he moved along as cautiously and quietly as possible, he made and cast aside several plans. The last thing he wanted to do was to put them at risk with a fumbled attempt at rescue. Morris might not be a real threat to them, but the two men guarding the door might not care who got hurt as they fought to escape any punishment for their crimes.

A man half-asleep in the hall caused them no delay. Iago had him unconscious and securely bound with an efficiency that made Orion decide to request a few lessons. Once at the door to the room they sought, they all hesitated. On the other side of the door were two guards, and it would be necessary to take them down as quickly as possible. Then Morris's bellowed words caused Orion to stop worrying about the guards. He had to put all of his concentration to the matter of fighting the urge to barge into the room so that he could immediately, and violently, shut the man's mouth.

"That brat is no de Warrenne!"

"I begin to see that," said Catryn, and Orion had to get closer to the door to be certain he heard her clearly. "Just who was Aeddon Vaughn, Morris? You knew him. Tom knew him. And now my son knows him."

"He cannot know him," protested Morris in a voice that shook as much with fear as with fury. "The bastard is dead! Dead and rotted, damn his eyes!"

"I know he is dead, but who was he? Why does my son believe the man is his father?"

"Because he was. He was, and that is why the title and all that goes with it should be mine."

Orion could only imagine how Catryn must feel.

It was a truth he had begun to suspect, but he could not bear her having to hear it from Morris. Signaling his companions, placing Bened at one of the doors and himself at the other, he counted to three. The moment he raised the third finger, he and Bened slammed open the doors. It did not work as perfectly as he had hoped, but well enough that there was only a brief struggle before both men were secured.

When Orion looked up from binding the hands of one of the men, his heart sank. They had not been quick enough. Morris held Catryn tightly against his front, a pistol pressed into her side.

"Let her go, Morris," he ordered after sending Gethin a look he prayed the man read correctly.

"No. You have no right to interfere here," Morris said. "She is *my* family, not yours. Just because the two of you have been rutting like rabbits as you chased me all over the countryside does not change that. You are not her family so you have no say here at all."

Out of the corner of his eye, Orion watched his relatives slowly begin to encircle Morris while Giles went to Alwyn and tugged the boy back, further out of Morris's reach. "You have to know that your plan can never work."

"It can if I can shut her father up."

"We have the boy now, so you have nothing left to make Catryn do as you want or, I suspect, to make her father obey you, either."

"I can make the boy come back to me." Morris looked at Alwyn. "He would not want his mother to get hurt, would you, Alwyn?"

"No." Alwyn took a step toward Morris but Giles held him back.

"You will come here, boy, or I will put a bullet in her."

"Then you will have no shield," Orion said quietly and watched the way Morris's eyes narrowed as he tried hard to think of a way out of the mess he was in.

"I will get the bugger to let her go," said Alwyn.

Orion started toward the boy, fearing that Aeddon might be pushing the child to do something that could get him killed. He had just put his hand on Alwyn's arm when the strangest feeling flooded his body. The combination of being too full and a chilling nausea nearly brought him to his knees. The last clear thought he had, the last one that was solely his own, was that he really did not like ghosts.

Catryn stared at Orion when he turned from Alwyn and glared at Morris. There was such hatred in his eyes, such a dark murderous fury, that she barely recognized him. The snarling smile on his face actually frightened her, yet she had never believed she could be frightened by Orion. Then she noticed that his eyes were wrong. They were no longer blue but almost black.

"Orion?" she whispered as he stalked toward where Morris held her.

"I will give him back to you in a moment, m'lady," Orion said. The voice was not his, but rougher and deeper. "I but need to have a little revenge on this mewling piece of scum."

"Aeddon?" she asked in a voice she could not keep steady, for she was awash in shock and utter fascination. "Is that you?"

"Aye." Orion/Aeddon looked down at Orion's body. "A fine man you found yourself, m'lady." He looked at Morris, all that furious hatred returning to harden and twist his features. "Let her go now, you bastard."

Catryn realized that Morris's hold on her had loosened and the man was shaking so hard he was making her body tremble from the force of it. She lunged forward, breaking the last of his grip, and ran to where the three men who had come in with Orion now stood watch over Giles and Alwyn. They looked an odd mix of intrigued and concerned.

"Can ghosts do that?" she asked them as she watched a panicked Morris run around the room like a fool while the Aeddon-possessed Orion easily blocked all escape. "Can Aeddon truly possess Orion?"

A handsome man with thick black hair and hazel green eyes smiled at her. "I am Iago Vaughn, Baron of Uppington, and Orion's cousin. And, to answer your question, I rather have to say yes, although this is the first time I have ever seen it done."

"Gethin Vaughn, m'lady, and I have to agree in most ways," said the man with beautiful silvery blue eyes. "Did see what might have been a possession, but I fear all the smokes and potions used to bring it about affected me enough that I cannot say with certainty that that was what I saw. This certainly appears to be Aeddon borrowing Orion's body for a while."

"He will give it back, will he not?"

"Aye," replied Lord Uppington. "He cannot hold it for long, as it takes more strength than a spirit has to spend. I can feel it weakening him even as we speak."

"Best be ready to deal with Morris if need be," said the biggest of the three men and then he smiled at Catryn. "Bened Vaughn, m'lady."

"Papa has him now," said Alwyn.

Catryn put her arm around Alwyn's shoulders and sighed. "By the look coming out of those eyes, I suspect he is about to kill Morris, and then I will not have all the answers I seek."

"Morris, stop running around like a headless chicken," snapped Aeddon/Orion as he grabbed Morris by the front of his shirt and slammed him up against the wall.

"This is not right, not right at all," Morris babbled. "Tom! Kill this abomination."

"I am tied up, you idiot," said Tom.

"Go away!" Morris screamed as he sank to the floor and pressed himself into a corner. "You are not real. That is it. You are not real. That bitch gave me something because she was mad that I never returned to her bed after taking first blood. Or one of you witches has done something. Ha! I know what you all are! I understand the joke, too. Calling yourselves Wherlockes. Ha! Warlocks and witches. Sorcerers."

"You are a pathetic pile of goat droppings, Morris. I would kill you now, but it would leave a problem for this man." Aeddon/Orion slapped Orion's chest. "Cannot have that. But I just want you to know I am watching you, you murdering bastard."

"I did not kill you! Henry did. Well, he had those men do it."

"You did not even look to see if I was alive when you and those bastards tossed me in the river. I was, you know, just a bit. Doubt I would have survived all those cuts and the throat slitting, but it was just damned cruel to then leave me to drown. And what you are doing to this poor lass is sickening."

"What *I* am doing?" Outrage gave Morris a moment of courage and he sat up to point his finger at Aeddon/Orion. "You are the one who bedded her for money, slipping in to do the deed with no frills and then sneaking away, night after night."

"That was a debt owed, and you know it. If I had guessed my throat would be cut the minute she was with child, I would not have agreed. Least then I would have met my death with no new sins on my soul." Aeddon/Orion glanced back at Alwyn. "Although, I have no regrets when it comes to the boy. He is a good lad and will be a far better man than I ever could have been. Not a bad legacy."

"He is stealing what is mine!" Morris squealed when Aeddon/Orion grabbed him by his neckcloth and shook him where he sat.

"Not yours. Never yours. Never will be yours. Heed me in this, Morris. I would like nothing more than to use this body to rip you apart, but not the best thing to do. I will come back, however, if you do not cease this plaguing of the lady and my boy."

"And we will help him keep that promise," said Iago as he, Bened, and Gethin stepped up to look down at a quivering Morris.

"You are more of them. I can see it," whispered Morris, his fear widening his eyes as he looked at the four men.

"Lady Catryn and her son are now under our protection. You would be wise to always consider what that would mean for you if you decided to trouble her again."

Morris looked at the men and vigorously nodded. Aeddon/Orion let go of him and turned toward

Catryn. She watched as he walked toward her and realized that even the way he moved was different. Aeddon had clearly spent a lot of time as a sailor. She started when he cupped her face in his hands and kissed her.

"There. That should keep me happy for a while. Never had the chance before." He frowned and staggered a little. "Will have to go soon. I am sorry, lass. It was a bad thing I did to a good woman, but at the time I thought there was no choice. There was. I just did not have the courage and honor needed to make it." He gave her a faintly roguish smile. "If things had been different, with ye aware of all that was happening, and Henry, may he rot in hell, not standing near to kick me out in but minutes, I might have given ye a little pleasure to remember."

"Most of the blame lies with Henry, sir," she said and realized she meant it.

"You are a fine mother to my lad," he said.

The next thing she knew she was moving as fast as she could to catch a falling Orion. The Vaughns rushed over to help her get him situated comfortably on the floor. She gently stroked his brow, worried about how pale he was, and watched until he opened his eyes. Catryn was relieved to see the dark blue she so loved had returned.

"No, do not move me yet," Orion said when Iago attempted to help him sit up. "I need to allow my stomach to stop roiling." He reached up and placed his hand over Catryn's. "You and Alwyn are well?"

"Yes," she replied and then blushed so fiercely her cheeks burned uncomfortably as she recalled all these men had heard. "I thank you most kindly for all you have done," she began.

"Hush, pretty idiot. We heard, but no shame lies with you. The shame is all on them, on Henry, Morris, and even cousin Aeddon. He admitted it."

"You know what he said?"

"I know what he said and have been left with a good idea of what he was and why he did not live to a ripe old age." Orion cautiously sat up but knew he was in no state to go anywhere under his own power. "I was rather looking forward to being the hero in the end, but Aeddon took the laurels. A shame he is only a spirit. I have a strong urge to punch him in the nose." He eyed her mouth. "He had no right to kiss you."

"I believe it was an apology, for all he made light of it. I could see the regret and shame in his eyes, Orion."

Orion cautiously nodded, still not certain he could hold everything in his stomach if he moved wrong. "And I could feel it in him just as I could feel his need to confront Morris and to end this trouble that dogs his son." He took her hand in his and kissed her palm. "Catryn, this has left me feeling as if I have been run over many times by a drunk driving a carriage. You need to get home and reassure your father that you are well and that this is over. He missed you at Radmoor and must be deeply concerned despite letters sent to reassure him. Go home, love, and once I get some matters settled, I will come for you."

* * *

Catryn was still wondering what he meant by the words *I will come for you* as she entered her father's home with Alwyn at her side. Her father was so obviously relieved to see them both, she was comforted enough to spend time telling him most of her adventure, carefully avoiding all hint of anything other than friendship between her and Orion. Only once did he start to ask some pointed questions but was easily diverted by the tale of Aeddon and the way Alwyn's spirit friend had taken over Orion's body. As she made her way to bed, she knew that would keep her father busy for a very long time as he searched his books for information on such happenings.

She settled into bed and stared up at the ceiling. *I will come for you.* What did Orion mean by that? Was he going to find her so that he could renew their affair, or for something more lasting? And why did he have to settle some matters before he could even come and visit her, if only to talk over the unusual happenings that ended their adventure together? Men, she decided, had no business complaining about how women made no sense; from what she could see, they did no better at making themselves understood.

All she could do now was wait to see if he really did come for her. Catryn vowed to herself as she started to go to sleep that she would not allow herself to pine for him if he did not. She had her pride after all.

Chapter Nineteen

It was not easy, but Catryn did her best to swallow a sigh. The way her father looked at her, however, told her she had not hidden it as well as she had thought. She hated how morose she had become. It was embarrassing to be behaving like some lovesick fool, but it was also difficult to throw off the sadness that swamped her from time to time, drowning all hope. So much for her pride, she thought wryly.

This day marked three full weeks since Orion had left her with a promise to return. She had received the occasional gift but no explanation as to why he himself had not brought the gift to her, or even just stopped by to have a cup of tea. He had even sent back a fully healed Sorley. Her heart wanted to believe he would return as promised, but her mind was very skilled at filling her head with doubts, questions, and fears. The worst one was a flicker of doubt concerning her trust in the man, a trust so newly recognized, which she clung to as she waited.

So now she sat in a window seat in her father's library, staring out the window at the garden being slowly killed by approaching winter, and behaving like a heartbroken maiden in a bad play. It did not help that the garden was fading too quickly; a few bright flowers might have lightened her mood. Nor did it help that she could find no interest in the usual invitations and entertainments, despite her relief at discovering that her adventures had not been revealed to make her persona non grata in society. She wanted to see Orion. Catryn knew it was what she needed, but even as she acknowledged it, she resented the fact. A man should not be the only source of happiness for her. Unfortunately, in her current mood she could not find the strength of will to rebel.

A new concern had been added, one that she fought mightily to ignore. Her menses were late and she had felt so ill this morning she had had to remain in bed for an added hour until it eased. A small, foolish part of her was thrilled with the possibility that she was carrying Orion's child. The sensible part of her, however, recognized the trouble she could be facing if Orion did not return. It was certainly not a good time to disappear to the Continent and then return a few months later with a baby, claiming a hasty marriage that ended too soon with the tragic loss of her husband. If nothing else, there would be people who would recall that she had disappeared from London about eight months before the baby's birth and put that together with her trip, abrupt secret marriage, and swift trip to widowhood.

"Why do you not just write to the man?" asked her father.

"That would be too forward," she replied, turning in her seat to look at him.

"Dear, you spent days with the man chasing Morris around the countryside, got kidnapped by that idiot, have met many members of Orion's family who now write you regularly, discovered we have a blood connection to that fascinating family, and his son Giles is here near every day." Her father counted each point he made on his fingers. "I do not believe he would think it forward if you wrote him a brief note. Well, not unless you tell him to come here because you sit by the window sighing like some forsaken maiden in a bad play."

The fact that he made the same unflattering comparison about her behavior as she had irritated her and she said, "I will not write to him. He said he would return. Just because I thought he meant in a few days and not a few weeks is no reason to prod him."

"It sounds like a very good one to me. You are going to marry him. A brief note would not be forward coming from you."

"He has not even asked me to marry him, Father. Not even hinted at it." And the fact that she kept dreaming of a perfect, picturesque future with Orion when he had not even spoken vaguely of love or a future was yet another thing that irritated her.

"He allows his son to come here regularly. If a man wants free of a woman, he certainly does not allow that to continue. He sends you the occasional gift, things that are not common gifts men give women. Even I can see that they are the types of gifts a man buys because he caught sight of them and thought of one particular woman."

"Truly?" She sternly told her heart not to cling to that as a sign of hope, but it ignored her.

"Truly. A book on herbs? A scarf? Those are not ordinary gifts. I would wager you know exactly why he would think of you when he saw them and why he thought you would appreciate them."

"I can." She sighed and stared down at her hands. "But . . ." She fumbled for the right words.

"But what?"

"He heard everything, Da," she said softly, falling back on the name she had called her father as a child. "He heard all about Aeddon, about Henry drugging me, about Morris. It was all so sordid. I still cringe when I think about it, even though I know I am not to blame for any of it." She started slightly when her father sat down next to her and took her into his arms, but then sank into his comforting hold.

"The man knows that you are not to blame, that you had no choice and no say," Lewys said as he patted her back. "He lets his son come here whenever the boy wishes to."

"You keep saying that."

"It is important. And I do commend you for never pressing the boy for information." He kissed the top of her head when she laughed.

"It has not been easy. I think that one thing which troubles me about the whole business with Henry, Aeddon, and Morris is that, quite often, I just do not care. It was sordid, wrong, and humiliating. It was a violation of the worst kind. But it all gave me Alwyn. Every time I begin to sink into shame I think of Alwyn, and it is as if the very thought of him washes it all away."

"So it should. In your heart, you know full well that you have nothing to be ashamed of. *You* did not do it. It was done *to* you. You know that, I know that, and, trust me in this matter, Sir Orion and his relatives all know that. He will come for you. I am certain of it. Just be patient."

Catryn just nodded. She would be patient, even though she was no longer as certain as her father appeared to be. If what she suspected was true, however, if she carried Orion's child, then all patience would have to be cast aside. She could wait another week at the most, and then she would have to decide what to do—go to him or begin to work on an elaborate lie.

Orion waited for the butler to take his coat and hat, his stomach knotting with nerves with each passing moment. It had taken him a lot longer than he had expected to arrange his life to accommodate the step he was about to take. The captain had not been too happy about his request to step back from the amount of work he did for the country, even though the man understood that it was for the best. A man who already had three children and was planning to add a wife who would add another child to his household had too many weaknesses that an enemy could take advantage of.

There had also been his finances and his home to tend to. Both had needed some hard work to prepare them for a family; he had been very lax in tending to them for far too long. He was far richer than he had realized, which was a relief as well as a pleasant surprise, and now the final repairs on his home were done. It was without doubt ready for a woman's touch. If Catryn wanted a country home, he was well able to provide her with one, and that eased his mind as well. In many ways he was marrying above his station, and it had suddenly been very important to him to make absolutely certain that Catryn would never be cut by some society matron because of him.

As Eccles led him to the parlor, leaving him there to cool his heels while Catryn was informed of his visit, Orion fought to calm himself. He knew why he was nervous. He had never offered himself, all of himself, to a woman before. He had charmed, seduced, and bedded more women than he wanted to recall at the moment, but it had all been shallow, flirtatious play, and never serious. This was no game, and he realized he was terrified that Catryn would refuse him.

Thinking on all Giles had told him, Orion was able to relax a little. The boy would not lie to him, and had shown the power of his gift of knowing how a person felt often enough for it not to be doubted. Giles said she was watching for him, waiting for him. Orion could only hope that he had not left her waiting for too long.

"M'lady, Sir Orion Wherlocke is here and requests that you join him in the front parlor."

Catryn pulled away from her father and stared at Eccles in disbelief. "Orion is here?"

Eccles nodded. "As I said, he awaits you in the front parlor."

She looked down at the plain, serviceable gown she wore and grimaced. For a brief moment she thought of having Eccles tell the man to wait while she ran up to her bedchamber and at least changed into a prettier gown. Orion deserved to wait for her now, if only for a short time. Then she told herself not to be foolish. She had been waiting on the man for three long weeks and needed to have matters settled between them. He had also seen her in plain gowns for the whole of their time together as they had chased down Morris.

"If you could see to some refreshments, Eccles," she began.

"They have already been seen to, m'lady, and will probably arrive about the time you do." Eccles bowed when Catryn did not move and just stood there biting her lip. "I will wait for you at the door of the parlor."

"Why do you hesitate?" asked her father the moment the door shut behind Eccles.

"Just nerves."

"Do you begin to doubt that you really want this man?"

"No. You see, when Morris took me, I realized I trusted Orion as I have not trusted a man for many years. There was my faithless husband, his brother, who soon showed he could never be a worthy uncle for my son, even Grandfather, who nearly brought us to ruin."

"And me," her father said quietly. "I am so sorry for that, love."

She hugged him. "No, you did nothing wrong, not

like the others. It was all childish hurt over actions that were perfectly understandable. It just took me a while to accept that. Then, after I married and even more so after I was widowed, I suddenly hear all about men who betray their wives, gamble away their money and marry just to get more, and all of that. It robbed me of my trust for any man. I no longer believed, well, in finding that perfect companion, someone who would stand by me at all times, help me, and watch my back." She stepped back and looked at her father. "And when Morris kidnapped me and Alwyn that final time, all I kept thinking was how I had to keep us alive and not give Morris what he wanted because I knew, deep down inside, that Orion was coming for us. He was watching my back."

"A very important thing and high praise for the man."

"Yes, so I had best go and see why my comrade-in-arms was gone for so long."

"Do not make him suffer too much for his manly ignorance," teased her father and he winked at her.

Catryn headed for the parlor, reaching it just as Eccles opened the door for the maid. She was not sure she shared her father's obvious confidence that a happy future with Orion awaited her. Despite knowing it was unwise, she had given in to a morbid curiosity during the weeks she had waited for him, and discovered some of the women his name had been linked with over the years. They had all been tall, voluptuous, fashionable, elegant women. She was none of those things.

Obeying a signal from Eccles, Catryn entered the parlor in front of the maid. It was for the best that a tray of pretty cakes and strong tea was set down on the table between the two settees. It kept her from doing something witless such as immediately demanding to know where he had been for so many days. Now, after dismissing the maid, she was able to bury that urge beneath the mundane etiquette of serving a guest some refreshment.

The intent way Orion watched her, however, began to make her nervous. His voice stroked her as it always did, even though he was uttering no more than polite words in response to her polite words. She sat back on the settee facing him, clasped her hands in her lap to hide how badly they were shaking, and finally met his gaze straight on.

"Such a proper little hostess," he murmured and took a bite of a delicate little spiced apple cake, enjoying the way her eyes narrowed.

"One should always present one's best manners when greeting the rare visitor to one's home," she said and smiled sweetly.

Orion decided that three weeks without Catryn must have disordered his mind. She looked as if she could leap across the table between them and beat him over the head with the teapot. He should be thinking of the best way to soothe her, ease any bruised feelings she might have. Instead he was fighting the urge to laugh and nudge her into a show of temper. After all, he thought, if she did leap over the table it would then be easy to get her into his arms, which was where he desperately wanted her to be.

"I had a great deal more work to do than I had anticipated," he said.

Catryn hated how her curiosity could rule her but still heard herself ask, "Work for our government?"

"Ah no, that was but one knot that I needed to untie. I informed them that, although I would always be willing to help if I am sorely needed, I can no longer be sent hither and yon on a whim. I have responsibilities now, and what I was deeply involved in for so long can quickly turn responsibilities into weakness, vulnerabilities. What happened with Morris made me see all too well how those closest to me could be used against me, either to make me do something I have no wish to do, or just to inflict hurt on me."

The way he was looking at her made Catryn think that he was including her in the list of those closest to him. Then she told herself not to be so vain. It was also the sort of thinking that raised her hopes, and she knew all too well how that could lead to the sharp pain of disappointment.

She nodded, silently praying that her ill-advised spurt of hope did not show on her face. "Your three sons."

"Enough of this," Orion said and swiftly moved to sit beside her and pull her into his arms.

Catryn heard herself squeak in surprise. She barely had time to toss her cake aside before he was holding her. It felt so good to be in his arms again that she could almost forget that he had left her alone for three long weeks. A few gifts sent with a blunt note did not make up for that. She put her hands on his chest, valiantly fought back the urge to start undoing his clothes, and met his gaze. His eyes narrowed and she knew she had to speak her mind quickly before he had the chance to weaken her resolve.

"You have been gone from my life for three weeks to the day, Orion," she said. "Yes, you sent me a few gifts and I thank you most kindly for them. Although, I did wonder if that book on herbs was actually a gift and not, perhaps, a little slap for deceiving you that day."

"A bit of both actually," he said and grinned. "A reward as well. I have never been so thoroughly gulled. And I sent a note with the gift."

That smile of his could easily break her determination to say what she needed to say, so Catryn hurried on. "Each one did have a note with it, true enough. A very brief note. The longest was six words. You did not even come round here once, Orion. Not even to drop the gift off at the door."

"I allowed Giles to come round here whenever he wished to."

"Somehow I do not believe your permission was truly requested."

He laughed. "True. I am sorry," he said seriously, all laughter gone from his voice and expression. "I should have at least come round now and then, no matter how short a time I had to stay. I had planned to, but I had far more that needed to be done than I had thought. It embarrasses me to admit how much I had simply ignored or had left completely to others. Working just to understand the state of my own finances cost me days. And nights. But you shall be pleased to hear that I am financially well set up."

"I never suspected otherwise, for you are far too clever for your own good at times, but I am quite pleased for you. It must be a true comfort to know that you are able to give your sons all they need."

"And you."

"I beg your pardon."

Orion cursed and placed his hands over hers where they had clenched his waistcoat. "Forgive my clumsiness. I have never, not once, even considered doing what I am desperately trying to do now. I was much more erudite and calm while speaking with your father."

"You spoke with my father? He never told me that. Whatever for?"

"I believe it is customary for a man to speak to a woman's father before he expresses his intentions directly to her."

As the meaning of his words settled into her mind, Catryn was surprised that the front of her gown was not bulging in and out like a bellows because her heart was pounding so fiercely. She fought to calm herself despite how easily she could see herself screaming yes and hurling herself into his arms. He had to say more, much more than simply asking for her hand in marriage. She would not lock herself into another loveless marriage.

In fact, it would be so much worse with Orion than it had ever been with Henry. What she had felt for Henry had been no more than infatuation, something shallow and fleeting that had died quickly at the first hint of strife. What she felt for Orion was so much deeper, she was not sure she could ever explain it clearly, not even to herself. He held her heart in those skilled, elegant hands and she wanted, desperately needed, him to care for her. If he was asking her to be his wife for any reason less than a true, deep caring for her, she would have to find the strength to say no to him.

"Catryn?" Orion refused to unleash the fear growing in his heart as her silence continued. "I am asking you to be my wife."

"Why? It is not because you feel you should do so in order to preserve my reputation, is it?"

"Ah." He relaxed now that he understood why she hesitated to say yes. "Cat, I am not that good a man. If all I felt was lust, I would simply work to continue our affair until that feeling passed. Then I would give you an expensive bauble, probably without a note or one that just said farewell, and then meander away to find another who stirred my lust."

"Ouch." She inwardly shuddered at the thought of him ever treating her in such a way. "Yet, I have heard that that is the way many an affair is ended. It just seems a bit . . ." She hesitated, unsure of what word to use, especially since she had no wish to inadvertently offend him.

"Cold?" Orion smiled faintly when she nodded. "It is by that time, which is why I would walk away." He leaned forward and brushed his lips over hers. "That is not my intention nor would I discuss the doing of such a thing with your father, which is probably why I left my meeting with him still breathing and unbloodied. Although I was sweating something fierce."

Catryn had to smile at the image of her father thrashing Orion. "Come now, it could not have been so very bad."

"Orion thought on the hours-long interrogation he had endured and murmured, "You can have no idea." He stood up, bringing her to her feet along with him.

"Now, come with me. I have something to show you. It may help you in taking me and my proposal much more seriously."

Before she could think of a way to reassure him that she always took him seriously, she was being bundled into her coat. Eccles just smiled when Orion said he was taking her somewhere, and that puzzled her, if only because Eccles rarely smiled at anyone other than family. The carriage he settled her in was much nicer than the one she had recently spent so much time in, more elegant yet still inconspicuous. She had finally wrestled her way through the mind-clouding realization that Orion wanted to marry her and was ready to speak to him more thoroughly about it when they stopped before his town house.

She frowned as Orion helped her out of the carriage and escorted her to his door. There was something different about the house. At first Catryn shrugged that puzzle aside by telling herself she had not gotten a good look at the house when she had stopped to *borrow* his carriage. Just as Orion opened the door for her to step inside his home, she knew what she was seeing that had been changed. The house was much brighter than it had been.

"Oh, you painted your home," she said as he tugged her inside and shut the door behind them.

"Painted, washed, patched," Orion said, idly wondering why something as simple as Catryn actually noticing the work he had done should please him so much. "It was something that had been long overdue when I bought the house, but I was a laggard about tending to it. Now, come and see what else I have done."

Orion led her inside. Despite how nervous he felt about how she would react to the home he had planned for them, he also experienced an intense sense of satisfaction when she crossed his threshold. Now that he had her in his home, he had no intention of allowing her to leave.

Chapter Twenty

The bed was huge.

Still reeling from the tour of the house, Orion cheerfully pointing out to her all the work that had been done, it took Catryn a moment to catch her breath. The way he had also made repeated reference to how the house still needed decorating, a woman's touch, had left her speechless. She finally, wholeheartedly, believed the man was completely committed to marrying her. And now there was this massive bed.

It was made of a dark wood, each post as well as the headboard and footboard beautifully carved with vines and flowers. It was an odd choice for a man, even though it did not look feminine. The bedding itself was plain, but as she recalled the rest of the house, that was undoubtedly intentional. She could tell without touching it that the mattress and pillows were all expensive down-filled ones.

"Hang a few heavy oilcloths up there and a family of six could make that bed a home," she said.

Orion laughed. "I insisted on it being big."

Catryn suddenly had all too clear a vision of Orion romping in that massive bed with several buxom women.

"It was not easy to get it made to my specifications in only three weeks, but since my purse proved to be fatter than I had expected, I persuaded the men to do it." He kissed her cheek. "A bride should have a new bed even though the one I had never held anyone but me. I had that bed moved to another room."

Embarrassed that her sordid thoughts had been so easily guessed at, she turned her attention to the massive stone fireplace the bed faced. "You could roast an ox in there."

"Is it not truly magnificent? The fireplaces in this home were the main reason I bought it. This area of town was growing less and less fashionable. The people who owned this house were finding it more and more difficult to rent it out, at least at a price that made maintaining it worth their while. And, since my family is buying up any property in this area that is available, I will soon be surrounded by them."

"And thus have a place where none of you have to be continuously on your guard," she murmured.

"Exactly. We will not only bring this area back into its former state of glory but make it ours. This is the master suite. Go, have a look around while I see to a fire for us."

She decided not to ask why he would build a fire in the bedroom when she was supposed to be there just to see the work he had done, to judge all he could offer her. There was a chance he would bluntly tell her that he intended to bed her, and she knew she would be easily persuaded. They needed to talk first.

If they fell into bed she would soon find herself agreeing to marry him without yet knowing what was in his heart, and that she could not do.

Catryn went through a door to the right of the fireplace and found herself in a large bath with all of the latest amenities. She went back into the bedroom and through the door to the left of the fireplace and found the largest dressing room and closet she had ever seen. Neither room was the sort a man would think of, not with the added touches she could see, and as she stepped back into the bedroom she found herself wondering if Orion had had a woman advise him.

"My cousin Olympia designed those rooms," Orion said as he worked to light the kindling. "She insisted. Said a man had no idea how to make them completely suitable for a wife. At that time I had no plans to obtain a wife, but I let her have her way."

"She has a true skill, for they are wonderful and filled with useful touches," Catryn said as she walked to the door across the room, biting back the urge to ask him if he could read her mind.

The room she entered was an elegant sitting room. Catryn could see by the trim on the windows, the fireplace mantel, and all the other woodwork that Orion had a love for dark wood with delicate carving. In that their tastes were very similar. She walked across that room to another door and found herself in what had to be meant for a nursery. From there she entered a room that could only be Orion's office, although the number of books she saw could easily mark it as a library.

What Orion called the master suite just needed a

kitchen and it would satisfy most anyone looking for lodging in the city. Catryn shook her head in amazement and headed back to the bedroom. Orion had proven that he was indeed very serious about marriage, about living with her and all the boys as a proper family. The only reason she still hesitated to say yes and reach for the ring she knew he had in his pocket was the continual lack of any true declaration from the heart. It was not until she stepped back inside the bedroom that she realized there was something missing from Orion's grand master suite.

"There is only one bedroom," she said.

Orion stopped admiring the fire he had built, stood up, and walked over to her. "My wife sleeps with me. There will be no separate bedchambers, no place for her to go and hide if there is some strife between us, and no place for her to lock me out of."

Catryn decided not to comment on that brief peek into what must have been his parents' troubled marriage. "Very well."

He reached out and slowly pulled her into his arms, his body immediately hardening with need. "Will you marry me?"

It was yes or no time and Catryn struggled with the fierce urge to say yes and leave all her concerns to be dealt with later. That was foolish and she knew it. It could end up hurting both of them. This time she would only enter into marriage if she was sure that there was shared affection and that their expectations about what a marriage should be matched in as many ways as possible. She rose on her tiptoes and lightly kissed him, pulling back when his hold on her tightened and he started to press for a much deeper kiss.

"I want to marry you, but"—she ignored his muttered curse—"you never answered my question. *Why* do you wish to marry me? I need to know, Orion. My first marriage was horrible, more so than I ever even knew at the time. And now you know as well, learning just how evil the deception perpetrated on me was. So I need to know why you want me for your wife. I—"

Orion put his finger against her lips, stopping her words. "I ask you to marry me because I need you at my side. I knew it before you went to your father to wait for me, and three weeks without you proved it beyond any doubt. You are my heart, my soul mate, my future." He frowned when her eyes shone with impending tears. "That makes you cry?"

She hugged him. "Happiness. Tears of happiness. Are you certain? Even knowing about Morris and Aeddon?"

"Your husband abused you, love. You were drugged, unable to even know what was happening when those men slipped into your bed. You thought it was your lawful husband. We know now, since the man's rude theft of my body for a while, that even Aeddon saw it as nothing more than rape and was shamed by what he had done. Alwyn is *your* child and that is all that matters." He put his hand under her chin and turned her face up to his. "And what a damned hypocrite I would be to condemn you for what you had no say in, when I myself willingly charmed my way into too many beds. All I care about is that *you* do not let what happened trouble you. You carry no guilt or shame for what was done *to* you, not *by* you."

"'Tis odd, but it only troubled me for a very short time, and after that only now and then." She wiped a

tear from her face, realizing that she had been more
concerned about how he felt over Alwyn's conception
than she had even admitted to herself. "I realized *I*
was not really even there, truly had no choice or
knowledge. And then I would look at my baby and
know, deep in my heart, that as horrible as it was for
them to do that to me, I would not ever wish to go
back and change it. Perhaps if Alwyn was not yet
born, I would feel differently, but now that I have had
him . . ." She shrugged. "In a way, the fact that I was
drugged and cannot really recall much of that violation may be why I am not more deeply troubled."

"True, but I will be there if it troubles you in your
dreams," he said as he started to nudge her toward
the bed.

Catryn struggled to keep her balance and then
laughed when he tumbled her down onto the bed. He
stopped her laughter with a kiss that quickly had her
trying to remove his clothes as hard as he was trying to
remove hers. When they were finally flesh to flesh, she
sighed with relief. She had missed the warmth of his
skin, the way it felt to be so intimately close with him.

She luxuriated in his kisses, in every touch of his
hands. It delighted her when he did not flinch as she
ran her hands over his strong, scarred back, for it told
her how deeply he trusted her. Catryn shivered with
pleasure as he feasted on her breasts and then began
a slow journey down her body, each kiss and stroke
of his tongue heating her blood.

Captured by the power of the desire he stirred
within her, she barely twitched when he began to give
her the most intimate of kisses. Catryn had one clear
moment of thought before she was completely lost to

the fierce need gripping her, and that was a sudden understanding of what those married women and wicked widows had been talking about. Then a blinding pleasure stole all ability to think.

Catryn was still gasping from the force of her release when Orion kissed his way back up her body. As soon as he was in reach she grabbed hold of him and pushed him onto his back. She could tell by the way he shifted his body beneath her that he expected her to immediately mount him. Catryn smiled and began to kiss her way down his strong body.

The way he whispered words of praise and encouragement, letting her know how she pleased him, made Catryn bold. Despite how the taste and even the scent of his skin renewed her own desire, she struggled to recall all those women had spoken about in those scandalous whispered conversations about men, what they liked, and how to give and get pleasure out of the bedding. By the time she kissed each of his muscular thighs, she had no hesitation about turning her amorous attentions to the matter of making love to him with her mouth. The moment her lips touched his erection and a shudder went through him, she knew he wanted it as much as she now desired giving it. She proceeded to put to use every single lesson taught by those women.

When he grabbed her under the arms and pulled her up his body moments later, she did not need to see the desire tauten his features to know that he had reached the edge. She had felt it building within him, even tasted it. Catryn did her best to join their bodies without too much fumbling. A shiver of delight went through her as he filled her and she leaned forward to brush her lips over his.

"I love you, Sir Orion Wherlocke," she whispered against his mouth.

Catryn abruptly found herself on her back, Orion kissing her as if he was starved for the taste of her as he drove them both to release with a force that pushed her up against the headboard. When he collapsed on top of her, she held him close, a pang of disappointment afflicting her because he had not returned the words she had whispered to him. She told herself not to be so foolish. He had already told her that she was his heart, his future, and his soul mate. Those words carried a lot more weight than one little four-letter word far too many people used with far too much ease and frequency.

Orion eased their bodies apart, turned onto his back, and pulled her into his arms. "That lacked finesse."

She laughed. "It was wonderful."

He held her close and kissed the top of her head. "I love you, Lady Catryn." He smiled when she tried her best to hug him. "And I think that, until I become a little more accustomed to the words, you might want to be very careful where and when you say them to me."

She was laughing as he left the bed to clean up, returning to do the same service for her, despite her blushes. Once back in bed, he pulled her into his arms again and smiled up at the ceiling. This was what he needed, what he had so deeply missed during the last three weeks. In one way, the separation had served a good purpose aside from allowing him to order his finances as well as his home. The very last hint of reluctance to give up his bachelor ways, his freedom, had left him. That particular freedom had shown itself to be an empty, useless thing. Even Beatrice, with all her sensual beauty, had not stirred a spark of interest when he had met the woman in a bookshop. What she could give him was shallow, a fleeting pleasure that touched little more than his groin.

Catryn *was* his future. She was friend, lover, and confidant. It was true that he had any number of friends and several of them were also confidants, but he would not want to lie naked with any of them in the night and discuss family or the events of an ordinary day.

Grinning at that image, he opened his mouth to tell Catryn but a sound caught his attention. They were about to have some company. He pushed Catryn away and grabbed her shift from where he had tossed it on the floor.

"What is it?" Catryn asked, only to be effectively muzzled as he yanked her shift over her head.

"We are about to have uninvited guests." He felt her tense as he did up the buttons on her shift. "Uninvited, annoying, but not dangerous."

"Best you don your drawers then," she said.

"Too late."

He watched with her as the bedroom door was eased open just enough for Giles to peer inside the room. When the boy saw them both watching him, he grinned and flung open the door. Behind him stood Hector, Alwyn, and Paul.

"I believe we need to have a chat about the courtesy of knocking on a door before you open it," drawled Orion, eyeing Giles as the boy walked up to the bed.

Alwyn studied the bed and then Orion's bare chest. "Are you naked?"

"Yes. That is how men sleep."

He almost burst out laughing when Catryn pressed her face into his arm and whispered curses about his idiocy against his skin. All four boys nodded as if his words were straight from some instruction manual about manhood. He suspected the first time Catryn caught one of the boys trying to sleep naked he would be blamed. Orion could not wait.

"Why are you here?" he asked, and then looked at Paul and Hector. "And when did they arrive, for I have not sent for them yet."

"I sent for them after you spoke to Lord Gryffin," said Giles. "I was afraid one of you might do something to ruin this and thought I might need help."

"Your confidence in your father's skill at hooking a bride deeply touches me," Orion drawled and was a little surprised when even Alwyn grinned at his sarcastic words.

"Well? I am thinking you did it right."

"Ah, of course. I have had some practice." Orion winced when he got a good pinch under the covers for saying something so risqué in front of the boys, although Hector and Giles hooted with laughter.

"I think we should make them tell us what is so funny," Paul said to Alwyn.

"No, we still will not really understand," said Alwyn. "Things are funnier when you understand. Papa agrees."

"Oh, is Aeddon back then?" Catryn asked as she sat up and tried to tidy her mussed hair.

"He went away?" asked Orion.

"He needed to rest," answered Alwyn. "It made him very weak to be inside you like that."

"Alwyn, why is he still here anyway?" Catryn asked. "He was here to keep you safe, but Morris is now gone. I doubt the man will come within miles of us."

"Papa says he has nothing better to do and wants to watch me for a little while more."

"Does he not trust his own kinsman to do so?"

"Yes, but he wants to help."

"As he wishes, but I hope he has no more plans to leap into Orion. It made him quite ill."

"He is not answering that."

"Which is an answer in itself," muttered Orion. "Well, it is a little early for Hector and Paul to be here, and I'm not certain the rooms are readied, but we can manage. Cody and Pugh Three will be back soon. I will let them know we need the beds made and all."

"Pugh Three?" Catryn asked.

"My butler. He is the grandson of my grandfather's butler. Same first name. Since at one time they were all in the same house, he became Pugh Three—or just Three."

"Do you know, I begin to think your various gifts might not be all that is odd about your family," she murmured, and laughed when he gave her a light punitive tug on her hair.

"So when do you get married?" asked Giles. "I will need some fine new clothes."

Deciding to ignore the hint for new clothes, something Giles had more than enough of already, Orion replied, "As soon as we can arrange it." He looked at Catryn. "Unless you wish something very fancy. Then we could wait."

His tone told her that he would not like waiting at all. "No, soon is fine with me. I am a widow after all. I believe another large wedding might be considered a little improper."

"Good." Giles nodded as did the other three boys. "You should get married as quick as possible so we can all be a family, all legal and the like."

Paul walked around the bed to stand next to Catryn and handed her a small missive. "This is from Pen. She says it will help you in the mornings. She will be happy you are getting married soon as she said you did not have much time to wait."

"Why do I not have much time to wait?" She opened the missive and discovered advice on how to settle a stomach upset by a child growing in one's womb.

Before she could fold it up and put it away, Orion snatched it out of her hand. She grimaced as his eyes widened and then he stared at her. It was hard to tell if he was just surprised or if he was horrified. The man probably had a right to some sense of impending doom since there were already four children to care for and they had not even discussed children of their own.

"You are carrying my child?" he asked.

"It appears so, although I am curious as to how Penelope knew, since I did not think her gift was the sight."

"It is not," said Paul, "but Aunt Olympia heard from Lady Alethea, who does have the sight. She knew my father was to marry and that he would have five children within the year." He looked at the other boys. "Well, here are four."

"You are carrying my child?"

Catryn looked at Orion again. "Yes."

"Why did I not see it? Why did you not tell me? We could have been married weeks ago."

"I actually did not realize it myself until I had to stay in bed for an extra hour the other day because getting up would have meant vomiting into a bucket for a while." She squeaked when he hugged her. "I suspect you did not see it because you have not seen me for three weeks."

"When were you going to tell me?"

"As I said, I only just found out for myself. I was thinking of giving you another week. It was either that or slipping off to some obscure village on the Continent where I would form an improper attachment, marry, and then have the ill luck to be tragically widowed a month or so after the child was born." She smiled when he laughed. "I know. No one really believes those tales but very, very few have the ill manners to question them."

The boys climbed on the bed, after obeying Orion's hasty instructions to remove their shoes, and Paul asked, "Do you want to know what the baby will be?"

"I assume it will be a boy. If I were a betting person, that is the bet I would make."

"Do you want to know?"

"Paul"—Orion looked at the boy—"do you know what we will have?"

"Yes, because Ezra told me. I do not usually see good things, but Ezra sees them sometimes. He told me but said that Lady Catryn might not wish to know."

Catryn thought about it for a moment. She had already had one child whose sex was much discussed, constantly guessed at and worried over, and she did not really want to go through that again. Fortunately, she knew Orion would not care. Yet, if she knew, she could be so much better prepared, could even have the pleasure of knowing just what she was preparing for, girl or boy. She looked over to find Orion staring at her. "Do you want to know?"

"I will go with what you want, as it does not trouble me one way or the other."

"Then, yes, Paul, I would like to know what Ezra had to say."

"You are going to have a girl, and Ezra says she will have a very fine gift, but he was not exactly sure what it was as the image was not clear to him. Do you want a girl?"

"Yes, I want a girl. I have four boys. A girl would be nice."

The boys all cheered and scrambled off the bed to re-don their shoes. Hector was the first to do so and he watched the others, acting very much the oldest, even though he was only a year or so older than Giles. Then, when everyone had their shoes on, he started out of the room, pausing in the doorway to look back at his father.

"Aunt Olympia says to expect her soon."

"Why?" asked Orion.

"Because she says you are to expect her soon."

"Thank you, Hector."

"I think I can hear Three and Cody, so I will tell them we need the beds made," he said. "Can we decide how we wish to split up, since we are to be two to a room?"

"I think that would be a very good idea," said Orion.

Hector nodded, walked out, and shut the door, the others following him. Catryn frowned as she heard Hector say, "And we are going to have to get busy learning how to fight like men."

"Why?" Giles asked. "I can fight good now."

"Because we are going to have a sister, and we need to watch over her like the ones at Radmoor are watching over Juno."

Their voices faded away and Catryn looked at Orion. "Oh dear."

He laughed and pulled her into his arms. "I noticed that same attitude amongst the boys at Radmoor."

"Well, I hope your daughter is a strong girl. This Aunt Olympia, she just tells you she will come for a visit?"

"Yes. She is not even thirty yet and has somehow managed to set herself up as a sort of matriarch of the family. You would be surprised how many tremble in fear when she says she is coming to visit."

"I see. Well, I will not tremble, but I will do my best to be cordial."

"Ah, you will like her, love. She is a very strong woman, has had to be, but none has a bigger heart. She cares for all of us, even if we sometimes wish she would not."

"But I do not want to sleep in the same room as Paul. He farts. A lot!"

Catryn recognized her son's voice and gasped. "I should go and sort that out."

Orion grabbed her and pulled her into his arms just as Paul bellowed, "Well, sleeping with you is no rose garden, either."

Orion laughed even as he kissed her, a kiss interrupted when there was a very brief knock on the door before it was flung open and Alwyn said, "Mama, since you are having a girl, Papa was thinking you might name her Catherine."

"Why would he want me to do that?" Catryn asked.

"Because he says he has some very fond memories of her. He says she was the first woman he ever . . ." Alwyn's last words were muffled by Giles's hand.

Giles smiled at them even as he dragged Alwyn out of the doorway. "I will have a word with him about repeating everything that rogue says. Do not worry." He slammed the door shut.

Catryn was still gaping at the door when a laughing Orion pulled her back down onto the bed with him. "Oh, love, we are going to have such a very interesting life."

She started to laugh. "Yes, yes we are, and I am so looking forward to it."

More by Bestselling Author
Hannah Howell

__Highland Angel	978-1-4201-0864-4	$6.99US/$8.99CAN
__If He's Sinful	978-1-4201-0461-5	$6.99US/$8.99CAN
__Wild Conquest	978-1-4201-0464-6	$6.99US/$8.99CAN
__If He's Wicked	978-1-4201-0460-8	$6.99US/$8.49CAN
__My Lady Captor	978-0-8217-7430-4	$6.99US/$8.49CAN
__Highland Sinner	978-0-8217-8001-5	$6.99US/$8.49CAN
__Highland Captive	978-0-8217-8003-9	$6.99US/$8.49CAN
__Nature of the Beast	978-1-4201-0435-6	$6.99US/$8.49CAN
__Highland Fire	978-0-8217-7429-8	$6.99US/$8.49CAN
__Silver Flame	978-1-4201-0107-2	$6.99US/$8.49CAN
__Highland Wolf	978-0-8217-8000-8	$6.99US/$9.99CAN
__Highland Wedding	978-0-8217-8002-2	$4.99US/$6.99CAN
__Highland Destiny	978-1-4201-0259-8	$4.99US/$6.99CAN
__Only for You	978-0-8217-8151-7	$6.99US/$8.99CAN
__Highland Promise	978-1-4201-0261-1	$4.99US/$6.99CAN
__Highland Vow	978-1-4201-0260-4	$4.99US/$6.99CAN
__Highland Savage	978-0-8217-7999-6	$6.99US/$9.99CAN
__Beauty and the Beast	978-0-8217-8004-6	$4.99US/$6.99CAN
__Unconquered	978-0-8217-8088-6	$4.99US/$6.99CAN
__Highland Barbarian	978-0-8217-7998-9	$6.99US/$9.99CAN
__Highland Conqueror	978-0-8217-8148-7	$6.99US/$9.99CAN
__Conqueror's Kiss	978-0-8217-8005-3	$4.99US/$6.99CAN
__A Stockingful of Joy	978-1-4201-0018-1	$4.99US/$6.99CAN
__Highland Bride	978-0-8217-7995-8	$4.99US/$6.99CAN
__Highland Lover	978-0-8217-7759-6	$6.99US/$9.99CAN

Available Wherever Books Are Sold!

Check out our website at
http://www.kensingtonbooks.com